Let That Be The Reason

Vickie M. Stringer

Let That Be The Reason

Vickie M. Stringer

published by

UpStream

a division of A&B PUBLISHERS GROUP
BROOKLYN, NEW YORK
11238

published by

a division of A&B Publishers Group
1000 Atlantic Avenue
Brooklyn, New York, 11238
(718)783-7808

First Upstream printing May 2002.

ISBN: 1-886433-85-2   Library of Congress Control Number

2001118106

Photograph/Art Direction: Helena Gilchrist Banks

Graphic Artist: Evangelia Philippidis

03 04 05 06   12 11 10 9 8 7 6 5

Printed in Canada

This book is dedicated
to all those doing time. and,
to my family, who was the wind beneath my wings....
at a time when i could not fly on my own

Not By Might, Not By Fate, But By His Spirit

Father, I Am, so Grateful

Mama, I hope that I have made you proud

In loving memory of Michael Easter2002, who planted a seed
for many.

Acknowledgements

Thank You's

Heavenly Father for revealing to me that my strength is made perfect in weakness, for blessings, mercy and grace

My family, whom I have dedicated this book to. I love you all.

My Publishing House A&B Publishers Group (UpStream division) Eric, Maxie, Wendy, Allison, Rawle, Karen and Marley. Here we go!

Chass Reed, mi amiga, for the title of this book and typing assistance

Diedre Johnson, I'll never ever, never ever, never forget the soap, lotion, books and visits.

Sister Tamera Kiwanis Fournier, friendship at it's best.

Lori, my lil big sis, you will always be my *Shero*. Your unconditional love gave me the strength to believe. Ma te da da!

Thanks to all the encouraging people at the *Holiday Inn Airport*, bar who listened to my dream of being a published author.

Linda F. Stringer-Earthman, Helena Gilchrist Banks, Evangelia Philippidis, Ashley Danielle Price, Ladies we did the first one and made it a success now we pass the torch to A&B to do the rest.

Clifford Benton, President of Audacity The Literary Consortium.

Columbus, Ohio-This ain't my hometown but you held me down like it was. The support and love from First Friday's (Greg Provo &

Jeff Gilliam), Minds In Motion Book Club (Ms. Dee Malone-Daniels), Black Women's Advocacy Group (Mechelle Harmon), Black Art's Plus Books, Sammy's Car Wash, Expressions Hair & Nail Salon, Visions Hair Salon, Naty's Hair Salon, Spirited Sisters Expo (Dawn Tyler), and many more

Valerie Hunter-Pounds, my publicist, See......Now! (Smile) Your support has been fuel on this journey. Without you, I would be out of gas. Thank U!

Cedric Stringer, Robert Gooden, Ivan Colbert, Arnell Hurt, Lloyd Black, Martin Whaley, Rob Chalfant, Franklin White, Men you have always been there for me

Young Ty, How does it feel to have a sister that has reach "Vet" Status?

Donald Goines, you set a path for those with a street story to tell.

Michael Haggen, my lifetime friend and Godfather of my son. Most importantly, My mommy, I survived because you took care of my son. You have taught me how to love myself. You are my star, always.

Valen, thanks for waiting for Mommy. I love you!

So many people have touched my life. I could never list them all. I receive all my lessons with joy!

Blessings,

Chapter

ONE

"Hello May I Help You?" –Click–
Ring…ring…
"Hello! May I help you?"
"You got any girls that speak Greek?"
" NO!"
-Click- (*what did he mean by that?*)
This was my first day answering the phones; my phones. I could not believe I had actually started my own service, my very own Escort Service. It seems like only yesterday I was working for Tony's Service.

I was living in a very expensive two-bedroom apartment with my only child, my beautiful son. He was seven months old at the time. My bills were getting taller and taller by the day. There was no help from his father, nor his father's family. It was very rough. My pride kept me from asking for help. I was receiving welfare. That alone tore my pride down. My son needed medical care. So I did what I had to do. I was just struggling to maintain the life I had with his father, Chino.

Chino was a self-made millionaire. Okay, maybe not a million-aire, but he was *paid*. He had *coins*! He also was a drug dealer. So,

1

it came as no surprise to all the material things we had together. But, now he has a new wife and a new life.

Shortly after our break-up, my leasing agent informed me of an offer to sell my hair salon. We, Chino and I, were owners of a wonderful full-service hair salon that we built from the ground up. We had rented space in an upcoming shopping plaza on Columbus' east side.

It started as drywalls and cement floors. I can remember the excitement we felt as we watched the salon take shape and evolve into the vision we shared. On a daily basis, I walked the square footage of the salon planning, dreaming and envisioning what it would become. By night, I browsed magazine layouts with the desire to duplicate the sleek images on the pages. With passion and complete faith, I communicated my particulars to the contracting team. Finally, a black and white color scheme blended with the state of the art salon equipment. We tried to include everything a salon should have. Deluxe European-style shampoo bowls with recline-like padded chairs fitting the contour shape of the client. Marble counter-tops and inlays to hold hair products. Open silver cage towel holders and brass magazine holders placed in reaching distance of the client from dryers. Individual oversized dryers with see through hoods lined the west wall of the salon. In the reception area sat an oversized black lacquer desk with a fresh cut flower bouquet for ornament. To show our clients that we appreciated them, we placed a break station complete with complimentary snacks. Our salon was fit for the pages of a magazine. A salon that was a trendsetter. And it was. It was the first of its kind for Columbus, Ohio. Something that they had never seen. And we did this together. One of my numerous opening duties included wiping the fingerprints off the windows. Fingerprints from the previous night of faces pressed against the glass peering inside to behold the transformation of the salon. We put over $50,000 into that place. Well he did, because after all, it was *his* money. But it was my sweat and stress that put it together.

In fairness to us both, one could not have succeeded without the other. We were a team, and L-O-Quent Hair Salon was our dream. A dream that came true.

Upon completion, prior to the open house, I can remember Chino and I in the salon. We were alone, holding hands and walking around when we felt the rush. Chino said, "Look Pooh, we did it!"

Breathlessly I said, "I know, it is so beautiful, thank you. Are you proud?" I always needed his approval. His opinion was every-thing to me.

Chino said, "Pooh, I am so proud of you, it all looks great. Put on some music." He then turned on the Sony surround-sound system, and jazz music floated through the air.

Turning off the lights, he took me in his safe and reassuring arms, and we danced on the lovely checkerboard floor. I tingled from his touch and felt as if I were floating. Right then, at that moment, success was already ours. And there were even more remarkable things to come. But, three years later, I sold my dream for $20,000; a give-away price. However, I was thankful due to the fact that I allowed the salon to diminish by refusing to go into the salon and unwilling to receive phone calls from the stylist seeking answers. Everything was jeopardized, the phone, lights, water, all threatened to be turned off. And, the staff kept working, looking for my return to work. Unable to face them and deal with my situation, I folded my hand.

The breakup was awful and very embarrassing. In solitude, while at my mother's home, I let go. Needless to say, I sped through the money. I lost everything when Chino left. He refused to allow me anything. I needed a budget and many other common sense values I had not been able to develop under Chino's controlling rules. His abrupt departure out of my life was so sudden. I stood alone for the first time in so many years. How could he be so cruel? I have asked myself this many times. Not willing to lend support for his son. Whatever the circumstances surrounding our break-up, he still should not have allowed our child to suffer want this way. This was not the man that I had fallen deeply in love with. Chino had become a stranger to me. His cold indifference towards my situation made me feel like I never meant anything to him. And, the child that we share was nothing more than an inconsequential result of a night's passion.

Though he had always been a very controlling man, he had never been abusive. I was attracted to his strong will. He was obviously punishing me by withholding support. It made no difference that I was his baby's mamma.

♥

"Chino, I can't deal with this shit! Bitches callin' the shop looking for you. What's up with that?"

"What are you talking about? I'm right here, right now, with you. I can't even walk in the door without you stressin'."

"Darling, it's three motherfuckin in the a.m. What am I suppose to say? How was your day?" As easily as he came into our home, he snatched up his coat and car keys to leave. Not wanting him to go, but to discuss how we had come to this, I asked the obvious. "Where are you going?" He replied, "Out!"

♥

As much as I was overwhelmed by feelings of vulnerability, I was even more compelled by maternal instinct.

The survival of my child was what mattered most. So, flat broke, I was unable to provide for my only child. My family had given me enough "I told ya so's," so I couldn't go there. I needed money fast, which meant fast money. I got a Sunday's newspaper and began a diligent job search.

I was qualified for a little of everything: public relations, decision-making, accounting, problem solving, etc. Problem was, I had no "Paper" to substantiate that fact. The importance of a college degree became apparent coupled with the regret of not continuing my college education. I became self-employed and a college dropout the day I met Chino. How could one trade in college so easily for a life of uncertainty? One who has never met Chino, only asks this question. He possessed the ability to persuade you that the sky was green when you knew that it was blue. The gift of gab was what this man possessed and eventually possessed me. It is called selling a dream. Or, in my case, purchasing one.

I bought into his ideas about how our life should be, blinded by my first love and only hearing his words. At age seventeen, I abandoned my courses for his vision for the family, for his created crew named The Triple Crown Posse.

I went on several interviews, though no one called. I couldn't fully understand. I ran a very successful salon. I won competitions; was even on TV because of it. I had a full staff of outstanding designers with two receptionists. I sold hair products, clothes, make-up and more. *Why? Why am I not qualified?*

In my desperation and embarrassment, I returned to the cosmetology community. It was slow and difficult for someone of my caliber to work in someone else's salon. But I had to feed my son, so I did it. Everyday customers never allowed me to forget that I was a has-been.

"Didn't you own L-O-Quent?" a snobby woman with a mud mask asked.

"What?" I replied with obvious contempt for this question.

"Did he take it from you?" Someone else would ask.

"Did Chino take your salon from you?" The remarks seemed endless.

It seemed like all the remarks cut close to home because they all seemed true. Basically, I lost my salon over a piece of ass and a nervous breakdown. I discovered Chino was having an affair as I wore an engagement ring that I thought symbolized our bond. Chino wanted to betray me, and I wanted to escape the pain.

Ultimately, he let go of me and I simply let go of everything. Then Chino would taunt me, "You know you loved that shop."

I reacted indifferently about it, but inside, it tore me apart in tiny little pieces that are still not together and may never be.

But, I had to go on, and one day, I pray I can let go, move on for the sake of my son. He became my strength and my motivation.

I did well in this other person's salon, and my confidence grew. I could walk into someone else's salon and not feel badly inside. I was healing.

It was not long before the salon owner began to demand longer hours from me. She was a very insensitive owner. Quite frankly, I did not care for her. Having been in the same position, I knew reasonable and unreasonable demands. I had an infant. His daycare lasted until 5:30 pm. I had no sitter for him; my mom lived in Michigan, the next state over. Therefore, I began to do nails at home. That worked better, but I still did not earn enough. In normalcy, it was enough. My hands ran through money. In my former life, budget was not in my vocabulary. Life with Chino was like, "Whatever my Pooh wants, she can have." So, I began to look for work again, do nails on the side, and be a Mom.

Sinking, I began to pawn things to try and get on track. I pawned everything. I even sold my son's bedroom set to a children's resale store. YES! It was like that. So, I returned to the newspaper. With tears in my eyes and a weight on my heart, I read "Help Wanted, Start Today, ESCORT, Great Money." I thought, *can I "date" someone for sex?* I didn't think so, but I called anyway.

A man by the name of Tony answered the phone and was so convincing. I went to the address and did not find a building like in the movies, all glamorous and glittery. Instead, I found a house in the ghetto off of Cleveland Avenue. I even wore a suit. Can you believe it? We talked while I heard phones ringing like crazy. As I sat there, he described me to a caller. Tony had the look of a retired playboy with a body that used to be in shape. He had a few cuts on his arms that were still visible as he took drags on his cigarette. Handsome light hazel eyes, but some facial scars like he had his ass whipped a couple times or two. He had a way with words, using them to get his way. I knew it was a Con (game). Chino had taught me a lot about it. Not enough to outsmart him, but enough for me to spot a con. He'd say, "Pooh, game recognize game." I was desperate, the perfect *mark*, so I went for it.

Tony said, "You can make $200 in fifteen minutes."

I got my paper and a pen out, and I went to what is called an Out-Call. An Out-Call is where the girl goes to the guy, known as a "John." The address was a Hot Tub Store rental place, and when I pulled in front of the building, my heart began to sink to the pit of my stomach. Feelings of shame swarmed over me until goose pimples surfaced on my arms. Dirty, filthy, tramp-like visions played tricks on my mind.

Please, I don't want to do this, God help me. Chino, where are you? I am about to sell my pussy. I am having sex for money. Something I vowed I would never do. Now look at me, I am a whore. I am a prostitute.

I thought about my mother. What would she think? What would she say to see her youngest child, Pamela doing this? I was raised to be better than this. Educated in the Catholic parochial school system, college-bound, and geared for success. Small tears began to roll down my face as I wiped them away, careful not to smudge my make up.

The client peered out of the window noticing me in my jeep. I took a deep breath and then another one. I closed my eyes and began to form a vision in my mind to focus on. I saw my son with new clothes on. I saw my stack of bills on my kitchen counter getting smaller. I saw the eviction notice torn into small pieces as I wrote a check for my rent. Then I saw me smiling; I knew what I had to do.

Reaching for the door and plastering a fake smile upon my face,

I walked towards this old, stinky, fat white man. He had requested a hand job for $150 or a blowjob for $250. I went for the hand job. Whitey flopped down in the chair behind a cluttered desk. He asked me to model for him. Turning around in a slow circle, I felt his eyes on my backside. They felt stuck on my ass. Rolling my eyes out of his view, I turned towards him with a Chester Cheetah-like smile on my face. I kneeled between his legs, looking up at him and thinking that his exposed dick looked like a piece of raw bacon. He began to rub his dick, stroking it up and down. Then he reached out to touch the side of my face with the same hand that he used to caress his now two-inch hard-on. Instantly, my mind went to how can I sterilize my face?

He said, "Blow on it, baby, make me come." I leaned in, to blow wind on his dick and began to caress it with one hand as I fondled his pink hairy balls with my other hand. He came squirting on my shirt, below my chin and all over my fingers. I continued to stroke him up and down as he moaned, head tilted back and eyes closed. He continued to reach for my face as I did a slow boxer bob and weave routine not wanting to be touched by him again. Three minutes of work. I was so ashamed, I felt dirty and so very low. I've never wanted nor had any desire to be touched by a white man. But, there I was, touching him, giving him pleasure.

This deepened my hatred for Chino. I just needed a little help from him. I would have been thankful for $100 a month. He was flashing, wining and dining while his son and I were taking a real live beatin'. It had my head all messed up. But, for my son, I'd do anything.

I blocked out the rest and focused on a "come-up" to help my son and me. I went on seven more out-calls: A well-to-do white businessman, a sixtyish black man in a wheel chair, another who was blind that only wanted to eat me out, a couple that wanted me to watch as they had sex, a diabetic with both legs amputated who asked me to climb into his bed and ride 'em like I was a cowgirl, and an elderly white man that wanted to be called "massah." I opted to call him "mister," and he just flipped up my skirt, got on top of me, fucking me, calling me "Kizzy." This sicko tipped me one hundred dollars. My last call was a young white doctor that had been poppin' pills and drinkin' Vodka. All he wanted to do was have me model and discuss all the dates I had. I made up sordid details as he jacked himself off.

Tony liked me because I had my own transportation. In four hours, I made $1,200. The first date was the hardest. I just rolled with the flow from there on out. I paid my late rent, electric bill, and got my VCR out of pawn. Then I rented a video, went to the grocery store, and finally had food in the refrigerator and freezer at the same time. I prepared a nutritious meal, picked up my son, and was back home by 4:45 p.m. We ate, and then I gave him a soothing, fun bubble bath. I took another shower to clean off the filth of those *John's*, and by 8:00 pm. we were playing. I had a lot less stress and gained a good night's sleep. I slept too good.

The following morning, I took the baby to daycare. Around 9:00 a.m. I called Tony, and it was on again. With more confidence, I requested more tips. I made $1,600 in about four hours. I paid my phone bill to zero, got cable TV, and got other backed up expenses in order. I purchased some much-needed clothes for my son. It felt so good to be able to *do* something. I even got a car wash, courtesy of a full tank of gas. I was surviving.

On the third day of this new career, I learned about "In-Calls." The girl or guy (yes men do this also) obtains a hotel room and waits for the client to come to him/her. Not quite familiar with this aspect of the business, I was nervous.

In order to save money, I shared a hotel room with a girl named Beverly. Beverly worked for Tony's service, which I guess made her my co-worker. She was a white girl that made over two grand a day. Beverly had the typical white-girl look. She had dyed blonde hair with a perm that she spent endless hours scrunching with hair spray. Her eyes were a beautiful green, and she constantly sprayed her body with that instant tan stuff in a can. Beverly was on the short side with very large breasts. We just clicked! Beverly had a six-year-old daughter she was supporting.

It was amazing to see how easy sex sold. The old adage that "prostitution is the world's oldest profession" is true. And it will always be. Simply put, Sex Sells: Fat Sex, Skinny Sex, Black Sex, White Sex, Male-to-Male Sex, and Yellow Sex-it all sells. This was my third day of work, but I was bred to be an entrepreneur. No one can pay me better than I can pay myself. I wanted my own. I informed Beverly of my plan to open my own service. She looked me straight in the face, took a drag on her cigarette and said, "Hell, go for it! Send me some calls, I'll work for ya." Bet! One employee.

I took the money I made that day, went to Cellular One and bought a pager. Along the way, I bought a newspaper. Then I went to the Columbus Dispatch and placed a help wanted ad in the adult section directed to my pager number.

Later, I picked my son up from daycare and headed home to make a voice message for my pager. In my most professional voice, I recorded, "Hi, are you looking to make lots of money with a safe, reliable and stable service? Well, you've called the right place. I am hiring models for full service sessions. Please leave your description, measurements and number, and I'll contact you for an interview. Please, no drug users. Thank you, bye."

Why I said no drug users was naiveté. The majority of women working for services have habits, not all, but a lot. They work to support their habit, their families, their man and *his* habit. There are a variety of reasons, yet the goal is the same: MONEY. I was learning more and more everyday. It was on-the-job training.

By 8:00 a.m. the next morning, the vibration of my pager woke me up. The message read full. Thinking, WOW! I told myself, go for it! This is my come-up. Chino always said to be for self because self-preservation was the nature of man, and I intended to survive.

I returned the calls and selected a variety of applicants. I set up twelve interviews at the Knight's Inn Hotel. I was surprised by the turnout, and they were surprised that I was a woman (most services are run by men). They also liked my professionalism. I was dressed in a sleek pantsuit, offering coffee and doughnuts. The response was great. I just held one open, informal interview. I had very good managerial skills acquired from my salon, so I communicated well. I explained my rules. Especially, the "no stealing rule." I kept it all very simple. After all, we were here to make money, not relationships.

I scanned the room with the mind and eye of a man. What would make me turn my head? What would make me spend to be with them? Experiencing Tony's service, I knew I needed a variety. I chose nine of the twelve girls. Three of them were hit! And if I were not so pressed to get paid, I would have taken my chances with these dogs to see just who in the hell would fuck with them. But I chose the best and began to qualify them for my purpose. Shapely, curvaceous, sensuous, child-like, innocent, well-groomed, easy listener, not too talkative were the qualities that gained these ladies acceptance to be my first employees. Some were experienced. Some were first timers. Only two had their own transportation. One young lady who was new to this business had her own transportation, no children and no habit. She was very attractive. She puzzled me. Why was she here? But I hired her and continued on. I wrote down all the girls' information, and I also changed their names to working names.

The half-black-half-Chinese girl, I named "China." China was absolutely beautiful with olive colored skin, an oval face, slanted coal black eyes and silky curly hair. She just had a lot of street in her. Every word out of her mouth was fly. She had an hourglass figure with an aggressive attitude, which I liked right away. I knew she could talk someone out of some money. I liked it in her. Problem was, she had a crack habit out of this world. China had a $1,000 a

11

day habit. China was up front and open about her habit and everything else about her. She said, "Stay out of my business, and I'll stay out of yours. I work 24/7, so let that be the reason you send me all the calls you want." Taking a liking to her was the reason that I bent my no drug rule. China was worth this violation.

Then there was Gabrielle. Gabrielle was very top heavy and statuesque. She was a young caramel tender with 44 double DD's. The men would love her. Also among the array of tempting treats whom I chose were: "Renaye," "Spice," "Sheela," "Toy," "Shy," "Chrissy," "Sugar," "Cinnamon," and "Pie." Pie was petite and very flat chested. She looked like she was twelve years old. The men would love her, too. Perverts!

When Gabrielle asked, "What's your name? I rolled *"Carmen"* off my tongue. It came from nowhere. From that day, I became Carmen, my alter ego. A totally different person from Pamela. Carmen was strong, emotionless and untrusting. Pammy, well, she was the opposite. Weak, emotional and trusting.

The interviews were over, and I asked them to report in by phone of their locations by 10:00 a.m. or pay a $25 fine.

Chino taught me so much. I knew the way you went into something was the way that you came out of it. Thus, I went in hard. I always kept in mind all the things that I had learned from him. Lessons of the streets. Rule #1: Get Paid; Rule #2: Don't trust nobody, not even yourself; Rule #3: Stay Free. It was time to accept the fact that he had raised me as far as the streets were concerned. He turned me out. But now it was time to raise myself.

When they reported in, they were to give me their locations—hotel and room number for In-Calls and availability for Out-Calls. I also informed them of my work hours. Phones off at my house by 4:30 p.m. This was when I got off work, and I gave my time to my son. This disappointed them because they wanted more hours, more flexibility. China just wanted to work. She wanted 24/7, and her favorite saying was "Let that be the reason" I send her some calls.

Next, they asked about working for other services. I informed them that it was no problem as long as it did not conflict with my "calls."

We dispersed, and I went to the newspaper to place my ads for the following week. I placed one exclusively for African-American girls. It read:

"CARMEN'S BLACK MODELS"
Then one for:
"SUGAR & SPICE" they were my bi-sexual white girls who did one on one and threesomes, (Two girls, one guy).
Then one for the petite Cinnamon and one that said:
"A TASTE OF HONEY"

All the ads were listed with my pager number. I went home and changed the message on the voice mail. With jazz playing in the background, the new message was: "Hello and thank you for calling Carmen's. We offer full service sessions, $200 an hour, $150 for a half-hour. We cater to your every need and all of your wants. We want you to call 555-1212, come 555-1212, enjoy 555-1212. We are waiting." I had an extra phone line installed in my home so that they could call and I could arrange the dates. I knew they would not leave a number for a return phone call. The wife or girlfriend might answer or something.

It was important that the phone was answered, the dates arranged, and calls made to prepare the awaiting lady. I spent the evening playing with my son. The next morning the phone was ringing off the hook, so was the pager, which meant I was getting a lot of inquiries. Under normal circumstances it would have gotten on my last nerve, but today, it was music to my ears.

Each tone of the ringer filled me with excitement and a compelling desire to dance. I ignored it, got the baby dressed and off to daycare.

I returned home and prepared myself for a day of answering the

13

phone. Seven of the girls called in and gave me their locations. I had read up on the sex business and all the desires of men. Golden showers, balls in the butt, anal sex, titty fuckin', peep shows, you name it. Freaky desires. Normalcy was for the wives of my callers. Erotica was for the girls and men with a vivid imagination. If only the wives knew how much. If only they knew. So I began my first day on the job. The first day owning my new business, **"CARMEN'S ESCORT SERVICE."** I do believe it had a nice ring to it.

Chapter

TWO

"Hello, May I Help You?"

"Good morning," a masculine voice chimed.

"Good morning, May I Help You?"

"I'm Dave. What do you have, say, around 11:00 a.m. in the North End?" the caller inquired.

"Dave, I'm Carmen. I have Black girls and White girls. What's your pleasure today?"

"I'd like a blonde."

"Okay, I have a petite blonde. She's 5'3", 115 pounds. Her measurements are 38-24-36. Her name is Sugar and she's sweet. We have a special on DOUBLES today," I offered enthusiastically.

"No. I'll take Sugar at 11:00 a.m."

"Okay, please call me from the pay phone near the Continental Plaza. I'll instruct you from there."

"Bye."

"Thanks!"

"Hello, May I Help You?" I said to the caller in my most professional voice as if I were merely working for a large corporation and this was just another day at the office. -Click! This caller must have thought that he had the wrong number or they lost their nerve because my question was answered by a dial tone.

15

Ring…ring…

"Hello, May I Help You?" Click. Imagine being comfortable with annoying calls and people hanging up on you. The calls were coming in, my business was booming, and I was excited. I was making a come-up, and it felt good.

Ring…ring…

"Hello May I Help You?"

"Are golden showers in the forecast today?" a deep voice, thick with lust, queried.

"They sure are, from light rain to a thunderstorm. What's your pleasure?"

"I like it when it is a light drizzle," Deep Voice replied.

"On the east end of the city, you can experience this. Gabrielle is waiting, off Hamilton, near the Eastland Mall. Contact me from there, OK?"

"Thanks," he whispered.

How someone gets off getting pissed on is beyond me. But for $300, we will do it. Spinning a pencil around the notepad in my lap I answered my next phone call,

"Hello may I help you?"

"Your line stays busy. I've got jungle fever. I like them plump and juicy."

"Great, Big Guy, I have something special for you on the North end. Call me from there. Bye."

Click!

My pager was buzzing. I've always been told what a nice phone voice I have. So I added a hint of seduction to it. I figured, always put your best foot forward. So I gave the service my all. I thought of an idea for a tantalizing business card. The card cover was neon pink in color with a silhouette photo of a curvaceous female figure. This way the clients could keep my number with them, and I could pass them out. I also decided to place them on cars in parking lots wherever I went, just like I did my salon business cards. Hell, I may even place one in one of those fish bowls at a restaurant trying to get a free company lunch or something. I realized that I was at the lower end of the escort business. There were services out there charging double my price. But I'd do better when I could.

"Hello May I Help You?" I answered.

"Do you offer male-to-male?"

"NO!" -Click- Hmmmm… an idea.

Ring…Ring…

"Hello, May I Help You?"

"Who has the best head on her shoulders?" the caller asked, and I confidently responded, "Renaye, with her full lips, she definitely has the best head on her shoulders."

"Ok. I'm ready. Where?" I directed him to a business and residential area on the north side of Columbus known as the 161 area.

"What is your name?" I quizzed

"Steve."

"Great, Steve. Please call soon."

As the day continued, I thought about all the services I could offer. Maybe I should try, "Male-to-Male." I made a note to place that ad tomorrow. I was stuck in the apartment. I needed mobility, which meant a cell phone. In between rings, I called Cellular One, gave them bogus information, and it worked. They wanted a $500 deposit. "Damn! Phone don't fail me now. Keep ringin'. I need some loot!"

Ring...ring...

"Hello May I Help You?"

"Hi, it's Dave. I'm on 161."

"Great! May I have the number to the pay phone?"

"It's 555-7787."

"Okay, I will call back." The clients provided the pay phone number in order to determine proximity to the hotel. If they were at the particular pay phone, it was a sure call and they were only minutes away from the hotel. Immediately, I dialed the number to the hotel where one of my girls was waiting.

Ring…ring…

"Cross Country Inn." the receptionist answered.

"Room 112, please."

Ring…

"Hello," a voice whispered. Sugar was her work name and the name that she went by. I found it ironic. She said that her father gave her that name when he would climb into her bed at night. He started climbing in her bed at night not long after her thirteenth birthday. So, she had the callers calling her the same. Her father died of cancer, but she missed him greatly, despite him taking her virginity. This followed nights of sexually pleasing him, her father. Just hearing a man call her *Sugar*, reminded her of the same feel of love she got when her father stroked her hair, called her name, as he held her head tightly between his legs, giving him oral sex. When I met her and gave her this name, I had no idea of the story behind it. I saw her as Sugar because she had such a sweet personality.

"Sugar?"

"Yeah."

"Dave is on his way over. He's an hour."

"Thanks, Carmen."

Ring...ring…

"Hello, may I help you?"

"Carmen, it's Sugar. Dave is here. I'll call again."

"Be safe," I instructed.

"I will," she assured. I marked $75 in my ledger for my commission from sugar.

Ring…ring…

"Hello, may I help you?" Listening to China's voice, I trailed my phone cord with my finger as she began to talk.

"C, it's China. I have a problem."

"What's wrong, you okay?"

"Yeah, I'm okay but my client doesn't want to see me."

"Why?"

"Guess?"

"I don't have times for games, China."

"Let's just say our mothers are sisters."

"Huh? I'm not getting it. Just spit it out."

"I don't have a problem seeing him, but he has a problem seeing me."

"Ask him if he wants someone else."

"C, he's embarrassed.

"Why?"

"Because he's my cousin."

"Damn! Girl, we never know who will use our service, huh? That's is so funny."

"Yeah, I know, and my family talks about me being in the streets, and here they go getting some ass behind his wife's back. Imagine that."

"China, keep ya head up girl. I'll mark off that call and get you another one. Okay."

"Thanks, C."

"Bye."

Ring…ring..

"Hello, May I Help You? Yes sir, I have a China doll, she's beautiful. Your name is Peter? Okay, Peter, I'll call you back." I made the call back and then called China.

Ring…ring…

"Yeah?"

"Hi China, it's Carmen."

"Hey girl, I need some calls."

"Well one's on his way. His name is Peter."

"Let that be the reason, bye."

Ring…ring…

"Hello May I Help You?"

"Carmen, he's here."

"Be safe!"
"Let that be the reason." -Click!

I marked China for $75. Already, I had made over $1,000 in commissions. I kept immaculate records. This had my head on swole. I was envisioning loot stacked to the ceiling, and I liked what I saw.

Around 4:30 p.m, I headed to all the hotels to pick up my money from the girls. Every opportunity I made improvements. I encouraged the girls to stay at the same hotels and perhaps share rooms to split cost. When one had a session, the other excused herself. My interest and professionalism were really appreciated by the girls. As I began to make more and more money, I began to do fewer and fewer nails. How could I explain my ringing phone? I wanted to save enough money so my son and I could leave Ohio. I only remained in Columbus with the hope of returning to college and establishing some form of relationship for my son with his biological father. I soon realized it would not happen. So I just hoped for another plan. I'd keep the service until something else worked out.

Time really flies when you're making money. Fast money. I couldn't believe how open Columbus was to the sex market. The newspaper is vital in a sex market. The ads were very reasonable. There was lil' doubt that an adult entertainment section was a big money maker.

Then hotel managers were cooperative. Many wonder how a person becomes a criminal. We learn rules from our childhood years, from our family. Then, as we get older, society is our family. We tend to adopt its views and perception of law and order.

When a person sees that rules can be bent, this is encouragement. We all like to be encouraged, to be a part of things that foster our beliefs. Newspapers fully supported me and enabled me an outlet.

The hotels were accommodating to say the least. I found little discouragement in running my service. There were very few obstacles. I can't say if I was not allowed to place ads or rent hotels that I'd not have pursued this. As we all know, challenges can be used as motivation. I was a person who loved challenges. I had professional men as clients. The majority of them were white. Granted, our society is *racist*. However, in the sex game, inhibitions fade away. True, the white girls make more money. Perhaps, because there are more white callers. In fantasy, the forbidden is the desire. Many, many white men desire the dark meat. Just as many, many black men want the white meat. This was about fantasy, and I was determined not to be outdone.

On Tuesday, I hired a driver, a young Ohio State University student, for weekends. He drove the girls to Out-Calls and delivered my commissions. I paid him $20 dollars a call to ensure the girls safety. He was happy because it beat pizza delivery. Instead of delivering pizza, he delivered pussy.

I hired a new girl that could have been Mariah Carey's twin. I named her "Ashley," a half black, half Italian young lady that was totally confused. She wanted to be accepted as Italian, but was often referred to as a Dago. Then with the black community, the women hated her because of her beauty, and the men wanted her because of her beauty. Feeling unaccepted and often used, she turned to drugs. Her chiseled figure began with a 44DD bust line, bangin' backside, full brown eyes, ringlet curls of light brown, and full lips revealing a perfect smile. She was a big money maker. A big draw. Men love breasts, any size. But the bigger breasts were,the more popular, especially if they were real. Falsies did not get good points (I know, surprised me also). Clients loved her. On a bad day, she had twenty calls. I extended my hours to accommodate the calls, the girls, and my pockets. In the streets, in the hustlin' game, I'd soon learn that more was never enough.

I placed China and Ashley in the same room. It was a mistake. I didn't know Ashley was an addict. Well, she was. So, I had one who adored (girl) The Cocaine Pimp, and Ashley was in love with

Dog Food (Heroin) The Heroine Pimp. Two addicts. They became inseparable. Realizing that this was a lethal combination, I decided to play it cool. Had I attempted to separate them, it would have been a mistake. The common interest in getting high was stronger than any rule I could try to enforce. Due to the earning potential, they became my high stakes gamble, and they were worth the risk. Neither of them had a home. Their families turned their backs on them. Or, they turned their backs on their families. Depends on who is telling the story. They had misused their families so much that the ties were broken. In essence, we became sisters. I was like the big sister.

On Saturday mornings, I'd take the girls and my son to breakfast. We all began to lean on each other. I had isolated myself. It was just me and my son. So, I didn't mind the bonds we began to form. This is also when my life began to change.

I received a lot of calls for private parties. The businessmen would call for bachelor parties. I'd send Ashley and China. Soon, they started turning the clients out and on to drugs. Bizarre, but it happens.

Ashley and China had the same dope dealer. They'd page him, and he'd bring cocaine, crack and heroine to them. His name was G-Money.

One time I called the room, and the girls told me he was there. I'd heard so much about him from Ashley. How he had it goin' on and how he stopped by to see them and how he was fun to hang out with. G-Money also sold them hot items like clothing. He asked to speak to me. Reluctantly, I agreed and heard a soft baritone voice come through the phone.

"What's up Carmen?"

"Hi." The phone felt silent for a moment and then he continued, "When am I gonna meet you?"

"You know that's not possible. I don't do dates and I don't spend. We don't need to meet." I played this unknown short, 'cause I didn't know him. Why was this nigga trying to get to know me?

"How about lunch?"

"NO!"

"How about dinner?"

"NO!"

"OK, Ashley told me you like clothes. I want to show you some clothes." You can always break a woman down with the enticement of clothes.

"Oh, I'm interested, tell me more."

"You got some good game, Carmen. I want to talk to you."

"NO!"

"Are you looking for a partner?" he demanded and sounded a little aggressive, so I raised my voice an octave to counter his.

"NO!"

"Well, I'm going to leave some things with Ashley. Tell me how you like them."

"Why?"

"Anything for you, Carmen."

"Yes, you know game recognize game? What do you want?"

"Nothing but lunch." He got a smile out of me.

"Ok, I'll check out what you left and see how bad you want lunch." I hung up the phone and began to think of my next move.

The following day I went by to collect. G-Money had left me some very beautiful clothes worth over three grand. I was impressed as my eyes checked the labels revealing designer names, and my hands felt the soft fabrics of linens and silks, bringing back memories of Chino's gifts. After his road trips, my bed would hold piles of leather outfits, purses, shoes and pantsuits that he purchased for me.

Driving down Livingston Avenue, I got a page from Spice. I pulled into the Brothers Carryout, ordered a perch sandwich, bag of Grippo Chips and Tahitian Treat soda, and called Spice.

"What's up, Spice ?, it's Carmen." With a pissed-off tone, she deepened her voice, raised it and said, " Carmen, I don't think we should do all the fuckin' and you collect all the money. I think—"

I immediately cut her off, becoming defensive, "Hold up, wait a fucking minute."

She continue to try and talk, "No, I won't wait. I—"

"Look Spice, I said slow your roll, Boo, hold on." I placed my cell phone in my lap in case she continued to talk 'cause I wasn't trying to hear it. I swallowed the bite of food I had in my mouth, popped a chip in, and swallowed my drink as I began to think of how to handle this.

Now let's see, she feelin' herself 'cause she's made about two thousand today, and off that 2 grand, I'm getting eight hundred, and she has a problem. So, what are the choices? I can tell her to fuck off or I can try to silk it, cause she makes money for me. Do I want to miss out on my cut of what she makes? No, at this point, she's of value. But this disrespect shit got's to go. So, I gotta flip on her.

"Spice, okay, I was eating my lunch, but I understand you don't feel it is a fair cut. So, this is it, okay, we straight. Leave me what you want me to have and then go work for someone else."

"Now, Carmen I am not saying that. All I am saying is that I think you should get less because you ain't the one fuckin'."

"Spice, you can have an opinion, but you came to me for a job and for clients. If you think you can do better on your own, so be it. If you don't like how you getting treated, so be it. I hate to see ya go, but my fee is the same for all of you, and it ain't negotiable. You pay for my clients, and you pay to be hooked up. If you don't like my program, Boo, stop ringing my phone for dates. Now I gotta go. Take Care." Click! *I reversed that shit.*

I won't go get the money, and I won't send her no calls. She'll think about what I said. Her thoughts right about now are, can I get the same amount of dates without Carmen? Can I make two grand a day, almost everyday without Carmen? And, if Carmen, can afford to let go of eight hundred, then she getting money and plen-

ty of it. She'll still want to be down, or I just lost eight hundred bills. I ain't trying to lose no money. But in a matter of time, she will call me, and when I go collect, I will chin-check that Bitch about callin' my phone trying to front on me about Carmen's escort service.

The following week, Ashley called me.

"Carmen, G wants to talk to you."

"Put him on the phone."

"Hello, beautiful," he whispered into the receiver.

"What's up, G?"

"You like your clothes?"

"Yes, they were nice. Can you get me some 'Victoria's Secret' panties for the girls? I need a lot of them. At least 200."

"Damn! Why so many?"

"It is for a promotional sale."

"You a real business woman. I like that in you. Yeah, I'll get some for you."

"If you do this, I will meet you for lunch," I said teasingly.

"Promise?" G, asked desperately. I had him. He was open.

"I promise," I said thinking what good was the promise of a complete stranger.

The next day, I had over 300 pair of panties, including thongs, G-strings, leather and lace, many with matching bras, and camisoles. This shipment reflected the entire Victoria's Secret line and then some. I gave the girls gifts to show my appreciation. I also gave Ashley $100 for her referral, and I told them of my new promotional idea. We would sell worn panties to our customers for $20. They'd keep $10, and I'd get the other $10. I sold out of the scented panties in one day. Some men, just like dogs, love the scent of women's undies. Now I was really brainstorming and stacking dollars.

I met G in the Radian Hotel lobby for lunch. He was in his mid-thirties, brown complexion, dressed very trendy, and was sportin' a Polo outfit with fresh sneakers. Not bad looking, but not handsome either; average is the best way to describe him. Cautiously, I approached him with a nod of my head and spoke, "Finally, I meet G-Money."

Glancing me up and down, he replied, "Carmen, ooh, this is the day I have dreamed of."

"Playa, you are full of shit."

"That's right, I am. I wanted to talk with you about your escort service." He wanted to get in on my escort business.

From years of schooling, I basically ran a lot of drag (con) on him. "Oh, is that right, what you want to talk about?"

"I want to talk about you and get to know you. You said that you don't date, but you own a service. I know you date or dated. I mean how else would you know about a service?" He asked that question like he was a psychiatrist and I was his client.

"Well, whether I did or did not is none-ya. Feel me. So tell me about what you do?"

"I want to open an escort service or buy into yours. I think it is interesting, and I know that men will always purchase sex. I also work as a fence. I purchase stolen items and re-sell them." We continued to have small talk as we enjoyed sandwiches on the patio of the hotel, and I strung him along and said that I would consider going into business with him. To show his sincerity, he offered me $3,000 and promised $2,000 more. We were gonna buy a Sex Spa. A Sex Spa is an In-Call location that fronts like it is giving massages. But, they give much more.

I told him I'd like to be a "Fence." He informed me that he was the best fence in the city. He said that some of his customers and addicts were boosters. Seeing an opportunity and not being one to refuse a chance to make money, I listened intently and then I made my request known.

"G, I want in," I demanded.

"Certainly. We can work something out, Carmen."

So, this was my introduction into my next level of crime; becoming a "FENCE."

Chapter

THREE

The Boosting Game

A *Fence* is a person that buys stolen items. Any and every stolen item, from the kitchen sink to the car's spare tire. I, of course, wanted to be selective in the merchandise I purchased. But the name of this game is supply and demand. A fence will purchase items at a third or fourth of the ticketed price. They will then re-sell them at any cost, based upon supply and demand. I tried to offer half price of the ticket. In any event, whatever brings a profit. I also never purchased items stolen from someone's home. I only wanted store merchandise. I did try to hang on to some morals. I believed the purchasing of stolen items from another's home would do two things: One, support break-ins; Two, be an act of Karma, and my home would be burglarized. G-Money purchased any and everything. You could bring him a used baby's pacifier. He'd not only resell it, but ask for more of them.

I had made a nice savings on the escort service. With my savings, I purchased my fenced items. I normally purchased clothes and perfumes. The volume of stolen merchandise really amazed me. I came to realize that although these boosters were addicts, they had skills. I was purchasing on an average, three garbage bags of clothes a day and had no problems reselling my clothes. I sold to the girls, and I'd campaign out the trunk of my car at local bars, hair salons, and nightclubs. I was gettin' my hustle on out there makin' ends. It's a resource, outlet formula that equals success. Once you build a rep for having things, people find you.

Like myself, G tried to be a professional with his venture. Every afternoon, I'd have my driver pick up the clothes. I gave the girls first pick over the items. It was apparent the boosters favored Victoria's Secret, Neiman Marcus, Cache, 'Saks and Henri Bendals'. I wondered what the stores felt. Are these boosters *that* talented or aided by staff? How can they remove such items and not be detected?

Constantly, I was being cautious about pitfalls. Watching out for the vice squad with the service and now being careful not to sell to the wrong person catching a receiving stolen property case.

Chino introduced me to this hustle when we first met. He financed his drug hustle with proceeds from stealing clothes. It was on-the-job training. He also taught "Young Mike" this trade.

Young Mike was a shortie he found on the streets and added to the posse. He was excellent with smash and grabs. A smash and grab is a technique that is used on stores and small businesses. One move would be to drive a car into a freestanding jewelry store, smash the front door and then the cases. Then comes the grab move—grab all of value in sight. All this is executed in split-timing seconds. He had skills. Then there were times when Young Mike would just simply grab. He would walk into an upscale department store and simply grab a rack of clothes or empty a sweater case like Versace and run out of the store to an awaiting vehicle. Smash-and-grabs are after-hour moves, but on a humble or if it was 'sweet,' Mike would do it during store hours.

I miss Young Mike. True, he was in the streets pulling capers, but I knew more of him. I knew him at my kitchen table studying for his GED, trying to get an education that his youth outgrew. I knew him as someone trying to take care of his mother and crippled younger brother. At age 23, Young Mike took his life when living became too much for him.

When he was released from prison after serving two years for a petty case, he returned to society broke. His girl was doing another money-making mother fucker in his absence and searching for a come-up. Mike got involved with another crew from down South that was up north getting money, and after two months, found himself a co-defendant on their federal drug case. He got indicted, implicated on some he-say, she-say, they-say shit, placed on house arrest, and was, shortly later, found dead. The coroner removed one nine-bullet from his dome. A tall, handsome young man, who could have been anything in this world. It's like, when the streets get you, there is no getting out. Young Mike got out. He took himself out. Or so they say. Young Mike's story is buried with him. May he rest in peace.

Chino turned me out to every hustle he knew and would later invent. He would have me go into stores and pull the clerk to the side or gain their attention. This would allow the guys to *creep* and move the merchandise. They were good. These guys were great. Some say drugs impair your senses and make you paranoid. I am still astonished at the volume of clothes they moved. But, if I'm amazed, quite certainly the storeowners were also.

China loved the fact that she never had to leave her hotel room. Nor leave her crack pipe. She had it all delivered to her doorstep. Going to China's room was like visiting a crack house, and sometimes I would sit and visit with her, which was like sittin' in a crack house. I would wiggle and squirm the first ten minutes, trying to get comfortable in a place where drugs were plentiful and had thoughts and feelings that at anytime, vice could kick the damn door in.

I questioned China if this was her concern, and all she would say was, "Carmen, I wish any mother fucker would run up in my shit. They'd take me down handcuffed getting my last drag off my pipe. Besides, I don't keep enough dope. I smoke it too fast. The worst I am looking at is a drug abuse case. I can lie down for a weekend while I beat that shit. Sleep right through it if I have too."

Other times, she would call me and say, "Yo, C! Bring me some food." I'd say, "Is Chinese ok?"

She would then say "Let that be the reason." That meant cool. Eating Chinese food was the only thing China held onto related to her heritage. So, I'd take food to her, and we would sit and talk. I really enjoyed talking to her. She was very intelligent. She just had a lot of street in her. Plus, she got a fake hair weave. There was one I wished she would have gotten rid of. It was blonde. The blondest blonde I had ever seen.

"China, I hate your hair, girl. It is flaming."

"Don't worry, I keeps me a *'Hooker Helmet'* nearby," she squealed smacking her lips.

"A hooker helmet?" I inquired devouring my egg roll.

"Yes, Ms. Carmen! A wig. I have a black one. Check it out." She began waiving an object pulled from underneath the bed.

"I like it."

"I don't care if you tell the callers I'm blond or brunette. Just get me some calls."

"And you know I will."

She would show me all the items she purchased. I told her, "China, please take care of your things. You have purchased some nice stuff."

As I glanced around the hotel room, I saw a photo of a beautiful little girl who looked just like China. She had the same eyes of her Chinese heritage.

"China, she is adorable. How old is this princess?"

"Four."

"Girl, let that be the reason you stop smoking," I said sympathetically.

"My grandmother keeps her. My old girl is still mad at me for stealing her checks and for having my daughter in a crack house. I took a hit and was like "DAMN, this dope is DA BOMB!" I felt like I had to go take a shit. The next thing I knew, I was on the toilet and out came my daughter. She looked like a wet Chinese rat. She was so tiny and so pretty. I was scared. I called my old girl, and she took us to the doctor. I left the hospital to go get my friend, first name '*C*' and ends with a '*K*'. My old girl picked up the baby, and we've been at odds ever since."

"China, she really is precious, and I think she should be the reason you turn your life around."

"Look C, don't make me check you 'cause I respect you and all, but we live in this real world, and you out there just like me chasing the dollar. Just like I chase my highs that I'll never catch. I may be a crackhead, but I am far from sleep. You think I wanted this for my life? You think I didn't try the traditional route. Shit didn't work for me, so I got down for mine. Was dating someone I thought was special, and he enjoyed the fact that I got freaky in the bedroom. So much so, he bragged to his friends and told them all we did in the bedroom. One day, his friend stepped to me and offered me a C-note to sleep with him. I was so mad that my special friend told our bedroom business, that I took the nigga up on his offer with the hopes that he went back and told the guy I was dating. Sort of a punishment for telling our business.

Boyfriend had a lil' paper in his pocket and didn't mind spending. I sucked his dick like a lollipop and even gave him some back-door action. Had him sayin' my name and whose is it. Hmmm, instead of telling and me getting revenge on my dude, he kept it to himself and kept coming back. I kept fuckin' both of them. I would suck the one's dick, swallow his cum and then later that day, go kiss the other in the mouth. But they were calling me nasty. Shit, I was making them fuck each other on the down low. Eventually, the nigga fell in love with me, the neighborhood freak.

"That was when I began to see that niggas are tricks for some pussy, and then other shit happened in my life, experimenting with alcohol, drugs and I just got caught in the streets. My motto is Bitch Gotta Get Paid!

"I live by the smoker's creed. Our nights are our day, and the daytime is our night. We smoke all night for several days at a time. Carmen, I have been up for three days. I'm gonna eat this food, go into a crack comma sleep for about 12 hours, and hopefully be awaken by the ringing of my phone, a call from you with a date for me. Take a hit, pop in the shower and make my money by what I do best, flat backin'. Carmen, I see you stackin' that cheese. So, what is your excuse?"

China hit a spot I was not trying to feel, and when I didn't want to feel, Carmen came out. "Carmen, your son is so handsome." China continued.

"Thanks, China and I hear ya. Do ya hear me?" We both smiled and hugged each other. China and I, for some reason, saw a lot of things eye to eye. I looked over at her and said, "Alright girl, you've checked me. Now I got work to do. No time to sit around and complain. I'm about to go campaigning and get you some calls."

"Now, that is what I'm trying to hear, and this food is good as hell. I will be sittin' right here in this room waiting on my men."

As I was leaving, she was slammin' on her food and watching TV. I left and drove off in silence. I just kept telling Pammy to stop thinking and for Carmen to stay in control. Besides, I had to meet G for more clothes, which meant more money. I turned the music up loud and sang along to Tupac's "Keep Ya Head Up."

Six in the morning, someone's at my front door. It was my boys from New York, T-Love and his brother, Abdullah. I met these money getting hustlers through my friend Erik. Erik and I met at Ohio State University as freshmen. He was from New York, and I was from Detroit. We both became curious about each other due to the rep's both of our cities held. New Yorkers were known for being trendsetters, and the men were known for their jewelry, gold fronts, clothing, accents and money. Me, hailing from Detroit, and him, believing the women were known for their dressin', hairdos, game and taste in automobiles; we searched each other out to see if the stereotypes were true. Hangin out after class, he introduced me to his crew and two of which were T-Love and his brother Abdullah.

When they were in town, they would stop by to see me. They were "BALLERS." A Baller is a person who hustles by any means necessary. It's sort of hard to explain. But, it is a person who views life from a sink or swim perspective. They are just looking for a chance, waiting for a chance, and willing to take that chance when they get it. In the streets, there is a philosophy that says: everyone gets a chance. What will you do with your chance? Sometimes you get that thirsty person, and they try to take the next person's chance. Then they get out there and ball. Run full-court with their opportunity, whatever that may be, to the best of their ability. That's the basics of a Baller.

I also sold them clothes for their girls, wives, or babies' mamas. I always got a little jealous as I watched them fuss over the clothes. They took time to select the perfect ones. Here I was, somebody's baby's mother, and no one cared. I only had myself to depend on. Here I was in the streets scramblin' for me and mine. Their BM's (Baby Mamas) were home safe. Every time Pammy went soft, Carmen came out hard. *"Fuck it, just tax them. Stack your own dollars."* So that's what I did. Carmen used every opportunity and created new ones. One of my escort service clients had a M3 BMW for sale. Peter said, "For you, Carmen, $15,000 cash."

So I stepped to T-Love about it. "Yo, T, I know where you can get a nice BMW. Cash, no questions and in whatever name you want." I'd learned long ago that "BALLERS" always looked for the easiest, less hassle-free way out. They used my house, phone and my car. Ultimately, Carmen had had enough. T-Love was like, "No Doubt! I want it."

"He wants $18,000 for it, plus give me $500 to do the title and tag registration." I also knew someone who worked at the Auto

Bureau registration. It is all about who you know.

I set the deal up with my client. Come to find out, my client worked at the car dealer auction. So he got the car for a bargain. This was another valuable connect, so I was determined to make good on this sale. I wanted to buy my mom and myself a new car one day. A shiny mother fucker rollin' right off the showroom floor.

T-Love had me 18 G's by nightfall. I spoke with my client and proudly told him, "I got $12,000 today. All cash."

"DEAL!" Peter screamed.

Bet! I made a $6,500 profit. Who ever said the middleman gets the worst deal? Plus, I was able to sport the car for a week. They automatically assumed that I would keep it, and it would be safe with me. I never went anywhere.

I began to resent the blatant disregard they had for me. See, at first you try to be a trooper and do all you can do for the team, doing your part going that extra mile, etc. Then you realize that it is not appreciated. Chino did this all the time with the fellas.

They just assumed I'd be there and available. I guess I had a major attitude. But only time would take care of it. Carmen was not having it.

I'd read in books how children could be so traumatized that an alter personality takes over to protect the child. Granted, I was not a child, but my mental state was child-like: *trusting*. I had been traumatized in my own way.

Betrayal is a very big pill to swallow. Two very important things in my life were gone: My Chino and My Salon. I felt like I had no control. I am learning that you always have control of your life by doing the best you can with what you have. What will be will be. God got it like that. When God says *"Be"* it is. And everything does happen for a reason. I would grow through this. Only way I can explain Carmen was that she appeared and saved me. She took over my life. Carmen had plans. Big plans she'd only just begun. Unbeknownst to Pammy.

I picked up my cell phone from my Coach bag and answered.

"Hello, may I help you?"

"Hello, sweetheart." G's voice faded in over background rap music.

"Hey, G, what's up?"

"Wanna meet for lunch?"

"No!"

"I wanna talk to you. I'm in a bad mood and need someone to talk to." His voice had a hint of sincere depression.

"In that case, I'm available. Where?"

"The Cooker Restaurant at 12:30 p.m."

"No, 1:30 p.m." *He don't run shit!*

"Ok, 1:30 p.m. Carmen, you don't give a brother nothing, do you?"

"Nothing he doesn't earn. Just like I got to earn it, so does the next man. I'll see you at 1:30 p.m."

I went to collect from the girls, and at 1:30 p.m., I was running late. So What! "You press hoes and clothes. You don't press me." I laughed. My Chino used to say this all the time when I tried to press him about things. As I pulled into the restaurant parking lot, there was G waiting in his champagne colored Honda Accord, rims sittin' on 20's, with the music playing.

"Hey, beautiful, you're late." He raised his sleeve, displaying his Rolex diamond studded watch. And for flossin' fun, I raised my arm displaying my diamond studded Ebel watch and said, "I know, I know, I had to make some stops."

"How are the girls doing?"

"That's a $2,000 question. Where is the rest of my money?"

"Come on, let's go in, That's what I want to talk with you

about." We walked into the restaurant and patiently waited for our turn to be acknowledged.

"Two for lunch?" asked the restaurant host.

"Yes. Thank you," I whispered.

We were seated near a window. Gazing out, I playfully said, "G, I am starving like Marvin." I noticed he was not his usual self.

"What's up? I like this place. It has fast service. Here comes our waiter. We must look hungry," I said laughing aloud.

"May I take you order?" the polite waiter asked.

"Yes, I'll have the lasagna and salad with a glass of your house white wine."

"And you, Sir?" Turning to G awaiting his response.

"I'll have a very tall glass of your best Cognac," G replied rubbing the sides of his face. That's it? Normally G, gets his eat on. As the waiter left, I kept my eyes focused on G's face. We had grown together, so I knew his moods. G and I basically came up together on different teams, but we watched each other grow. Over a short time span, I watched him go from a Honda Civic to an Accord. He watched me go from a white Jeep Cherokee to a black Range Rover and Silver BMW. In the streets you watch people grow by their gear and their rides.

"Carmen, my connect got knocked. I never told you this, but I work for someone else." *You frontin' fake-ass nigga.*

He continued. "Well, I had my own 'girl' connect, but he got knocked. I didn't do much with him, but what I did allowed me a lil' more freedom. I work for this dude named Jay-Jay. I push Heroin for him, and he pays me."

Just to break the mood, I said, "Oh, so you on commission. You a sales clerk." I laughed, but this was serious. "Damn, G, it is not like you will starve. You still have the Boosters."

"No, not really. They work for drugs. They want to unload and score all in one stop, ya know."

"Yeah, I hear you. It is all about service, convenience and another hit. Just give me one more hit!" He still didn't smile. Ain't shit funny when you on the verge of broke.

"I'm gonna lose them, C. I got bills. I don't know what to do. Can I get my $3,000 back?" I could not believe my ears. Next, he looked me dead in my eyes waiting for a response. I leaned into the table and replied through gritted teeth.

"Hold up, this ain't no refund counter. You want that, then go to Wal-Mart or someplace." Time for one of my timeless lectures.

"First, stop all that whining," I demanded. "You've totally flipped on me. Where G at? 'Cause Gregory is trying to fold like a card table? Money don't make you, you make money. Remember this! I gotta go to the bathroom. I'll be right back."

I excused myself, and as I walked from the table, I heard Carmen in my head. *Look, game is sold not told. Remember the price you paid for it. This is an opportunity, so take it. Fair exchange ain't robbery. This shortie's looking for a sponsor, so sponsor his ass 'cause he ain't getting his money back. He ain't your friend. Ain't no friend shit in this. You already know that, don't forget this. You down for Yo Crown, fuck da rest.*

"OK, OK, can I pee now?" My mind was really starting to play tricks on me. I was really talking to myself. Yes, it is normal to talk to yourself. But, I was answering myself also." *G, is a wimp. Who doesn't have problems? Get in line. He is crying because the next man really was "making" him. That's why I chose to help myself.*

I returned to our table and cleared my throat. "Ok, G. Explain to me what you need and what you are trying to do."

"Well, I was getting an ounce of powder, and I'd rock it up and sell it to geekers. Slang me some rocks."

"Okay, how much do you pay for an ounce?" *I don't know what*

I'm talking about, but he will never know. "Anywhere from $950 to $1,200, it just depends on my plug. You know how it is." *No, I don't.*

I took another deep breath and responded confidently, "I'll see what I can do for you. I'll contact my people on it and get back. Now do you feel better?" He slowly nodded as I continued, "Now order 'cause you ain't getting none of my food."

Finally, we both smiled.

Chapter

FOUR

Ring...ring...

"Hello, May I Help You?"

"Hi, Carmen."

"Hi, whom am I speaking with?" Wondering who this was getting too comfortable with me.

"This is George. I've been a very bad boy." I was relieved to hear one of my favorite clients that I call "George."

"Yes, George, you *have* been very bad. I want you at Toy's hotel room in ten minutes or you'll really be in trouble."

"But I can't make it in ten minutes. I need twenty minutes." He pleaded getting into the role-play of his session.

"NO! You be there in ten minutes, up North on 161 at the Cross Country Inn in room 212—or else. Now go!" -Click!

Toy also worked as a dominatrix. George was an excellent and generous client that liked to be dominated. He was a very successful investment banker with a prominent financial institution. He got pleasure from being dominated. He liked to play house and would portray the child in need of correction. He never touched Toy, and she was never allowed to touch him. She only used her whip, belt or paddle. At the end of her session, George would masturbate to satisfaction.

Ring...Ring...

"Hello, May I Help You?"

Click! I reminded myself to call Toy and tell her George is on his way before another call came through.

Ring… Ring… Ring…

"Cross Country Inn," a scruffy voice answered.

"Room 212, please."

"Hold on."

Ring… Ring… Ring….

"Hello?"

"Hi, Toy. It's Carmen."

"Hi, Carmen."

"George is on his way over, and he has been a very bad boy. So, give him what he is looking for."

"Carmen, I'm getting uncomfortable seeing George. The last session, I beat him so bad that it scared me."

"What's up with George?"

"C, he likes it rough."

"Girl, if it ain't rough, it ain't right for him. Just complete this session, and I'll find him a replacement. He really likes you Toy. What does he look like?"

"I know, I like him too, Carmen. He is sorta scrawny looking. Very pale in color like he never sees the sun. Black rimmed glasses, short curly hair, very conservative in his dress, and rather thin. He's fun, and I get rid of my frustrations."

"Then there are the tips." The tips always made the session go better. An incentive.

"Carmen, I know, it's just—let me see how this session goes. Maybe I'll keep him."

"Be sure to let me know so I can find someone else and get them the equipment for his sessions. I'll beat him myself for the money."

"C, you are wild."

"Yeah, I have a wild side too. I'll let you go. He will be there soon, and remember, he is late no matter when he arrives. Here's a new punishment for him. Have him drink a lot of water and make him hold his urine. Be creative. Use those devices."

"Okay, C, I'm waiting for him."

"Great! Later, bye!"

Ring…ring…

"Hello May I Help You?"

"Carmen, this is Toy. George is here."

"Good, I'll mark it. Have fun."

With a smiling voice Toy responded, "I will. I don't know about him."

"Call me when he leaves, and I'll get you some regular calls."

"Thank you, Carmen."

"Bye!"

Ring…ring….

"Hello May I Help You?"

"Carmen, this is Gabrielle."

"Hi Gabby."

"I have a problem."

"What's up?"

"My client is still here, and his time is up."

"Wait, let me check. Mmmmmh. Yeah, it is up. They never stay the full time."

"I know. Well, he hasn't—you know what yet. And I'm tired."

"I guess so," I said smiling.

"This is serious, C. He wants his money back."

"Whoa! This is serious. Is he threatening you?" I began to search Gabby's voice for seriousness in her phone call. Also trying to decide what I could do feeling helpless on the other end of the phone line.

"No, but he's not happy."

"Are you uncomfortable?" Feeling out her level of fear would

41

help me determine what advice to give her.

"Yes."

"Gabrielle, are you dressed?"

"Partially."

"Tell him he can have his money back, and I'll still pay you for this call."

"Hold on…C, he doesn't want it. He wants service."

"Put the money on the bed."

"I can't…"

"Did you hide it?"

"Yes."

"And you don't want to retrieve it?"

"Yes."

"I understand. Let me check my book. One second. Gabby, Renaye is in the same hotel. Listen, tell him I'll send someone else down to the room to complete his session."

"Hold on. No, he wants me. *JACK RUBY*". Our code word for trouble.

"Gabby, you will have to place the phone down and hit the door. Renaye is in room 160, and I'm ringing her room on my other line now. Hold on." I placed her on hold and called Renaye's room.

"Renaye, go get Gabby in room 180 "Jack Ruby." –Click-

"Gabby, she's on her way. Hit that door and call from Renaye's. She is coming for you. He is not a maniac or you'd know by now. When you leave, he will too. Trust me. Then you will come back later and clean your room up. I'm sending the driver for you both. I'll move you to another place. Gabby, are you ready?"

"Yes."

"HIT THE DOOR NOW!" I found myself yelling at the top of my lungs.

Clang! The phone falls and there is yelling. "Please God protect her."

Ring…Ring…

"Hello, May I Help You?"

"Carmen, you paged me?" the driver asked anxiously.

"Yes, go get Renaye and Gabby ASAP! It's a Jack Ruby. They are at the Cross Country Inn. Take them to the Hampton Inn, get them settled and call me."

"No problem. Peace!"

-Click!

Ring…ring…

"Hello, May I Help You?" Answering the phone the receiver was filled with silence. The silence was finally broken with hard breathing. "Carmen, this is Renaye, and I got her," she said breathing hard.

"Good girls, hold on, I'll call her room to see if it's clear. Renaye, the coast is clear, so pack up everything, get her things, and the driver is on his way to move you. Be ready! Call me."

"We will."

"Bye!"

Ring…Ring…

"Hello May I Help You?"

"I WANT MY MONEY BACK!" An angry male voice yelled.

"We tried that and you did not cooperate. Use another service." I furiously slammed down the phone. Click-!

Ring…Ring…

"Hello May I Help You?"

"BITCH!" - Click!"

Just another day on these phones. This was happening with greater regularity. It made me think about getting out of this. That was close.

Thank you God for keeping Gabby safe.

Chapter
FIVE

I found me a luxurious condo to rent on the northwest side of the city. I always admired and drove past it when I would go to the Designer Shoe Outlet, and I told myself that one-day I would live there. *One day* finally came and there was a sign out front that said "For Rent." This was rare, because in this area, condos sold well and were seldom rented. They were very reasonably priced with a six-figure ticket, considering all it offered. The unit included two master bedrooms, a sunken living room with wood-burning fireplace, and gourmet kitchen. It had a finished basement with laundry. This place was nice. I received lots of sunlight because of the skylights throughout the condo. Plush carpet of emerald green relaxed my feet as I entered my front room. Then followed by white marble tile that led me to my enclosed patio with French doors. It was not bad, not bad at all for a come-up.

T-Love was staying with me as he usually did and still hustling. We were in my den when T approached me.

"Pammy, this guy I do business with is going to stop by."

"This is my home. How are you gonna bring someone to my home?"

"Calm down. He's good people, he really is. Too late to stop it." Shit, I guess I had to let T-love have his way. He'd done enough

44

favors for me, and we were like brother and sister, arguing, sharing secrets and playing cards late at night talking shit. Yeah, in the streets he was becoming that nigga, and he was my boy, for sure.

I learned the hard way. You must roll with the flow and do the best with what you have. I was upstairs getting dressed, when I heard the chime of my doorbell. T-Love let someone in. I assumed it was his friend. Moments later, I heard my son's laughter. I came downstairs, and that's when I saw *him* playing with my son. My son was laughing like he only does with me. Plus the guy was very handsome. He was tall, thick and tempting. His mere presence reminded me of Chino. The way he stood, self-assured, shoulders back and looking you in the face when he spoke. That is how my Chino was, a dead-in-the-eye kinda guy. The shapes of his lips had the look of softness and made you imagine the feel of them on the sides of your neck. The way he shifted his weight back and forth from one leg to another was something else that Chino did all the time. This motion gave you the impression that he was impatient or ready to go somewhere. I wondered if his lips hid a set of perfect teeth like Chino had?

♥

"Out? Please Chino, don't leave, you just came home." I ran to block his exit. He began to push me aside.

Giving me a grimacing look he spoke, "Every time I look at you I think of you and Erik. Of all the niggas in the city, why did you need him for a friend when I was doing my bid?"

"What are you talking about? I didn't have any friends because you wouldn't allow it. So, when you were away, he was just some-one to talk to." Tears began to well up in my eyes from the pain of the exchange of words. This was not our character, not how we related to each other.

Chino, tightened his grip on my arm and continued, "Fuck that! Did you think I wasn't getting out? You were supposed to stick to my program and wait. Did you think I wouldn't find out that you was fuckin' that nigga? You just like the rest of these gold-diggin' ass bitches. Pooh, you will not get another dime. You've booked yourself. I do more for you than you can do for yourself. I taught you finesse. I clothe you. I take care of you. I made you. Look at those jewels on your fingers, I put them there. Look at this house, you can't even pay the damn light bill, let alone the phone bill. Bitch, I put you in this place. If it wasn't for me, where would you be?"

Those words cut into my heart like a knife. Chino had never called me out of my name. He knew I was a virgin when we met and that I had never been with anyone but him. We built TCP together. What type of shit was he on?

"How in the fuck can you say some simple shit like that? I have never been with anyone but you. Can you say the same? Chino, you went to prison, and I was left out here all alone. None of your crew would help me. And mother fucker, you came home from the penitentiary with everything that you left with. Not one lock was changed, not one phone number changed, your clothes hangin' where you left them. I put your precious cars in storage, visited you twice a week. You came home to all your loot. Every stashed dime. Nigga, what? I kept money on your books. I sent clothing boxes, food boxes in your name and any other nigga's name you gave me. I accepted the collect calls and made three-way calls for you and all them other sorry ass-niggas you met up in there.

Why are you doing this to us? Chino, be strong for us. I need you. Erik was just my friend. You know we went to school together..."

Cutting off my words, he pressed harder to get past me. "Pooh, that nigga getting money in the streets just like me, and you should not have been fuckin' with him like that. Save that drama for your momma. Them tears is because your ass is cut off. You on your own. I can't take it anymore. Besides, I am in love with someone else."

The pushing to leave and his resistance to my insistence that he stay was all removed. Once leaning against each other and talking, me pleading with him to stay, him pushing to exit the door, his words brought silence to our luxurious home. And we both stood straight up as if a drill sergeant yelled "attention." The words sobered my mind, and I really looked at my Chino for the first time that night and noticed hickeys on the side of his neck and exposed parts of his chest. My mind drew a blank as I felt the blood rush to my face. I wanted to rip his shirt off and examine his dick, but the obvious was clear. He had been fuckin' someone else.

"What, Chino, what did you say? You said you're in love with someone else?" I raised my hand and smacked the shit out of him.

♥

At the sight of him, there was a flutter in my heart. I thought my heart was frozen.

"Hi. My name is Delano." His eyes roamed my body from head to toe. Delano began looking into my eyes until I could not hold the stare any longer. I was feeling super self-conscious, wanting to be as attractive to him, as he was to me. Blushing inside, I felt as if though I was standing before him in the nude. I began to tingle inside, holding onto whatever words were about to come out of his mouth. With my heart beating faster than an addict's after a hit, I believed that God has placed before me the man of my dreams. T-Love eagerly said, "And this is Carmen."

"Hi. Umm…T, I want to talk to you now that you're back in town for the weekend. It is really important."

"A'ight, no problem. My boys and me gonna crash in the family room for a couple of days."

I interrupted. "I need to go get my hair done. Can you watch the baby?"

"The baby?" He turned looking at me with surprise.

He's about to get put out. "Yes, the baby!"

"Uh, How long?" T asked irritably.

"Three hours max." I held my hands as if in prayer.

"Well, that's cool. Me and the 'lil man will watch the Playboy channel."

"No way!" My mind raced to the fact that T-Love would be irresponsible with my son. I had an expression of concern on my face.

"Nah. We will take a nap," T smirked as he looked over at Delano and asked can you drop Carmen off?" T-Love continued to control the room and he turned to me and said, "Carmen, I might need to make a run, so I'll take the baby with me."

"What type of run with my son?" I did the sister-girl routine and placed my hands on my hips.

"No, it is not what you think. I had something made by a jeweler for my wife the last time I was here. It's supposed to be ready for pick-up. So, I may have to just run and pick it up. So, Dee, can you give Carmen a ride?"

Dee and I both looked of surprised, but Delano casually said, "Sure. No problem."

Now this will be interesting. We walked over to a very ugly hooptie. A hooptie is a car that is on its last leg. This car definitely qualified as one. It was silver in color with dents on every side. The passenger door stuck as he attempted to open it gracefully. None of the tires matched, and the rims were non-existent. It didn't look like it would get us to point B. "Don't be laughing at my car or I won't let you in," Delano said jokingly.

I thought, well, a sense of humor. I had gotten to the point of constantly amusing myself. I had to focus hard on motivation because of the pain inside of me. Most days I laughed to keep from crying. I hated the streets, the constant lies, and mind games. You could never forget that your life was in danger all the time. I was making some money, but it was not enough to be out of skid-row reach. So, I had to keep stackin' dollars. I didn't want to get hurt out here in the game, especially since my past drama, I wouldn't. Then, I couldn't imagine life without my son or doing time behind bars. Noticing the manicured lawns that surrounded my neighborhood, I had the urge to knock on the doors of these homes and ask the question, "What do y'all do for a living (for real) or What kind of job you gotta have to live in a place like this?"

As we rode, I thought of my Chino and realized all he went through to provide for us. You know what they say, unless you walk a mile in someone else's shoes, you may never understand all they go through or are going through.

Well, many nights, Chino and I would talk and talk. Chino was so wise. He would use stories and parables to teach me many life lessons. He shared his experiences and his pain. One of the many memorable stories that he shared with me was one about the loss of a friendship. Chino was around eight or nine and was playing with a kid from a supportive and financially secure family. During one of his playtime visits, Chino decided to remove something from the home that did not belong to him. In other words, he stole from this kid's home. As a punishment, the parents of the kid forbade him from playing with Chino. Chino related how painful this was for him and how his actions were definitely not worth the loss of his friend. His lesson was that you weigh the consequences of your actions. Nothing is worth the loss of a true friendship. I also was learning everyday that all that glitters wasn't gold. Now I was beginning to make sacrifices and overcome the same challenges to provide for my son. I was entering another level. The same level that sealed our fate.

"Carmen…Carmen! You are in another world. Can I give you a penny for your thoughts?" I snapped out of my thoughts and answered his question.

"No. Just daydreaming."

Staring out of the small Honda window he continued, "Are you married?"

"Why?" I snapped defensively. *Do you want to marry me? Did you know that I was almost married, scheduled to be married two months before the drama?*

"Because I want to know if you are single."

"You are very direct."

"I believe honesty is always best, and distrust is the number one reason relationships fail."

"Well, I'm just getting a ride from you, and I *honestly* need to get my hair done."

We both laughed. We just fit so easy like a puzzle piece, like we had known each other forever. I hadn't felt this comfortable with anyone since I met Chino years ago. Delano was handsome and had beautiful eyes. Not beautiful because they were another color besides brown. But they were beautiful because they were deep brown, very full with a sparkle. The eyes are the mirrors of the soul. I wonder what I really saw in his eyes. He was so much more than outward appearance. His vibe just felt right to me.

"Hey, that's a nice reggae tape," I whispered.

"Don't tell me you like reggae."

"Yes, I do."

"They have a reggae spot here open late on Fridays and Saturdays. You want to go tonight?"

"Dee, it sounds good, but no thanks."

"NO?"

"Yes. Have you not been told *no* before?"

"Yes. I have, but when it is something that I want, I won't take no for an answer."

Time to change the topic. "Where are you from? You drive like a maniac? As I clutched the non-existent door panel, he glided the corner with one hand and replied, "Brooklyn."

"I knew you drove like a wild New Yorker."

"What do you have against New Yorkers?"

"Nothing," I said defensively.

"Do you want me to come and pick you up?" He pulled beside the curb in front of the salon.

Reaching for the door, I responded, "No, I'll get a cab or call T-Love for a ride. Thanks."

"You can page me if you need a ride."

"I'm okay, really. Thanks. Drive safely."

I gave him a wave, then dashed across the street already twenty minutes late for my appointment. I was getting my hair done around the way on Long Street. I was under the hair dryer reading a magazine when my hairdresser came over. Tiki said, "I think you're finished and you have a phone call." My first thoughts were of my son. T-Love would have paged me, though. As I walked to the phone, I checked my pager, no messages from T.

"Hello?"

"Hi, Carmen, almost finished?"

"Who is this?"

"You know who this is. I'm on my way to pick you up, so don't call anyone."-Click!

He had the nerve to hang up on me. Inside it felt good to be waiting for someone to come get *me*. My hair looked great, every strand in place. I decided to put some make-up on while I was waiting, but changed my mind because I wanted a man to accept me as I was, this time around. *If he can take me at my worst, then he will appreciate me at my best.* I felt good about myself.

Delano walked over admiring my hair and said, "Carmen, you look good girl." His entrance into the salon caused a quiet rush and neck turns in his direction. The patron seated to my right leaned over and whispered into my ear, "Girl, where did you get him at? He got a brother? Is that a sock in his pants or what?"

I blushed and responded to Delano, "Thanks." I turned to my hairdresser and asked, "Tiki, how much I owe you?"

Unexpectedly, Delano said, "Don't worry I got ya. How much Tiki?" With my peripheral view, I noticed women applying lipstick and walking, no, sashaying past Delano to the magazine rack attempting to gain his eye. However, this gentleman kept his eyes on me. Tiki did a pretend calculation of my bill.

She taxed him. She charged him $95. Delano flipped out a crisp $100 bill and added a $50 on top of it for a tip. Tawanna and Tiki gave each other the eye and looked at me like, "Damn, can I be you for a day?"

That is how hairdressers are. Tameka (Tiki) Baytops, hair designer from Jersey, was the best stylist in town, and she knew it, and you paid for her expertise. She cut and styled your hair like no other. I have tried to figure it out. I even purchased the same sort of hair comb she uses trying to duplicate the style at home. Tiki styled your hair so pretty with soft, flattering looks that frame your face and compliments your personal look. My appointment was standing twice a week. Tuesday and Saturday's, a guaranteed three-hour wait. Insanity, but you gotta do what you gotta do. During my wait, it was business as usual. I would sit in the reception area, telephone and notepad in hand, answering calls and arranging dates. G, would come up to the shop and bring me lunch; then we would sit in the parking lot rappin' about getting money while I sported a shower cap getting my locks deep conditioned. I definitely did not do split ends, dry hair, or curls out of place. G would say, "Damn, Carmen, it takes all this to look good? You need to get a fro or some damn braids. You live up in this piece."

Beauty is pain sometimes. Then, you got the absolute best fashion tips from her assistant, Tawanna (*ghetto-ass name*) from Detroit. So, during your wait, she would try to sell you something or up you on the latest styles. Tawanna would shampoo you in some Gucci boots and Prada jeans. She kept you laughin' while you simply waited on your turn in Tiki's chair. There were some perks. Plus, if they smelled drug money, they upped the prices. Who could blame them? Everyone wants a piece of the pie. If Dee wanted to be Big Bank, then be Big Bank.

"Delano, thanks for my hair. You didn't have to."

"I know I didn't, but I wanted to do it. Your hair needed some help girl." We smiled as we walked to his car. "Are you hungry?" he asked.

"Yes."

"I know where we can get some delicious food made like Mom makes it." *Wow, he is asking me out on a date? Courtship isn't' dead, huh? In his presence, I feel special.*

"Now that is good because my Mom can cook. Let's go."

"They have good music. One concern, it is in the hood. Is that a problem?"

"No, just as long as I don't get shot."

"I'll protect you."

The food at Boopsey's was great and the music was good. They had a jukebox that pumped the latest in R&B. Upon entering,

there was a row of booths for seating to the left and a bar equaling in length to the right. They also had pool tables towards the rear of the building near the restrooms. It was a smoking environment and that was an understatement, as I got a breath full of indo. The tables were equipped with not only salt and pepper shakers, but with all needed condiments for the soul food menu it offered—hot sauce, mustard and ketchup. Dee and I played a few games of pool, and he gave me some quarters to play the jukebox. I felt like a schoolgirl on a date. He led me to our table.

"Well, you already know from my driving that I'm from New York. I am also the proud father of two sons. They are by two different women from my younger hay-days." *I knew it was too good to be true. Not one baby's mama, but two baby's mamas.* "I have a nice friendship with them, and I spend a lot of time with my sons. I am single and have been for sometime. I am looking for Ms. Right. I'm not actually looking, but I asked God to bring her to me. Carmen, I see something in you that I like."

"Oh, really?" I gave him a screwed-up face and raised eyebrow.

"Yes, really, despite your attitude."

Keep your walls up, your guard up and keep your heart locked.

"Life has taught me that the things worth having come with a challenge and I am very patient," said Delano confidently.

"How old are you?"

"Thirty." *Great a man with wisdom.*

"Well, I'm not interested in being chosen." Needing him to understand where I was coming from, I wanted to make myself clear.

"You always talking fly. Carmen, you need to understand that I am in the streets on a mission. But I'm not classified by Baller, Player, none of that stuff. So talk to me like you talk to a man because that is what I am. I will always talk to you like you are a woman."

"Now will you stop talking so I can eat, sir?" *I do not want to like him, but I do.*

We sat, ate and talked for hours before I realized I'd been gone longer than I wanted. It was my first time being out on anything close to a date. It was fun. I lost the pool games. All of them. I promised I would beat him next go 'round. I returned home and told Dee I would call him. I knew I would not. Well, I knew I did not want to. I was on a come-up, and love was a monkey wrench in my program that I did not need.

I walked into my den a little after 9 p.m. and found T-Love and my son asleep. Music videos were playing low. I took my son in my arms and kissed him as I walked him to our bedroom. He never really used his room. We always slept together. My son was my life, my force, and my motivation. For me, he represented all the good in this world. He was my blessing from God. I just wanted his life to be better. I just wanted to give him the best. Was this so wrong?

I went downstairs to talk to T. I had money on my mind and my mind on money. I really didn't know what to say to him. I knew nothing of the Dope Game. Although I had been exposed to it, I really knew very little. I knew G purchased "O-Z's." That's all I knew. I had an outlet and was determined to find a resource. That resource was T-Love. I touched his shoulder.

"T, wake up. I thought you had a date?"

"Yeah, I did but you jetted. You were gone forever."

"Well I didn't mean to be late. And I thank you again 'cause I really needed to get out."

"Watch yourself with Delano. He has a lot of women interested in him. Plus, I hear his babies' mothers are crazy."

T, had my back and I appreciated that.

"Don't worry. I will. It is still early if you wanted to use the jeep to go out. Were you at least able to make some runs?"

"Yeah, but Abdullah and 'em will be here, and I need to be up and here at the house to get his page and give him directions to your new fly-ass condo."

"T, I am going to stay up and watch a movie. I can get his page, return the call, and give them directions for you. I can wait up for them, get them settled and squared away. You leave your pager and take mine. I'll page you when they get to the house. Go out and enjoy yourself. You go back home to your wife in two days. You know you wanna get your freak on. Besides, I need to take some calls and make some money."

The more I talked, the faster he moved. All T saw was ass. All I saw was opportunity.

"Mmmmmh, T," I said as I followed him around the house. "You know I am a single mom and out there hustlin'."

"Right, right." He nodded in agreement.

"Well, I need to buy some *'girl.'* Can you help me?"

"No way! Keep your service." He shook his head in disbelief.

"I need a house for my son and me."

"You living nice, you're making money. Shit, I want to leave my wife for you. What's up?" he said smiling sheepishly.

"Yeah, Silly, but I spend a lot of money, and I am renting. I need security."

I quickly saw and knew that I could not get any sympathy over my situation, so I went to the jugular vein. His pocket. "I'm talking dollars."

Aw! A raised eyebrow. Now, I had his attention. "Listen, whatever you're movin', I can help you move double."

"I'm moving a kilo to a kilo and a half. No problem," he stated proudly.

"Next week, bring me one," I pleaded.

"Umm. I need some money up front," T, responded staring me in my face.

Damn, he's sleepin' in my den, driving my jeep, and I've never asked for anything. I was hurt, really about to cry because all this time I am thinking that we closer than that. At that point, I vowed to get independent so I'd never need anyone. I knew he didn't get money up front from the other people he dealt with.

My anger brought out both strength and weakness. In my strength I said, "No problem. But tax me and I'll tax your ass."

He was like, "A'ight, next week it's on, and I'll see what you can do."

With that, we exchanged pagers. I handed him my car keys and waved goodbye. *Yeah, T can bounce my jeep around town and make it hotter than a firecracker, tryin' to use me. Okay, T-Love, everyone get's a chance, and my turn is coming.* As I ended that thought, I turned my phones on and settled in my den watching TV with my pencil and notepad. Back to business.

Ring…Ring…

"Hello May I Help You?" I paged some of the girls for their locations. Then began business.

Ring…ring…

"Hello May I Help You? Yes! Renaye is 36-24-38. Out-calls are $175. No problem. She'll be there in 30 minutes."

Click!

I called back to verify his number and address. Then I called Renaye to set her appointment. A video by Janet Jackson came on. The same song that I heard in Boopsey's. Why was I thinking of Delano? Why was I thinking of him? Well I paged him. Why? I don't know. I figured, why not?

In 15 minutes, he called back.

"Someone call a pager?" He sounded anxious as if this were a call for a potential buy.

"Hi, it's me. You don't recognize my number?" Instantly, I began to feel uncomfortable because he didn't remember me.

"No. You did not give it to me, remember?"

"Oh, I remember. What's up? My brain is not always the best when it comes to remembering."

"I've been thinking of you," he smoothly responded with that Brooklyn accent.

"Yeah, right." I began my habit of twisting the cord of the phone as I was mesmerized by his soothing voice.

"No. I really was. I'm at Boopsey's playing pool. I'm at the outside payphone, and it is very cold."

"Well, I can call you later." I didn't want him to hang up the phone, but I couldn't let him know that.

"Can I come over?"

"No, I just wanted to call and say Hi. Maybe we can do lunch this week. I'll call you."

"Carmen."

"Yes?"

"Goodnight."

"Goodnight, Delano-Click!" Talking with him reminded me too much of Chino. His Brooklyn accent sent chills up my spine, and I longed for him to be sitting beside me on the couch talking to me as I laid my head in his lap.

Ring...ring...

"Hello, May I Help You?"

"Hi, sweetheart." I recognized this voice as G's.

"Hey, G."

"Can you help a brother out? I am pressed."

"Yes, it is on for next weekend. I'll see you and discuss more about it."

"Thanks, C." –Click!

Now, how in the hell could I sell a kilo? More research was needed. It would all work out some how, some way. It had to. If not, I'd be out of my savings on skid row again and have enough coke to snort for a year. Weighing the odds was too depressing because the deck was definitely stacked against me. I had come so far, and the escort and fencing was a slow-roll hustle. The potential earnings thrust me to believe in the unknown. I had to take a chance and ball. The come-up is always the greatest challenge. And I loved a challenge.

"Beep, beep!"

"Oh, shit! It's them." I got the page in the middle of washing dishes. I'll never forget it. Abdullah and the fellas from New York.

My door entry into the Dope Game.

Chapter
SIX

"Hello, Infa, this is Carmen. T asked me to direct you to my home."

"Where he at?" asked Infa

"Where else? On a *booty call*." We faded in like a rap group.

"You got anything to eat?" My grocery bills alone supporting this crew was in the four figures. Damn!

"Yes. My fridge is full. Want me to fix you something?" I knew he did. They always want service.

"Yeah. Do Dat," said Infa.

"How about some Philly steak sandwiches with onions, peppers and mushrooms with some Heinekens to wash it down?"

"We're on our way," he said, and the phone line went blank.

I grabbed my cordless and went to check on the baby. I just enjoyed watching him sleeping. I gave him a tender kiss on the side of his face. Tracing the outline of his eyebrow, down the middle of his little nose, over his lips noticing his first teeth coming in, and smelling his scent underneath his neck. Going downstairs to the kitchen, I got all the items out of the fridge. I got a bowl and put some chips in it. I got some blankets, linens and pillows, and stacked them by the stairs.

I saw the lights from the kitchen window as they pulled into my garage. It felt like déjà vu because I had gone through this with Chino and all the fellas. I did the same things for them. Then, they turned around and cut my throat. I am not forgetting that. Everyday I heal. But this go around would be different. Trust and believe me. I would not get hurt this time, nor would I be forgotten. Carmen would make sure of this. It was all about me and stacking some dollars to buy us a new home.

For a split second, I was standing in my old kitchen, Chino and mine. I could see a pile of tennis shoes off the garage kitchen door. I really miss the fellas. I hate to admit it, but I do.

They would watch basketball game after basketball game. There was Rock, the athlete of the crew. Wherever you saw him, a basketball was near by. He would dribble and talk, talk and dribble. Getting down on the court was his thing. Chris J, the tallest of the team, standing 6'4, thin, gentle and a definite follower. Ant, the model type, good looks, that handicapped him and confused. All he wanted was some money. Cory, nerdy, reared for more out of life, chasing the excitement of the streets and my Chino, leader of the pack. Talk about some niggas looking good ridin' four deep in a 500 SEL.

Just when I began to feel a sudden sadness inside of me, Carmen popped in, greeted Infa at the door and took control of the night. Infa was sexy, sexy, sexy. He was half black and half Panamanian. His skin was smooth cocoa brown outlined with a thick trimmed beard. His thick eyebrow accented his thick kissable lips. My mind thought of *ooh wee* when I saw him. He was also married to a Spanish Momi that would definitely kick your ass for thinkin' about her man. So I left that one alone and gave him the utmost in respect because of her. We, all the women lusting after Infa, were afraid of Mamacita.

They came, and we kicked it hitting the club. Arriving in a white Lincoln Navigator limo, chromed-out rims, black piping throughout the seats, TV's in the headrest complete with play station, fully stocked bar and fridge. We were flossin' and profiling as we pulled into the valet section for drop off. Infa handed me his nine to place in my purse to get past the security pat down. Problem was that my shoulder strap purse was too small. Infa started cursing, "Why in the fuck you carry such a small ass bag. You know the drill. How am I gonna get my piece up in the spot."

I ignored his complaints and looked at Abdullah as his nine was now in his lap looking for a hiding place to get up in the club.

I quizzed, "Okay, my fault, but do you got beef with anyone? Y'all from Uptop, and we in Ohio. Let's just stay for a couple of hours." I convinced them it was cool. This was a new nightclub that hadn't been broken in with a notorious rep yet for violence. They stashed their nines underneath the seat.

I emerged from the limo sportin' Versace. White leather hip-hugging shorts with knee-length white Durango boots with three-inch heels. My matching white halter rested against my skin. The leather was so soft, you had to get up close to determine if it was material or leather. Infa bounced from out of the tinted glass door wearing a black Armani suit, and Abdullah followed wearing the exact same suit, only in white. All eyes were on us as we strolled into the club, giving shout-outs to people that we knew. The Pulse nightclub was on jam. Swinging my hair from side to side and pulling it behind one ear, I sipped on my drink listening to the music. The club was sponsoring an open mic contest, and the contestants were going for the gold. Rippin' shit up on the mic. Ignoring the stares from the jealous females wondering how I had it like that, I was enjoying the men eyes glued on my backside. We were having a good time. Abdullah motioned for two nearby chicken-heads to join us. He pulled out a wad of cash, and their eyes were glued. I looked at his wad. *I want my wad to be bigger and better yet, for it to be mine.*

"How about some bubbly?" Abdullah motioned the bartender over.

I didn't get any play due to the fact that Infa stayed glued to my side with a mean look on his face. Any interested suitor knew that to approach me was to approach Infa. Infa called it his club look.

He felt he didn't have time to get played anywhere, especially up in a club with an audience. We stayed up in the place for about two hours and began making our way to the exit. Abdullah smacked a c-note on the photo booth counter, and we began a photo session. We clowned and hammed it up for the cameras. I gave up some booty shots, and they broke out with some penitentiary poses. I got tired of being silly and just stood on the sideline as the chicken-heads joined them allowing total strangers to cup their booty and tah-tahs. Infa even stuck his tongue down one girl's shirt. I stuffed the photos in my purse and headed for the exit.

We returned to the limo and headed downtown for dinner at Morton's. We ordered Steak & Lobster and drank on bubbly all night. After the third bottle of Cristal, we just started crackin' on T-love and his booty-call adventures.

Abdullah got it started, "Why won't T-Love use some of that money and buy his girl a new hairweave? Her shit is unbeweave-able."

I elbowed him in the side and said, "When I first saw her, I wanted to reach over and feel T-love's forehead and take his temperature, 'cause his ass was near death and desperate when he picked that one out of the bunch. And you, you can't talk. Don't your girl got a weave or do you not think that latch hook is a weave?"

Infa started on me, "You the only girl I know OK wrap her hair up at night so damn tight that you got lines on your forehead and have to press your face in the morning. What the fuck is a wrap?"

I got an attitude and said "Oh please, if you dated black girls, you would know what a wrap was."

Infa responded, "It ain't enough aspirins in a bottle of Tylenol for me to date a black girl."

Abdullah took another sip and said, "Shit, I don't see how T-Love dates Lashawn. Her damn voice is irritating."

"Playa, he ain't dating her voice, and I don't think her pussy talks back," said Infa.

I broke in and said, "Well, she getting paid. Don't T know that they call it trickin'. How does it feel to have a brother out there trickin'?" I asked.

Adbullah spat his bubbly on the table. Infa and I both screamed, "Damn! Nigga."

He began to wipe his shirt and said, "Ms. Heidi Fliess imitator talking about trickin', you run an escort service. Come on, tell us, do you be doing them dates?"

I replied, "Back up off me. You can't afford this." I pointed to between my legs and traced his lips with butter from my little finger.

The waitress approached the table with a monster size dessert Infa dreamed up. I asked Infa what it was. He responded, "Look, Wrappy, just eat it. You ain't never turned down chocolate."

We grabbed our forks and dug into the plate and all started nodding. "This some good shit," Abudllah said.

We closed the restaurant, and when the bill arrived, we kept passing it around and around the table like no one wanted to pay for it. Abdullah was so drunk, I slid my hands into his pants, clipped him for $300, and paid the tab. Infa saw every move, and we just laughed at his drunk ass. We hoisted him into the limo and headed back to my place to crash. The following morning, they were back on the road, headed home to New York. It was a fast weekend.

I tried to remember all I saw Chino do. He never involved me in his drug hustling, so I had no past recollection to draw from. Another tip I gained from Chino was relationship building. People do business with people they like. So, you gotta entertain people and make them feel comfortable with you, and you will keep your clientele. 'Cause there is always someone around trying to take your "custic" once you groomed them. I take care of my people.

The next morning, I got my son dressed and ready for daycare. I always hated saying good-bye to him. I've learned, you must do what you must do and that's just how it is. Because I was seeking knowledge, I went to where knowledge is found; the library. I didn't want to ask anyone for anything. I got a book on weight, then read and copied all the things associated with a kilo. I learned how many grams are in an ounce. How many ounces are in a kilo. It was not difficult to figure out a big eight's amount. Then I went to a drug paraphernalia store on Cleveland Avenue named Cloud 9, and I purchased a scale for about $100.

I must remember the rule of keeping the scale in the kitchen. Rumor in the streets have it that if the Po-Po find a scale in the kitchen, then they think you measuring food with it. So, you keep it in the kitchen for baking purposes not drug selling.

I also went and purchased some rubber gloves from a hair supply store and plastic baggies from the grocery store. Shit, Chino use to count money in gloves, his ass was so cautious. I had everything I needed—I hoped.

As I began cleaning my house to music, the pagers were buzzing off the hook. I ended up checking messages and answering phones, the usual hectic day, including my bi-weekly hair appointment. Hustling is very hard work. Most people don't know this. They think it is easier than working a real job. It is not. Your nerves are a wreck. The only soothing balm is the money. The harder you hustled, the more money you made. I would soon learn that with money came all sorts of dramas. Motherfuckers makin' your money short.

Short money brought excuses. "See, see what I'm sayin'. I got stopped by the police, and the money was in the trunk of the car, and the police towed my car because I don't have a valid license, and when I went to pick up my car the next day, the money was gone, so I am short, but I am gonna make it up."

Or, "I was gonna pay you, but my mom had an operation." Or, A whore talkin' about. "I can't fuck 'cause I am on my period." Or, An escort talkin' about, "I got a headache, so I can't fuck."

Then comes the friends that think you gettin' money and want to borrow money that they won't repay. Or, the time, a heroin addicted booster sat on my front porch ringing my bell for hours in the rain until I let her in to sell her wears. You had the salesman at my favorite sound system store, Mobile Electronics, on Morse Avenue trying to upgrade your shit for his commission to be higher. If you check out Pretty Toney at Mobile Electronics, his ass is the bearer of bad news, "I'm afraid to tell ya, because you own a BMW and are a drug dealer oops, I mean have an expensive car, it will cost you triple to install your system."

Then you got the rival drug dealer worried about you tryin' to get their block. I wasn't interested in no blocks, nor territory. I wanted to sell weight and let them worry about where they sold it. I intended on being that girl. Do me, be loyal to myself, and get paid.

I was a Madam. More like a *"Pimpadam."* I was a Fence, and now a Drug Dealer. This was not how it was supposed to be. I just sat on the floor and cried. Things were going better for me financially. But I was sad inside. I missed my Chino. It wasn't supposed to be this way. Before tears could fall, Carmen chimed in. S*nap out of it and get over it*. That voice and the ringing of the phone snapped me out of it. I suppressed the pain.

"Hello May I Help You?"

"Yes. Do you have girls that speak Greek?"

"Yes, I do." Greek is anal sex. The Hershey highway for lack of a better word. Most men like to get down like that. Responding to the caller's question, I chimed into the receiver, "They are fluent in it, and for three hundred dollars, you can be tutored." I set the appointment and told myself China's line, "Let that be the reason I get over my past."

The weekend came super fast and I was ready. T-Love arrived late Friday night, so I told G-Money I'd meet with him early Saturday at the hotel after I collected from the girls. He was very anxious. I didn't know what to charge him. T-Love gave me my package and told me my ticket was $24,000. 24 G's. I was like,

Whew! My own 'bird,' my own 'brick.' I had 17 G's in a shoebox upstairs, but I was thinking, *Now what? I'm short so, I must think fast. I've got to make some moves.*

I impressed T-Love with my confidence and shiny new triple-beam scale. I had practiced using it. All I knew was I had a sale for a Big 8th, and that four Big 8th's equaled a half a kilo. So I could package four Big 8th's. I weighed and measured as T watched me. I was very nervous but decided not to show it. This was my pre-requisite for tomorrow's performance with G-Money. Yes, I was ready as ready could get. I immediately took the conversation to one of his booty-call adventures. I was hoping he would not ask for the money up front.

"So T, when are you leaving? Sunday night or Monday morning? You didn't finish telling me about your hoochie LaShonn. Why she be tryin' to pronounce her name 'La' Shone' like it got an 'e' on the end? Like her shit is French or something. I call her LaShawn, which is it? When she call, she be like, tell him LaShone called."

" I'm bouncing on Sunday night. Yeah, she be trippin' about her name. I just call them all Boo. You can't never go wrong with 'Boo' or 'Shorty' because it is easy to remember. Every girl I date will be shorter than I am, and everyone is a 'Boo.' So, I just call all them chicken heads the same. But Lashawn got something special. She is not as pretty as my wife is, or as intelligent. I kick it with her because of how I feel when I am with her. Lashawn swallows, if you know what I mean, and wears some sexy ass lingerie. Have you ever seen those bras that got the nipples exposed? She rocks those joints," he announced fidgeting with his jean outfit. Smoothing the jacket as he laid it on the couch.

T-Love wore jean outfits everyday of the week with matching Timbs. He was a brother who sent his jean outfits to the cleaners after wearing them one time as if though they were business suits.

"Well, I'll have everything together by Sunday."

"No problem. I've given you the very best 'flakes' so your

'custies' will be pleased. Curiosity killed the cat, but satisfaction brings them back all the time. As China would say, "Let that be the reason." Our eyes met and we laughed together. The ice was broken.

"I need to use your jeep. Every time we ride around in the rental car with those New York plates on it. We get pulled over."

"I understand. T, I got you, I know one slip is a prison bid waitin', waitin' to happen."

"C, give China a call. I feel like eating some Chinese tonight."

"You are so nasty. China will be glad to see you. She said you're a good tipper. That'll be $200. I'll take it off my 24G ticket."

"No problem. I'm going upstairs to take a shower," said T.

I called G and told him to have the Booster get me some fly men's gear. But I'd take it off *his* ticket the following week.

"G, one favor deserves another," I pleaded into the phone.

"Carmen, it better be worth it."

"And you know it will be, man. Hook me up. I need it tomorrow. You bring yours to the table and I'll bring mine."

"Okay let—"

I cut G off before he could continue and proceeded to complete his line. "I know—that be the reason," he said, "Bye." Click!

I packaged everything and went to sleep. I said a prayer. *"God, direct my paths and forgive me. Watch over my son and protect me."*

The following morning I told the girls I needed to use the hotel that night. I had rented a townhouse suite at the Residence Inn Hotel. It had an upstairs and downstairs, two full baths, fireplace, and kitchen, a bedroom upstairs and one downstairs, both with large TVs, VCRs and cable. Damn, this place was nice.

I brought my clothes, therefore, I decided to shower and change to kill time. I decided to wear a beautiful white linen Armani pantsuit. Chino had purchased it for me. It was another "just because" gift. He had it custom tailored to fit me by his personal tailor Stephano who had a shop on High Street. I looked great in this suit. There is something about a woman in a tailored pantsuit. The fabric rested against my cocoa brown skin, hugged my waistline and accentuated my hips. I was just glad it was at my Mom's home when Chino and I separated, or I would have lost that also. I was nervous. It was six o'clock, and T-Love wouldn't miss me until later.

G finally paged me. This meant he was ready for the sale. My first drug sale. I called him and told him to come on through. I had his package all prepared. The dope looked great. This really was some high quality "girl." I had two Big 8ths with me. I still had not figured out what to do with the rest of that kilo I talked myself into. Anyway, there was the bell, so out of the corner I went. I took a deep breath and opened the door.

"Hey G. Want a drink?" I said smiling.

"Sweetheart, you look fabulous. This spot is tight."

"Yeah, yeah, let's do this. I'm expecting others. My schedule is tight tonight." My mind remained focus on being calm and not exposing the novice drug dealer inside me.

"I thought all this was for me, for us."

"Well, it's not, so come on." I pulled out the package and his eyes couldn't believe the chunks.

"Damn, C, I always get shake—powder. This is lovely."

"I am glad you like it." Next, he pulled out the money, and I began to count. I still didn't know the price. But I counted thirty-eight hundred for four and a half ounces. I took the money and prayed this was the going rate. I was so relieved, I rushed G to leave. He hesitated before exiting and said, "Sweetheart, is there more of this?" I asked.

"Yes!"

Nodding his head with approval he said, "I may be back."

"Just page me." With that, he turned to leave. I sat down and poured myself a glass of wine. I did it! I did it! If only my Chino could see me. A small tear fell from my eye. I quickly wiped it away, and I went for my pen and paper to do the math. *Okay, I can get*

$15,200 for kilo,. And for a kilo I can get $30,400 and with me pay-
ing 24 for it. That's a six thousand dollar profit. Great! I can do this.

Forty-five minutes later I got a page. Beep, Beep, Beep. *It's G*
paging me again.

"What's up, G?" I confidently whispered into the phone.

"C, it is great, baby. It is nothing but 'butter.' I'll see you in five
minutes." Click! He came back and got some more. This was great.

My client Terrance and his wife Tasha wanted a 'lil somethin',
an ounce. They were faithful customers of the escort service. They
gave me $1,000 for an ounce—unbelievable. T always said the
prices in Ohio were sweet. I could see how. This was sort of high.
In other cities, the cost was cheaper. But this was so good. Later, I
got a page from Tasha and Terrence. I returned their call, and Tasha
answered on the first ring.

"Yeah, C, there's a li'l problem. Let's meet at Damon's for a
drink."

"Okay. In 15 minutes," I said. Hanging up the phone, I paced
back and forth feeling my nervousness leaving. Regretting not taking
advantage of learning more of the drug game from Chino. I would
know how to handle this and not just have gut feeling to rely on. Shit!

What am I getting myself into? How do you know if the drugs
are real? I know Chino used a tester from time to time.

A tester is someone who is an addict, and they sample your pur-
chases for you for the quality. There were heroin testers whom you
could hire for a sample; they would shoot up a sample and tell you
if it was good or not. They welcomed the thought of a lethal near
overdose of something strong, which had no cut on it. If an heroin
addict read in the newspaper about a person being found dead from
an overdose, the first question that addict would ask is, "Where did
he cop at?"

Also, there were the cocaine samplers that gave a first hand
judgment on the quality of the coca. I was winging it and hopefully not so much that I've gotten myself into trouble.

Getting myself together, I took a sip of water and left the room walking at a slow pace trying to keep calm.

Damon's Bar & Grill was directly behind the hotel. I decided to front G two more Big 8ths since he had paid me for two. This way, half the kilo would be gone. I paged G and invited him to meet me at Damon's also. A.S.A.P. I went through the back parkway leading to Damon's. It was a beautiful summer night. Not too hot, not too cold, and I was enjoying the walk. Tasha arrived first.

"Carmen, smooches," She said, giving me play kisses on both cheeks.

"What's up?" I said backing from her embrace and trying to see what was up from the expression on her face.

"What are you drinking?" She waved the bartender over.

"I'm drinking Kahlua & Crème. Is there something wrong?"

"Well, yes and no."

Oh shit! Was it real dope? I didn't test it.

Climbing up on the bar stool I replied, "Yeah, let's talk. What's up?"

"Carmen, it is too strong. It is making our noses bleed. We didn't want to try and cut it ourselves because we don't know what to use. We heard of baking soda, but we don't want to mess this up."

Now what should I do? I don't know what to use. I don't know how to cut this stuff. My research revealed powder cocaine is most often cut with icetone to either stretch its volume, or dilute the potency without changing the texture. Whereas, baking soda is generally used in rocking up cocaine. But due to our collective ignorance, I'll elect to admonish Tasha to cut the powder with just a little baking soda.

"Well, just use a little."

"We did Carmen, and we are still high behind it. Terrance will probably be dead by the time I get back home."

"Please, don't say that." I placed my hand to my chest.

"No, he's ok. He has one of his friends over." *I am going to silk it.*

"It's like this Tasha, I don't cut my packages. I don't deal like that. So, I honestly don't know about cut. I give it like I get it. I like quality. Ask Terrance about my quality." I winked at Tasha, and she gave me her dentured grin.

"C, that's why we like you so much," she replied after gulping her drink.

"But I am meeting someone, and I can ask him what he uses, if you want."

"Yes, please. Terrance will wait. I'll finish my drink 'cause I want to get my snort on. Let that be the reason I wait."

That damn China got everyone saying that line. China saw Tasha and her husband last night. Tasha and Terrance had a great relationship. They did everything together. I guess that was why they've been together for 18 years. *That's what I'm looking for, a forever, everlasting love. Ya know?* We noticed G-Money walking towards the bar.

"Hi, sweetheart." G, reached to hold my hand and I raised my hand to introduce them to each other.

"Hi, G. G this is Tasha."

G reached down and kissed her hand. He is such a flirt. "Tasha, excuse me," I said and G followed me over to the phone area.

"G, I've got a lot of running to do. I want to leave you with nine ounces, and you work it during the weekend. This way, you'll be covered. I promised I'd do all I can to help you. So I'm trusting you."

G gave me a big hug and said, "C, I won't let you down." I could tell he appreciated it. I was not certain on the "let me down" part. I knew men were not reliable. I also knew G had been through some problems in the street. Plus, he recently got out of jail. He was doing everything to make it. We were very similar to each other in many ways. Nevertheless, I just didn't trust his ass. I didn't trust anyone anymore. Shit! I didn't even trust the weather, kept an umbrella in my car.

"G, my associate, Tash, snorts her purchase, and she said it is too strong. It makes her nose bleed. I don't cut my packages. I don't get down like that."

"C, your package is straight. When I rock it, it comes back even more. My pager is blowing up over this. Don't start cutting it, please. Tell her she can go to 'Cloud 9.' They have all sorts of stuff to cut with. She can try baking soda, but it will mess her nose up. I have some one hundred dollar packs of powder of some old, weak, bullshit that ole boy gave me. It may be good for snorting."

"G, check this out, I'll turn you onto her." Good. I won't have to see her for ounces. I am not about to start selling O-Z's. "I'll turn you on, but you must treat her right. Tasha is very good people."

"Great! I will work with her and take care of her. I am trying to get paid."

"She is all yours. I won't deal with her anymore." I gave him a wink, then we walked back to the bar.

"Tasha, G can take care of your needs. I'll let y'all talk. I've gotta go."

"Wait, Carmen, I want to ask you something." Tasha was whispering in my ear. "Is he with your service?"

"No. He will probably do you for free. But more than likely, not your husband."

"You know we do everything together. Terrance wants what I want." I just laughed and whispered, "Good Luck." Then I turned to G and asked,

"G, you got my tab?"

"Of course, C, goodbye."

I looked over my shoulder, and they were getting along great.

My jeep's clock read 9:30 p.m. Time to go home and be with my man, my son. I must get T's money together by Sunday night. I hope his booty call last for another night. But I am living for today, and today I am all right. After all, it gets greater later. I am at the bottom, but I am also on a come up. I popped in a Sherry Winston CD, and I knew I would somehow be fine. Nothing but my son on my mind and our new life. Safe in a suburban home, street lined with mature trees and me greeting his school bus at the corner. Dreams can come true. Two more miles, Bethel Road. My exit.

SEVEN

Sunday morning and there was still no sign of T-Love. Many thoughts were racing through my head. *I wonder what time it is? Where is my watch? Oh, it is only 6:00 a.m. Well, while the baby is sleeping, I might as well do my usual Sunday cleaning. I think I'll also go to the grocery store since I have some money. I'll splurge and purchase me some "Red Snapper." I can't believe I have acquired a taste for it. It seems like yesterday I prepared some for Chino and the fellas.*

Yeah, that was the first meal I prepared for him and Joe Bub. Old Joe Bub Baby, standing 6 feet even, brown skinned, large nose and dazzling smile. Clothing was this man's best friend. If you looked in the dictionary under dapper, he would be standing there, suited in Armani, with a cane smiling and smelling like Cool Water cologne. He was Chino's first partner back in the day, but they fell out over some bullshit. The same old shit we all promised on our lives that we'd never fall out over. Imagine that. Joe Bub was the smooth time playa-type kind of guy, or so he thought. Now, I liked old Joe and his fake ass, wanna-be-Chino, but then I couldn't stand to hear his voice. He had a voice on him, and no one could tell him he wasn't Gerald Levert. I swore if he sang "Casanova" one more time, I was gonna get my scrap on with him.

Damn, Chino why we gotta hate one another? Forget it!

I'll pass on the Snapper and take my Boo to Chuck E. Cheese. He will really love that and so will I. Forget Red Snapper! Forget Chino! And, forget the memories!

It was G-Money paging me. What did he want? I turned down the music before I called him back. *Dear God, please let it be good news.*

"Wuz up with ya, baby?" I confidently spoke into the phone.

"Hi, Sweetheart. How are you?"

"I am well and you?"

"I am sitting on top of the world."

"Oh, really?" I listened closely for a juicy come up story.

"Well, not yet, but I will bc. I need to see you."

"Well, today is Sunday, and you know what that means?"

"Yes. You and your Boo will be together. But this is really important."

"Check this out. I'll see you at 'Chuck E. Cheese' up north at 2:00 p.m."

"Come on, C. Why there?"

"Wait, G. First, you don't press me. Not now, not ever. You getting real comfortable. Do I need to back up from your ass or what?

Nobody runs me, and my son's quality time comes first." For a minute neither one of us said anything. The silence seemed forever. *Good. Screw him and anyone else. I've got enough stress. I do not need anymore.*

"Okay, Carmen at 2:00 pm."

"G, please don't page me this early again unless it's an emergency. This is not a good time." *I've turned into a real bitch!*

"A'ight. Peace."

I had to come down on him like that because I couldn't be soft. Only God and me got my back, and He was kinda up there and moving on the slow side those days. It was time to get the baby and me dressed to get some playtime in before the day got away. One p.m. and still no sign of T., nor a page. He really was getting his freak on, and I wasn't mad at him, that's for sure. Not that weekend. I needed all the time I could get. I wondered should I call him or what?

I decided to call him later. He had my pager number if he needed me. If he wasn't worried about this kilo I had, why should I be. I had been thinking, I really needed to get out and mix it up a bit. I really needed to set some sort of goals with this lifestyle. I wasn't trying to do this forever.

Dear God,
When I make me fifty thousand, I will stop the street life totally. Just nineteen thousand short. Okay God, I just need some things for my son and me. I mean, after Chino reached in his pocket and gave me two twenty-dollar bills for the baby, I swore I'd never need him or anyone else again in this lifetime. Piece of shit! Driving a brand new convertible Corvette and this punk gonna give me two twenties. The sad part of it is that I took it. I needed the money. So I've got to get myself established and together.

Amen.

"Boo, we are going to Chuck E. Cheese." My son started clapping his hands and so did I. It felt so good to be able to go out somewhere. I strapped him in his car seat, and we bounced the jeep down the street to see Mr. Chuck E. Cheese.

My son loved to play in those colorful balls at this place. I mean, it does not look like fun, yet the kids love it. I was tempted to get in them myself just to see what the big deal is all about. The children were running and screaming. This was really fun, and although I was sitting all by myself eating some pizza and sipping on some beer, I didn't feel lonely. Actually I was very content.

Money makes the stress go away.

It was the Chuck E. Cheese stage show, and the kids were going nuts. I heard all sorts of weird sounds coming from a variety of video games and music over the speakers. My son always wanted to run in the other room to see the big-ass rat. Yet, when the rat came over to him, he started crying and wanted me to pick him up. I still can't figure that out. But I could go through it as many times as he wanted to. One day he won't be afraid of the rat. One day he won't even want to see the rat, nor spend Sunday with his *Moms Dukes*, so I knew that we'd better enjoy it together at that moment. In walked G-Money.

"Hey, G, what it be like?" I extended a 70's handshake to him and he laughed.

"I didn't know what to expect from you, another cursing out or what."

"You know we all right. We in it to win it!" I extended my arm for some dap.

"You be acting crazy. Carmen, you won't let anyone get close to you, will you?"

"You're close as close gets to me. What more do you want?"

"You know what I want." He gave me that supposed-to-be sexy look, rubbing his silk shirt. He didn't know that I hated silk shirts.

"Yes I do. Money. I do too. So, how is it going?"

"Well girlfriend, I have all your money, and I thought you would want it. I promised to be straight with you. I've hooked up with someone, and I'll be able to do more if you can handle it."

"You know I can, man. What is more?" I replied for the first time feeling like a *Baller.*

"Maybe a kilo a week."

"Good. Right, right. Let that be the reason. I'll need money up front (*it was tried on me, right?)* or on the time of purchase. I may still be able to front occasionally. But it will go better for us both if you begin to save your money."

"The guy I used to work for wants to know if you can get some dog food?"

Eating my slice of pizza, I was cool and said, "Maybe. Who have you been discussing me with? Whom do you work for again?" *Time to put the baby back in the balls.*

"Well, he doesn't know that you are a girl, and I never told you I worked for someone because I didn't know how to tell you."

"G, it really is none of my business. I just mess with you. We all work together in the streets. 'Cause someone is always seeing someone. Just try to be on your own terms. Just do the best you can for self. That is what I do."

"I think things can work out for us," said G.

"I think things can work out between us. But ultimately for each other." *He had that hurt look on his face. I wasn't being a partner with no one.*

"I hear ya. I want to be solo also."

"Yeah, G-Money. Solo luomo is the only way to go."

"Well, the guy, Jay-Jay, knows I'm seeing someone, and he wants in on the mix of things. He is really looking for a good supplier of heroin. That's his thing."

"So, tell me of your arrangement with this guy and more about him," I said.

"He and I did time together. He sold lots of drugs in the joint. He got out before a lot of us and set up things. So, when I got out along with some other guys, he gave us some work. He put us on his payroll. The problem i,s he won't sell to me. But he will front me and this keeps me under his thumb. He is controlling. I know this sounds weak, but, C, that is how it is when you want to be put on."

"G, baby, I understand because I have jumped through some hoops myself. And I still may have some to jump through. So, don't even knock yourself. I see a lot of me in you. I heard some stories about the time you did and about you working for someone else. I just waited to hear it from you. That's how I am. I've never been one for rumors. Just save your own money, and this is what makes you your own man. When you are able to pay up front and not be fronted, it becomes your shit and not the next man's."

"So G, I really need you to be able to purchase your items. This will keep it all good between us and not place me in a position over you. I don't want you to owe me anything. We simply working together trying to make our money. This is best. Besides, no man wants to answer to a woman. Money will make you fall out real fast. I will be ballin' until I reach some personal goals, and then I'm out of this business and out of this city. Let me check on some things, and I'll decide if I want to deal with him. If I do, the first round will be on you. This is the only way I will do this, and possibly your boy Jay-Jay will appreciate the favor. It may put your relationship on another level. You got the plug. He could be coming to see *you*. Imagine that?

Listen, please do not bring me any more people or inquiries because we are not partners in this game. If you see some moves, please use some courage and faith in yourself to do some things for yourself and not for me, nor through me. You know a lot of people and have a lot of opportunities for yourself. This is your city. It astonishes me how guys will let out-of-town people come into their city and take over. New York boys come in and lock the places down."

"They got all the connects," he responded anxiously.

"So, What! This is still your city, and can't nobody do it better than you. Use your opportunities. You plugged in now, so get the ball and run with it. You big Baller, Baller." With that, I punched him in the right arm to close my pep talk. I could tell that I encouraged him. I either encouraged him or sold him a dream.

In the streets, it is either one or the other. Nothing in between. I was just trying to keep off ties and keep people up off me. No time for the clingy, hold-me, grab-me type bullshit. Ya know?

"G, this your last free conversation. My game is sold, not told. I owed you this one. I'll talk to you later in the week. Take care."

"Bye, C. Later."

Where is the baby? He is going to be worn out in those darn balls. *God, I thank you. It seems like some things are working out for me. If I can only reach my goals, I'd be safe.*

Arriving home was welcomed peace. That outing wore me out. Your home is your haven. Still there was no sign of T-Love. T, knew when you getting dirty in the streets, you needed to call somebody. Babies always fall asleep in the car, and mine was too heavy to be carried. He was such a big baby and was still growing like a weed. I really wanted to do the correct things by him, myself, and my life.

Beep, beep. China was paging me for some calls. I had not thought of the phones since this new gig ópened up. I needed to get settled and get her some calls. I needed to get all the girls some calls before I pissed them off. I knew they had been using other services. I just had not been working the phones like I used to, and they needed money just like I did. They were very faithful to me, and I tried in every way to show them I appreciated them also.

Last week, Toy got a little anxious because I didn't send her any calls in two days. I stopped by the hotel and gave her three hundred as an incentive to hang in there with me. I didn't want her to bail, and I knew they liked my clients because I mixed it up, and we had fun. I've been plugging in the Ballers with the service, and it was refreshing for the girls to date some young, money-getting- niggas besides all those older white collar workers. The other services didn't have the flavor I had. The wave was the sex scene with people that look like you. You got the Ballers going to the titty bars 'cause they go see the girl next door up in there. I was giving them Carmen's "girls next door"—for a small fee.

I thought I'd give Gabrielle a birthday party at the hotel next weekend. She would be 19, and she really deserved to have something special. If it were not for her 44 Double D's, I'd have starved, and she really helped me when I needed it. So, I decided to work on that and call all the girls with my plans and catch up on some chitchat. I would send the driver and have him pick up the money from the previous night's calls.

The vibration of my pager interrupted my thoughts. It was T-Love, finally. My mind was relieved that he was okay. I began to think of the proper way to approach T-Love. I wanted to build him up and make him feel relaxed. Immediately, I called his number.

"What's up ?, T-Love lover, player, big Baller, Baller. Man, where you been? I got a message from your wife on the machine and a message from her brother-your best friend Erik. Erik wants me to call him, said it was urgent."

"Yeah, I just talked to him myself, and he is hot, so I need to speak to you about a few things. I'm on my way to hizz-house. Will you be there?"

"Yes. I am staying put and answering some calls."

"Good. Peace!

Whatever happened to good-bye? Oh, I had to call my Mom. We talked every week. If she didn't hear from me, she would think something was wrong with me so I called her. If my Mom found out about my life, she would hit the ceiling, drop to her knees and call on Jesus. I wished I could tell my sister, Lori. Lori was my big little sis. I called her that because I got all the height in the family, and Lori was short and petite. She was six years my senior, and I still acted as if I were the oldest. Lori would listen, but not keep my confidence. The things I was into were too deep, and she would tell our Mom. Not out of betrayal, but out of wanting the best for me. Everyday I stuffed one more skeleton bone into the closet after the other. I phoned my Mom thinking that my parents had had the same phone number for almost twenty years.

Ring…ring…

"Hello?"

"Hi, Mom."

"Hi, Baby. How are you and my grandbaby?"

"Mom, he is very well. We just got back from "Chuck E.

Cheese. Now he is asleep."

"When will you send him up here to see me? I miss my baby. I miss both of my babies."

"I will."

"And you too. You can come for a visit."

"I'm coming for a visit very soon. I'm working on some things."

"Well, has Chino seen the baby?"

"No." The baby and Chino subject was my Achilles heel. I hated to go there.

"I told you he wouldn't care where you were. A sorry ass man is going to be sorry no matter what. He really doesn't deserve to see the baby."

"I know, Mom, but I'm just praying he will come around and be there for the baby and be a father. I never dreamed in all my life that he would act like this."

♥

Seeing the look on Chino's face had me filled with fear. I turned, moving just in time out of his reach and ran towards the stairs leading to the lower level of the indoor pool. With Chino in pursuit, I jetted towards the poolside chair and remembered what I had placed underneath the pillow the night before. A 380 with hollowpoint bullets.

"You stupid, Bitch! You just made my day. Oh, now you wanna be a man? You wanna fight?" He began to get excited, and I ran around the chair running near the pool table thinking of grabbing a pool stick, but afraid that he'd use it to crack me upside my head. I was dancing back and forth around the table, in my bare feet, almost sliding on the ceramic tile, he continued to rant and rave. Then, he became calm and removed his shirt in order to get cool. The removal of his shirt exposed his thick frame that held a slightly pudgy dope boy mid-section from one too many good meals. My eyes watched his face, and when I noticed his waistband, I saw the

handle of a shiny black 9mm. I became alarmed.

Chino never brought guns into the house. The rumors of him out in the streets wilin' were apparent. This was one of the reasons I secretly propositioned my brother for the purchase of a small 380. I wanted to feel protected. He added the hollow points thinking that if I shot anyone with that small caliber gun, I needed to take them out or they would beat my ass for not killing them. I began to plead as the look on Chino's face announced war. "Okay, Chino stop playing, I'm sorry." We continued the game of chase around the pool table as he breathed harder getting angry that he couldn't catch me.

♥

My Mother said, "I know, baby. No one could have told me this either, and I've been around for a lot of years. I'm praying also that the two of you work out your differences and come to some agreement for the sake of the child. He is a beautiful baby and looks just like him. Like he spit him out. The child doesn't deserve this. He is caught in the middle of the problems you have with each other."

"I thought we were closer than this."

"Like my momma always told me, 'Teeth and Tongue will fall out, and you can't get any closer than that.' "

"I know. I'm giving it to God. If it is meant to be, then it is meant to be, and sooner or later, something will give. I'll either give up or he will give in to his responsibilities," I said. At that point, I felt it might be a lost cause.

"I'm always here if you need to talk."

"I mean, I thought for sure someone in his family would have made it to the baby's first birthday party, but they did not. If Chino is mad at me, then they all are."

"That's just the way it is with them people. But God don't like ugly, and you don't make differences over children. It is not right," said Mom with extreme bitterness.

"I know, his family never did try to get to the truth. One day they loved me, the next day I was hated. And so they reject my son. But, Mom, I thank God for my son even if nobody else will."

"Amen!" said Mom.

"And I heard it on one of those rap records that you don't like. Imagine that?"

"That baby is not missing out on anything with relatives like that. Children are a blessing. They come when God tells them to come. Why can't people understand that? People love you in good times and leave in bad. That is how friends do you. Remember, I am not your friend. I am your Mother and I will be here until the end. You can count on me, Pammy. And you can always come home," she said with a hint of sadness in her voice.

"I believe they never cared for me and maybe dealt with me because of Chino. I never listened to you about things. I am trying to do better about that. See, I am growing up, Mom. I'm just trying to go on with my life, make some sense of all I've been through, and all I must go through."

"I am a woman, and ain't no real woman on the planet that don't understand. But you bend those knees and pray. God will see you through this. He never fails."

"What's for dinner?"

"I'm cooking your favorite, Bar-be-que Chicken with my special 'Star' sauce. I got my po-ta-tah salad and some greens with a side of macaroni cheese. Want some?"

"Yes!"

"I wish you were here. I worry about you all the time."

"I miss you too, Mom. I am being careful and trying to work out some internal and external issues."

"Remember to let God help. He is the Master! Have you gone past the hair salon? Who has it?" asked Mom.

"No, I haven't the courage to go past the shop yet. I will one day. This guy named Ricki has it. I hear it is not the same as when I had it."

"Of course, my dear, no one can do it like you."

"Mom, you always know what to say," I said.

"That's right, I am your Mom, Pammy, not your friend. You need to remember that. If you would only talk more, I could help you a lot more with your concerns before they become problems and all messy. Promise me you'll talk to me more."

"I promise that I will try. So, what's up at work? How are your students?"

"They are fine, and these kids are getting bigger everyday. It must be the fast food."

"The baby has more teeth in his mouth, and he is okay. He is trying to swim in the bathtub. One day I am going to buy him a swimming pool, and not a lil' plastic one."

"I know you'll be fine. Do you need anything?"

"No, I am fine. T-Love just pulled into the garage."

"Oh, he is there again? Where does he work at?" asked Mom.

"I know, Mom."

"Pammy, be careful. Don't get into that same messy stuff again," Mom reminded.

"I'll call you tomorrow, okay?"

"Okay, baby. Kiss my grandson for me and yourself too."

"I will. Mommy?"

"Yes?"

"I love you."

"I love you too. Remember to pray."

"I will. Good night."

I heard the garage door raising, followed by the sound of the disarming of the security system. Attempts of gentle footsteps glided across my kitchen floor. However, T-Love was too heavy for gentle steps. I knew the sound of his brown leather Timb' boots anywhere.

"Look at you. T-Love finally home. You'd better call your wife. She left three messages on the machine."

"I know. She has been blowing my pager up. First we need to talk."

• "Okay, remember the last time you didn't call her back? She got in her car, drove all the way here from New York, caught you in the bed with that sack-chaser and beat her and you down. Ha, ha."

"Well those days are behind me. She wasn't my wife; she was my girlfriend then. Now she is my wife and driving an Acura Legend, so she'd better sit her ass still, keep counting them dollars, and take care of my son."

Damn, T may be chasing tail but home is taken care of. Why can't that happen to me?

"So, what's up?" I asked curiously.

"Well, C, Erik does not want me to deal with you. He found out that we did something this week, and he is crazy mad, so we ain't gonna be able to do this drug thang. You know what I'm sayin'?"

"Oh, really?" Stay calm. "Erik has mo' money than God, but he wants me to starve, right? This shit is crazy. Why? I've got your money."

"I know, I ain't worried. But he just feels like I shouldn't sell to you. Why can't you go to Chino? He's in the same game."

"You know why I can't go to Chino. I went to him for help and couldn't get it, let alone some dope. And yes, I've asked him for that too, to try and help me, but he won't. I'm on my own. And now you want to dump me."

"Erik thinks you are getting it for Chino."

"Oh yeah, right. One kilo? What is Chino going to do with that? Erik hates Chino just as much, if not more, as Chino hates him over that fake affair he accused Erik and me of having. Look, I've got to take care of myself. No one is helping me, not you, not Erik, not Chino. So I must help myself and that is what I am doing!"

"I know, but Erik said 'no'!"

"So, is that what this is? Fuck me? Take your money and your shit and get the fuck out! I am not going to beg your fake ass! Okay, give me some money since I can't work for it."

Silently, T just stood in place unable to look me in the face. First, staring at the walls, then the kitchen floor. Here I was ballin' for mines. He knew I had no one, and now he was turning his back on me. Just when I began to trust again. Just when I began to think things could be different. I didn't get paid for thinking. I barked at him like he was a nigga on the streets and told him what I really felt.

"That's what I thought. Fuck You! I am an entrepreneur, and I'll survive all of this shit! Trust and Believe."

Chapter

EIGHT

I ran to my room and started crying. All I saw was opportunity going down the drain, and that was when Carmen kicked in.

Look, dry those fuckin' tears. He ain't the only store in town. You gotta campaign, not complain. What's really the deal? Obviously, T ain't his own man, but Erik is. So fuck it, go kick it. Money talks and bullshit walks. Go spit it at him. This ain't nothing but an illusion.

I rose from my bed, dried my tears, and got his money together. He was in the basement watching videos when I said, "Okay T, here is your money, and thanks for everything. When you get your own connect or become self, then I am here to deal with you, but I'm getting my serve on. And this is with or without you. From now on, you ain't bringing no drugs or flopping on my couch no more. I'm all for self, and actually, I've got work to do. I've still got my phones. Who needs Erik?"

I just made his fat ass money, probably twenty grand more than he had, and that had to be worth something. In the streets, money is worth everything. I knew there was no use in calling Erik. He was a Taurus just like Chino. Both stubborn as hell. Erik and Chino were so much alike, and I knew once his mind was made up, that was all there was.

Erik believed that, one day, Chino would come around and help me with the baby. I, too, believed that shit, but after a year of no help, I was seeing it for what it was—left for dead! I was on my own. I knew that too well. True, Chino was driving around sporting the latest in everything while I still had nothing coming but what I gave myself, and nobody could pay me like I paid myself. And, I liked paying myself. So I wouldn't try to call Erik. But I *would* try to work T-Love.

See, Erik came to Columbus from New York for school as an engineering major. He more or less pioneered this area with the New York trade, and the same custies that T now had, once were Erik's. So, Erik was in New York with the connect and sent T up here to keep the hustle going on. T didn't really have any customers. Nor did he have the plug. He more or less worked for Erik, and all the money T made was split with Erik because of what Erik had established. If you look and listen, you learn a lot. Not to mention if you get or got played the way I did, you also learned even more. So I knew what time it was. I just needed T to know he could be his own man if he wasn't so fucking lazy and was not the middleman. So I figured I'd take a chance on some convo. They were trying to dismiss me the way I saw it, so I might as well give them something to dismiss me for.

I sat next to him on the sofa and calmly said, "Okay T, check it. I know you share custies with Erik. But I can be *your* new custie and give you an opportunity to make money on your own strength. I can do more. In fact, I need some heroin also. A couple ounces of that."

He sat up and I continued, "Yeah, I know all about your clients and how y'all got them and what's what. You can keep tearing off Erik. But tear yourself off on some things you put together." Here goes another dream, but, oh well.

"Would you like something to eat?"

"Yeah," he responded eagerly. *Look at him rubbing that stomach of his.*

"Come on, let's go into the kitchen to talk." *I will not be cut off.*

"Let me prepare you something to eat while we talk about this." *At least I've got his attention.*

"C, you trying to get me cut off. Erik said *no*, and I can't get cut off." He opened the cookie jar filled with chocolate cookies. I noticed this and began to pour him a glass of milk. T popped the miniature cookies into his mouth, one at a time and listened to me plead.

"How is he gonna cut you off? That is your partner."

"I know, but you don't really understand."

"Well, explain it to me, and make me understand how it is. Don't you know the connect?"

"Yes, I do, but Erik mostly deals with him all the time," he said this like a scared kid who wanted no parts of that responsibility.

"Well, all you have to do is talk to Erik. I am not saying to cut his throat. All I am saying is that I need money and so do you. That's why you out here right? And I feel you owe me that effort. On my behalf, talk to Erik. I can't talk with Erik. You know how he feels about me and the streets. He don't want me in them."

During Chino's incarceration, Erik and I spent time talking about the streets, and he was sympathetic to Chino's absence from society. He understood it to be a price you paid in the game, and couldn't understand my willingness to wait on a nigga behind bars. He constantly tried to push up and get me to choose, saying things like, "You too pretty too struggle. Another nigga can pay your bills just like he was." His problem was not seeing that Chino was not a nigga paying my bills, but he was my friend, my first love, and I would wait on him for as long as it took. So, I resisted his advances even though I enjoyed hanging out with him. But he definitely didn't want me in the streets. He wanted more for me and that included him.

I kept trying to convince T-Love by adding, "I can move more dope and I need a connect. If not, take me to New York with you, give me my own plug, and I won't need you." I don't really know what I am saying, but when you are desperate, anything is likely to come out of your mouth. "Now eat this delicious steak and fries. Here, have a nice cold beer and count your money. All your money. Erik doesn't know about this extra kilo, does he?"

He looked startled.

"No T, I know and I understand. Why can't it be a secret between us? Okay? Also, call your wife and give her my love. I never tell him about any of your booty calls, so why tell Erik any of my business?" ·

T-Love knew damn well two things, and they were one, not to mess over Erik's money, and two, don't fuck around on his sister, Deidre. Erik hated him dating his sister because of how loose he was with his dick. But against Erik's wishes and warnings, his sister fell in love with T. Blind love, can't see shit and hear nobody but T-love. Now, I had his attention, taking the fight out of a now weak argument.

"But Erik knows the amount of them thangs I get."

I got confident and said, "Well, tell him whatever. But T, I don't want to see you without two kilos for myself and an ounce of your best heroin. Perhaps Shemeka would like to come over for a movie. Maybe you should take that extra money, go to the mall, and get her a gift. I can go for you." I leaned on the kitchen counter, folded my arms and gave him a wink with a sly smile. Then I showed a little cleavage and whispered, "T, baby, we can do this."

Yep, he took it, gave me five grand and told me to spend it on that bitch. I knew it. He really liked that girl, and people always love it when they have someone to be deceitful with.

I ran to the mall around 8 p.m. rushing against closing time to a store called Diamonds, Pearls and Jade. I talked with my favorite salesman, the same one who did my beautiful engagement ring Chino got for me. I saw the perfect gift for Ms. Bitch—a lovely tennis bracelet made up of solitaire and baguette diamonds with a beautiful clasp. The ticket was about four grand, so I gave the sales-man $3,500, had them gift-wrap it, and I signed a card for T-Love. I was a little mad because I could have gotten some earrings or something, but sack-chasers always want a tennis bracelet. It was some sort of status quo or something.

Anyway, I was keeping the change, and I knew he trusted my taste in things. The gift was beautiful, and I was on my way. I stopped at a bookstore on the way home and copped a copy of *K'wan's Gangsta.* I did a lot of reading in my spare time.

Yes, I would not be denied, and it would work out. I just need-ed to be more of an asset, and that meant all I had to do was make more money. Then, I could call my own shots. That was it. I also got some flowers for his girl. I could spare $35 for some roses. *One day someone will buy some for me. If not, I'll buy them for myself. Yes, I'll lace my home, every room with flowers. I can look around and remember that I got love for myself.*

Red lights. Why do red lights take so long when you're in a hurry? I glanced over and saw the gift resting in my leather pas-senger seat. The gift-wrap looks exactly like my engagement ring and roses that I received from Chino.

I remember when I was in cosmetology school, and he came up to the school with his boy Darren. Chino had on a very nice suit, overcoat and a hat—a big back-in-the-day player's hat. I was so very surprised and happy to get engaged. It was not really a pro-posal. We always claimed each other as husband and wife. But it was more like the final touches to our relationship. I had been wait-ing so very long for this day. He kept saying, "I don't have the money to get a ring yet."

Not that I ever pressed him. We rarely discussed it. The only time we ever gave it any conversation was when I was going to Orient State Prison to visit on his first drug dealing bid and when completing the visiting forms, I had to check the box marked "friend" all the time. He said, "Pooh, that is crazy. You coming up in here as my friend. You are my wife, and I am so sorry I put you through all of this. But I realize you really love me for me, and as soon as I get out, we're getting married. I promise."

"Chino, whatever you want is fine with me. Besides, we must really budget our money. This trip to the pen almost made us fold."

"No, ain't no folding with us. We got love on our side. So it will be alright."

And somehow it always was. We didn't lose anything. We thought of selling the salon, but we decided against it. Even though times had gotten really rough, I hired more staff and customers came out of nowhere. The salon really began to boom and do very well. We lived by faith, not by sight, quite similarly, to how I am living my life today. Just keep on going and striving. I missed my Chino.

Honk, Honk, the constant honking of an irritated motorist made me realize I had been daydreaming...

Okay, green light. When I arrived home, I found T and the baby playing and having fun. He decided to give him a bath for me, which I really appreciated. T was all right. It's just that the streets will change people. I know it has changed me a lot, and the influences I've been around have really done some lasting things to me and affected my life in profound ways. But who had time to think about all that stuff.

"Carmen, I love this wrapping paper," T said as he fondled and admired the appearance of the gift.

"Thank you. Your girl will love the gift."

"What is it?" He began to toss it up in the air.

"I won't tell you. You both will be surprised. Here, I'll finish the baby while you get ready for your date."

I kneeled down next to the tub and began to lift the bubbles from the tub with my hands, blowing them into my son's face. At first, he began to twinge and wave me away, but when one of the bubbles popped on his cheek, he began to smile. T-Love began to look through his denim pants pocket. He was again wearing another denim outfit. This one was gray, black and white, with matching Timb's.

"I have some last minute errands I need to run or could you help me out like you did last time? I need you to get some money for me from Delano and Paul-P. You remember P?" asked T-Love.

"Yeah, I remember him from when Erik was up here last summer."

"Well, if you could do that, then I could go out."

"I can do it first thing in the morning because I'm in for the evening. I'll page the fellas and arrange something with them." *T is so very lazy. He was like 'cool.' Anything, so as long as he didn't have to do it.* "Also, I'm giving Gabrielle, one of the girls, a birthday party."

"Who?" asking like he had never heard of her.

"Your favorite, Gabrielle."

"The one with the big titties?" He began to lick his lips.

"Yeah, that's her. She will be nineteen, and I want you to invite some of your fellas. My service could use the business, and we could mix it up a little. Sort of a toast to our new business venture. Besides, I want it to be very nice for her. I'm gonna invite Delano, Paul and his boys, if that's cool. I'm renting the party house at this one spot and making it like a pool party and cookout with music. We just gonna get fly. Bring your wife down here so she won't get too mad about things. I need you to go back to New York and arrange things. You need to keep everyone happy, so we can get down."

"I will, because if I start bringing kilos down here like that, I can't bring them in the trunk. It's too hot. But old dude that we see has these vans with hidden compartments and shit," said T.

"Maybe we can hook up with him and start using his vans. If you start moving things and let *me* spit it at him, then he will. Yo T, bring him to Columbus. Bring him to the party this weekend, and I'll talk to him. Bring Erik, and I'll talk to him, too. Or better yet, I can come to New York for the day on Wednesday and talk to whomever, if you hook it up." With every word, my fingers were crossed.

"I don't know... Erik said you were very manipulative and not to really mess with you because he knows Chino has schooled you."

"T, life has schooled me, and yes it is true, Chino taught me a lot ,but not too much about the streets. He taught me about people, and I'm not trying to take anything from you. I'm just trying to make some money. You got the plug, so let that be the reason we get paid."

"Is China gonna be at the party?" He moved his hands down to his pants and started rubbing his dick right in front of me. Nasty bastard. I ignored him and started polishing my toes with my favorite pink polish thinking, "Horny ass-nigga." The service just well may be easier than slangin' them thangs.

"You know she would never miss it," I said.

"Bet! Carmen, this shit just might work."

"T, I know it can. If only you just believe and have some faith in yourself and in what we are doing. Look how far faith has brought me."

"You've got a point because we've seen you with everything, then go straight to nothing. Now you on the come up, the rise, again."

"That's right, T, Maya said it best: like dust I rise. It always gets greater later. My son is the reason why I've got to get mines and move out. 'Cause ain't no man gonna do it for me, and ain't no man gonna ever again take anything back from me that he gave. Been there-done that shit, and I ain't even interested in it again. Now, go on and get dressed. I'll take care of Delano and Paul tomorrow. I'll spit some words at them also and give you a total to take back with you to New York. T, have a nice night."

"C, I sure will. Peace."

Chapter

NINE

I woke up early Monday morning with my mission on my mind. It
seemed like I've been craving rap music more and more since I've
started hustling. I don't know what it is but that music seems to
motivate me. Mostly because it is talking about things that are close
to home. Like struggling, the streets, death, loss and how you try to
make a dollar out of 15 cents as TuPac says in his music. Or, how
he tells me to keep my head up no matter what, or how Naughty by
Nature tells me that everything's gonna be alright. Or how the
"Above the Rim" soundtrack just talks about everything it seems
like I am going through. I really get into this rap thing, and those
who don't, can't only because they can't relate to the messages, to
the streets, or the struggle. But those of us going through it can
relate. It hypes us up and lets us know we ain't alone. Not hype us
up to kill, like the media portrays rap listeners. But hypes us up to
keep on keepin' on. Like MC Breed just reminded me that I need to
take my jeep to the hand car wash and shine it up good. Hell, who
knows? One day, I may get a ride and put Carmen on the chrome.
Ain't no future in my frontin'! And I love KRS-ONE, Knowledge
Reins Supreme. `Cause we all know that 'Boogie Down
Productions' will always get paid. I love all that stuff.

The new rap and the old school rap. Some of those rappers be
kickin' straight knowledge and some of it is straight bullshit. Like

Ice Cube, that's my boy. His rap is almost a form of gospel because it makes you feel stuff. You just want to shout sometime. That shit be makin' me want to jump and say, "ah yeah,'ah yeah." Say that shit, say that shit!

But a couple of years ago, I was an all jazz kinda girl. Chino was the one into the rap scene. We were on different pages. I couldn't understand why on our cross-country road trips, he needed some rap in the cassette player and nothing else. But then I understood it. I wish he knew that I felt him and all that he was going through. Everyday in the streets brought me to a closer understanding of his work and all he went through to provide for himself. How hard it is in the streets. People don't realize that this is a real job, and it is tough. People in the streets ain't people with no brains and no skills. On the contrary, you got coaches, organizers, sponsors, and CEOs. You got it all, just like in corporate America. Only problem is corporate America ain't trying to give a brotha or sistah a chance to really express themselves. Especially with no background, no legit papers.

When Chino got out the clinker, or belly of the beast as some of them Muslims call it, he got hired at MC Cafeteria due to his parole conditions. They gave his ass a hard time. I know you probably think I'm making excuses. I am not. It is just like this sometimes for some people, mostly my people, African Americans. I don't know the answer, but I want to be self-employed. The American Dream. Yeah, I want it. Maybe that is my problem or whatever, but I'll figure it out one day.

Paul was upset because he didn't want to wake up when I called him, said it was too early. T really had these people spoiled and just as lazy as his fat ass. But I could tell Paul was far from lazy. He had it in him to do some thangs. I could spot a winner when I saw one. So I was gonna focus on him. Delano had it in him also. T really had some good guys to work with. I've seen a lot worst. I was encouraged to work with these guys. To inspire them to reach some goals, thus my own.

P was to meet me at the bagel shop near his house, even though it was out of my way and he owed T money. It was all good because one day I would have it my way, and that day was coming. I thought I would get some iced tea for us.

Then he came, and he was still *fine*. I always thought that P was a real cutie pie. Silky chocolate with wavy hair, the voice of a temptation, luscious smile, perfect build, and a platinum diamond-filled cross on his chest. He wore trendy framed sunglasses all the time. He had a wife-girlfriend, and I think three or four kids. Too much baggage for me, but it wasn't even that type of party. Besides, I didn't want no man. Yet, it didn't hurt to look. I hoped he smiled a lot because he had a nice smile. I think I liked P so much because he had gentleness about him. I really trusted him, and there were not many people in the streets that I trusted.

"C, what's up?" He pulled out the chair, glided into the seat and scooted in close to me. I moved in closer for the privacy of our conversation.

"You, sometimes me. How have you been?" I asked.

"Just chillin', just chillin'." He remarked, slowly rubbing his chin.

"We need to talk about business. There is gonna be some changes. You bring the money?"

"Yes, but I normally don't deal with anyone else. Especially women. No offense."

"I know," I said softly. My mind wandered to one of the many memories that I have had to experience as a female in the *life*. Men are so threatened when they see a woman getting money. 'Cause they want to use money as a stronghold with women, and when a woman has her own money, a weak man finds it a challenge to gain a hold in her life. If she ain't depending financially, he feels weakened. Last Friday night, it was the ideal summer night, so I rolled up to St. Adelbert parish to watch the fellas play ball. A couple niggas startin hatin' on me. One, 'cause they knew I was out there tryin' to be that girl; two, I was fine; and three, I wasn't falling for that weak holla' they was throwing.

This one known Baller walked over to my jeep and asked me to step out and talk. I knew he was hatin', but I stood outside the jeep to hollar because I was in a position where I had to mix it up to gain my own rep. My rep of handling my business and myself in any situation. Not by murder or sexin', but by finessing.

So, I was talking to Dude, just kicking game, and then we drew a light audience as he tried to play me.

"What you driving, Baby Girl? Is this a new ride or a used one?"

I kept my cool and I responded by saying, "Baby, it is transportation for now, but it is mine and I didn't flat back and fake it to get it, you know."

Everyone knew he had purchased a high piece of pussy with his golden diggin' dress-n-rest whore he was sporting. She was pretty all right, pretty damn expensive.

"You out here kickin' with the men. Why you ain't ever with no man, or you can't keep a man, or do you like women?"

I calmly replied, "Love, I don't do women and I don't do broke ass men, so I'm out here paying myself."

Holding my own, all he could do was some foul shit. He stepped to the side of my jeep unzipped his pants, pulled out his dick and started to pee, saying shit like, "Can you do this, can you write your name with your dick?"

The stream of pee was the focus as he entertained the crowd with his stream control and aimed the urine to the edge of my shoe with one drop landing on the tip of my sandal. Now he knew this was provocation for a fight, or better yet, welcome to death. But because I was female, he wanted to offend me and teach me a lesson about coming to the court alone.

I stepped back, and he missed his aim. He zipped up his pants apologizing, acting like he was going to wipe my sandal with the T-shirt he had in his back pocket. I waved him away saying calmly, "Not a problem, Boo."

I bent down, took off my sandals exposing perfect pedicured feet that had all eyes on my toe rings. I walked over to the garbage can, tossed the barely worn sandals inside, then walked over to my jeep, reached in the backseat, and replaced the sandals with a pair of stiletto heeled pumps. I always kept a change of clothes in my car. It is called being prepared.

I winked at the guy that did the piss performance and told him, "It's okay, Baby. I only wear my shoes one time anyway." I looked over at the fellows, who now were giving me the nod, and said, "Stay up, have a good game. Next time, I'm gonna come out and put some money on the game."

I hopped into my jeep, applied some lipstick, picked up my cell phone holding it with one shoulder, turned up my bumpin' sounds, and drove off. The next time I went to the court, they gave me my props, and I just sat in my jeep waiting for the right time to make my move and let them know that I was that girl and I had the weight.

P continued, "I just heard that you were into this escorting service. Nothing else." Holding a look of seriousness on his face, he listened.

"Well, it is like this. I know a lot of people, and I mix it up. I am whom you will most likely be dealing with in the future. We are advancing. I need to know what it is that you are trying to do, and what you are looking for in a supplier," I said sternly.

He looked spooked. But I found on the streets that so many people don't have an agenda. They are just out to make some money, get some sex, and some clothes. Like G, all he wanted was the money so he could have the *honeys*. His conversation went no further. G, was also turning into a big gossip. He was in everybody's business. If I had listened to one more tale of his threesome fuckfest with China & Ashley, I would have screamed. Every time we met, no matter how many times I checked his ass, he wanted to broadcast how China sucked his dick while Ashley ate China's pussy. Or how Ashley sucked his dick, while he watched China eat Ashley's pussy. Or how he watched China & Ashley eat each other's pussies for a hit of dope. Now, why would you brag to another women, especially about fuckin' a sex pro, as China is classified? With no protection, no condoms, nothing. One day he would cost me. I felt this, and I needed to do something about G's gossipy ass. He had female qualities, and females will cross you up. But P could kick it. He just kicked conversation with me.

"C, I ain't trying to be no drug dealer all my life. I am in college and studying business. I hustle to support my family and stay in school. But I don't really make a lot of money. I basically turn others on due to my relationship with Erik. Some of my cousins and people I grew up with mostly benefit from what I get from T, or shall I start saying *you*?"

"No, it is not all about me. We do this together." *I knew I liked him. He understands the group and the family concept of things.*

"But I am making about four grand on each of them thangs I get. If you could get Erik to lower the ticket, I could do more."

"How much you paying now?" I asked this praying he would provide some answers.

"I'm paying 25 for a kilo, and I let it off for 29."

"That's it?" I asked trying to hide my disbelief.

"Yeah, because I am not breaking it down like I used to."

"How are you driving a Land Cruiser making one grand with three children and a wife?" I smiled, but was curious as to how he was doing this. 'Cause I wanted to work my hand, the best way I could, also. Perhaps, I could learn something from P. Everyone has something to teach you.

"Carmen, you funny as hell. That's my business. I'm trying to stick and move, and to be honest, it just ain't worth it."

"Well, what *is* worth it? What if the ticket was lower? Could you move more than what you are moving?"

"Well, I do now about five a week from various sources.

So, if I could get a new price of say, maybe twenty-four or even twenty-four five. I could do a lil' more."

"Have you ever talked to T or Erik about this?" I quizzed.

"I tried to talk to T, but he never has the time to really discuss it, and you already know that Erik ain't trying to come up off of nothing."

"In fairness, the price is not that bad because it is delivered to you in Columbus—" He cut me off waiving his hand to silence me and began to explain his view.

"Look, you don't have to go into all that. I know you got some debate skills. T has mentioned you a lot. He really respects you. I'm not complaining or trying to get hemmed up in a debate with you. I could make more. I'm just keeping it real."

I wanted to keep his interest, so I calmly responded, "P, I ain't here to work you over or debate your position. I really like your style, and I think we could do better. Why risk yourself for say five grand, when you could risk yourself for double that? What if I give you a ticket of twenty-three grand for less than ten of them "thangs" and 22,500 for ten to fifteen of them thangs? *His eyes just opened really wide.*

"How can you do this? Erik and T tell me they can only bring so many."

"I'm not Erik or T, and this is what we on today." I felt hot, so I took a sip from my drink.

"Bet, I can easily do 10 for 22,500." He gave me that sexy grin.

"Great, that is what I am looking for. I will have 10 for you on Friday, and we will see how it goes. I know you may be able to move it or maybe not, P. Nothing beats a failure but a try. So let's go for it! As long as you're trying, your ticket will be $22,500, and you can't beat that. And don't ever try to beat me." *I just thought I'd throw that in for scareface type-effects. Although, I know that P is not that type of guy.*

"So, it is all about Carmen now, huh? For years when we would talk on the phone, I wondered when you would come out. Well, Erik speaks very highly of you, and for you to set a price like that, you must have some pull. This is deep. A female drug dealer. I will give it a try."

Beep, beep-

"Is that me or you?" P asked, smiling glancing at his pager.

"It's me." I looked at my pager and pretended to be rushed. Besides, Delano would be here any minute. "P, also start saving your money so we can deal on a cash up-front basis. This will keep the prices down and ensure you all that you are looking for. I will contact you on Friday when it arrives. Just have your people in place because you will only have until Sunday morning to get it all together." *I know he knows what that means.* "Also, I am having a party on Saturday, and you and all your boys are invited to attend. It is going to be a cook-out and a celebration to celebrate our success."

"C, you are so positive that this will be a success."

"Yes, I am! I do things by faith, and faith *Is* the evidence of things not seen. The substance of things hoped for. Keep your faith at all times. We're doing wrong, but we still need to pray for each other and pray for ourselves."

"True dat, true dat." He stood and began to walk away.

"The girls will be there looking for work, if ya know what I mean, and you can come and get your eat on. It will be very fun. Bring some swim gear. I'll call with the details mid-week. Please come."

"For you C, anything. Carmen."

"Yes?"

"Are you married?"

"No."

"Are you with someone?"

"No P, I am alone. Just me and my son. If I had a man, I would not be in the streets. Why do you ask?" I am so tired of being asked this question. Wouldn't a man know that if a woman had a man, that she wouldn't be in the streets, hustling, going for broke, and risking her freedom. They call it throwing bricks at the penitentiary. Eventually, you build yourself behind a wall. Or, so they say.

"Just curious as to how you got into this."

"It is deep. We will talk one day. I know it is different dealing with me, but I'm here with quality and customer service. We about to become incorporated, a'ight?" I extended my hand giving him a firm handshake. It is important for women to give men firm handshakes. It lets men know that a sister is right back at ya and ready to do business.

"A'ight."

"P, this is our summer. Look for me on your hip. My code is triple zeros."

He gave me that sexy smile and said, "So, let's get it on!"

"Later. Bye!" I watched him walk out the door to his awaiting emerald green Land Cruiser. Sipping on my drink, I waited for my next appointment.

I looked at Delano walking up in here looking like Christopher Williams. This was a man I could marry, but not at that time.

"Why didn't you call me this weekend? I thought we were going out?"

"Hi, Delano. How are you today? I can't get a hello, a hug, nothing but drama?" Opening my arms for an embrace, he pulled in close and kissed me on the side of my face. Damn, he smelled so good. We returned to our seats, and he took a sip out of my glass of tea. Yeah, look at them lips on that straw. I wished I was that straw. I began smiling at the thought, and he continued with his questions.

"My fault. How are you and the baby?"

"We are fine, thank you. I intended on calling you, but we got tied up. I am having a birthday party this weekend for a friend of mine, and I want you to come to it. You may bring some of your friends, if you like," I chimed.

"Sounds interesting, when and where?"

"I am still working on some of the details, but I will let you know everything about it, okay?"

"Let me know if you need any help with anything," He said sincerely.

"Thanks for offering. I'll let you know if I do. Did you bring the money?"

"Money?" he said responding as if he didn't know what I am talking about.

"Yes, T's money." *Don't get brand new on me. I ain't in the mood.*

"Yes, and I do not like dealing with you on this level." He slid his chair away in order to look me head on in my face.

"Well, I am sorry you feel this way, but we need to talk about this level and some other things. You may have to deal with me because I am going to be helping T out with his business." *He looks really disappointed with that, but the truth is, I am not trying to date anyone at this time, especially not seriously. After my past experience, I am too tired of men. My lil' heart is worn out.*

I gave him the new price of $22,500, and he was very happy about it. He smiled and said, "I still don't want to work with you. I want to take you out to dinner."

"Delano, that won't be possible, and you know it. Let's try to be friends first okay?" My mind was on business only.

"We can try that. You know you like me." *He is really pushy.* I realized that the more I resisted him, the more he would want me. We always want what we can't have. It is the law of nature. I really enjoyed spending time with him, but at this point in my life, it was not a good time for this type of relationship. I wanted some money. That was it!

Delano and I finished eating and just talked about everything. I found him very easy to talk to, nevertheless, I did not trust him with my heart or my feelings although I really liked him. When I was with him, I didn't think of Chino—not ever. Delano and I could have been the power couple, hustle together, make moves together, do things together and—Fuck it, it wouldn't work. I was not going to try it. No way.

♥

"Stop playing. Yeah, Bitch, we gone play. I should have whipped your ass a long time ago. You kicked it with Erik with no fear. Straight larceny in your heart, like I wouldn't tap that ass for an infraction. Now you'll see. You'll see what I meant all those times I told niggas I'd be to see them. Pooh baby, it's your turn to get to know your Chino. You wanna curse and talk like a man instead of a woman, now I am gonna treat you like that." Darting passed him, he snatched me by my hair, bringing me to my knees.

♥

I told him I had to go, and he offered to pay for our tea and bagels. Then he leaned over and kissed me on the cheek. *Yeah, he smells so very nice. Time to keep moving on. No time to catch feelings with anybody.* I pulled out the parking lot headed for the freeway, and all I could think about was how to pull all this off.

I wished Chino were here to talk to me. If only he were near. But as always, I could talk to him in my head. We used to talk so much. I knew him so well that I could finish his sentences before he started them and vice-versa. As soon as I got home, I planned to send the baby to my mother's that week. It was to be a week of moves and a week of faith. I needed to get to NY, convince Erik and their connect, and get some transportation and some drivers. Then get this ball rolling. It was summer already. I wanted to be gone by the fall. I wanted to be in another state with a new home, with my son. Yes, four months or fifty grand. Whatever came first. This was all I was giving myself, and I had to move very fast.

The game was getting tight and competitive. Other knock- off escort services began to surface and attempted to match mine. Ballers from Gary Indiana, also known as the GI Boys, had infiltrated Columbus with stick-up moves, barbaric tactics, and gorilla schemes taking over blocks and small apartment complexes. One complex off 18th and Main, they renamed the Carter after the movie New Jack City. They slang rocks from that building's stoops and windows daring anyone, including the police, to stop them.

I didn't worry about what the next man was doing. I kept my eye focused on my prize. I knew in the streets everyone got at least one chance, and I was determined to play my hand when my ace card was dealt. I didn't want *all* the money, just enough to reach my goal. I would do the best I could with what I had. Get mines while the getting was good.

I began to think of a way to put this together: There is Delano who could do seven and then G, who could do two. Then there is Paul, who could do ten. That is nineteen. I'll ask for twenty-five. This was my most risky gamble to date. I had to take the roll of this dice to make this a deal maker. Who could resist a sale for 25 kilos?

If I could convince this man in New York that I could move 25 kilos every weekend, then there was no way he would not work with me. I was uncertain of the average move in the street, but 25 of them "thangs" a week is a lot to someone. Not to forget the ounce of heroin that I needed. I could remember Chino doing 200 of them a month so I know I can do half of what he did. I never saw the 200, but that was what he told me, and he was always counting money, so it must have been true. I mean, who cared about Chino? This was my life and my venture. I needed some money, and I was going to get it. I knew this was the right move.

One time, Erik told me that he could move more if he had the vehicles with the hidden compartments. He said he could lock Columbus down with sales. I almost met the supplier once. I was in New York, and I went with Erik to purchase some ganja plant to smoke. We went straight to a corner store in Brooklyn, purchased some weed, rolled up a phat blunt, and smoked it. Erik asked me if I wanted to come in, but I declined. He brought some guy to the car, and a Spanish guy waved his hand towards me. I knew it was *him,* but I had no further interest in meeting him. I was in one of my moods. But I was willing to bet that when I finally met him, it would be the same short Columbian or Dominican at the store. And one day I expected to meet him. "Dear God, please let me meet him," I thought. I needed a plug.

I told T-Love of my meetings and my need for twenty-five kilos. He grabbed his head and screamed at me.

"C, you are out of your mind? I can't get twenty-five kilos."

"Can you get twenty?" I was ignoring his raised voice.

"C, I told you I have to talk to Erik. It is not as simple as you think. My relationship, my partnership rides on my decisions."

"I can be in NY on Wednesday to talk with whomever. I have already put the shit in place. I spoke with P and Delano. I also got peeps that I deal with. The shit is already sold, quiet as it is kept. T-Baby, I am ready to Ball. Let's get it on!" I jumped into the middle of the floor acting like a WWF wrestler and screamed, "Let's get ready to rumble! In the right corner, you got a thirsty single Mom ready to campaign, never complain, and get down for her crown!" I continued with the drama and said, "In the left corner, you got my partner, T-love Babay! Waitin' to tag team Columbus, bring this bitch to its knees. Bow down!"

T really liked my ideas and the fact that I took the initiative to talk to Delano and P. After all, who wants failure? And T didn't mind using me as the front-line man. He would put me out front so that it all would be on me. Well, I had been a front-liner before. I could handle it, I hoped.

T said he had been trying to get this guy to work with him, using the transportation and everything, but he kept thinking about it and putting him off. I told T he was not bringing him the correct figures, and that 20 kilos would spark his interest. T also revealed that the guy was already aware of me. He said he wanted to meet me on the strength that I opened a service, provided housing to the guys every weekend, and supported them whenever they were in town. He recognized the fact that it takes a community of people working together to make this drug trade happen. So, I was almost in. He was familiar with my name, so I was not a complete unknown. I had a chance.

"Look, T, please call me. When will you see him?" I pleaded.

"When I get in town, I will talk with him. I am telling you now, C, Erik will not go for it." He continued to fold a two-inch cuff into the bottom of yet another denim outfit. This one was green, with the Timbs to match.

"Just please try. Now, let's get you packed and on the road."

"C, I will page you and let you know that I touched down safe."

"Don't forget because I do worry." The way to a man's heart is softness.

"I know you do, and I will hit you on the hip. I'll page around three a.m."

"Here, give me a hug, and no matter what, thank you for trying. Bye," I said.

"Peace, I'm gone."

I called my Mom, and she happily agreed to take the baby. I decided to arrange a connecting flight to drop my son off and continue on to New York, all in one day. I made the arrangements for the party, and hired a DJ and caterer. I rented the pool house at the

Lakeview Square apartments in upscale Worthington and began to prepare the menu. I decided to serve nothing but light and nutritional foods. I decided on chicken, shrimp shikabobs, and vinaigrette tossed salads. I would play pre-mixed tapes, for music. I had a lot of NY pre-mixed tapes so the music would be nice. I think I had covered it all. All I could think of was that soon it would be on. I could feel it.

TEN

I arrived at New York's LaGuardia Airport on Wednesday afternoon. I was so nervous that I didn't eat anything. T-Love had arranged for me to meet with his source. I finally got his name.

A driver was to meet me at the airport. I was anxious to get it over with. No turning back. This was what I wanted, right? I learned a long time ago that everything happens in cycles, in seasons. This was my season to reap a lot of the harvest of things that I had planted. So I was going to be blessed.

I noticed a man with a sign that read Carmen. My driver arrived on time. I knew I was dealing with some pros because they were on time. Lateness is a sure sign of an amateur. I made it to the car, which was a Nissan Pathfinder, not a limo—I was okay with that. Inside, I found T-Love and two other Latino men.

T introduced me to the driver Victor and the other passenger who was Capo. Capo sat silently looking straight ahead. He didn't even acknowledge me when we were introduced. This gave me an uneasy feeling and made me think it was all a mistake. We drove swiftly through the city towards a restaurant in Queens. I was told I'd meet *him* there. I took in all the sights, and it seemed like my nervousness went away and my appetite came back. I was starving. We went to an Italian spot, and I ordered some pizza and a salad.

As we waited for our order, three men came into the building. One was a slightly short and very young—the same guy from my memory of the corner store in Brooklyn. The two men took the table next to me, and I took the extended hand of the man before me.

"My name is Dragos."

"My pleasure. My name is Carmen," I replied releasing his hand and thinking of a way to stay calm. Dragos was a toasted warm brown in color with thin gold-rimmed glasses and a well groomed goatee that he rubbed from time to time. As he spoke, he continued to stroke the hair on his face.

"I am surprised, Carmen. I thought you would be more of a different kind of lady. More like a hip hopper. But no, you are a young lady. You look like a college student."

"So do you." We gave each other a grin. My order arrived, and he ordered some bottled water. Taking a few sips of the water, he asked, "How do you like Queens?"

"I like it very much. I wouldn't mind living here."

"I have apartments all over, and you are welcomed to stay at any one of them, anytime. I've heard a lot about you." *I am wondering when T-Love will join in. Instead, he just sits there stuffin' his mouth.*

"Carmen, go ahead and eat. Later we will take a walk. I like to walk. I like to walk and talk."

"I like to walk and talk also." I could not stop smiling.

"So, tell me about yourself," Dragos quizzed

"Well, I have a small son, and I'm a single parent. I'm just trying to make it in this world for me and my son."

"You don't have a husband? You are very pretty and gentle," he said curiously.

"No. I had one, but he left me for another woman." *I figure, why start with the lies?* "I've been struggling and just trying to put some things together. I have a lot of goals."

"Please, tell me of your salon." Deciding to put it all on the line, I gave my heart with an honest response.

"Well, I, or we, had a salon, a very nice salon, and when my life went through some changes, I just let go and walked away from everything. But, now I'm on my own, and I'm not looking for no man. I'm trying to be independent. Dragos, this is very important to me. Tell me about yourself." I had no idea as to what I was doing, and the wrong question could be a deal breaker. I held my peace and paced myself as I attempted to get in where I fit in.

"No one has ever asked me this before." Dragos held a look of peace on his face.

"I try to be personable," I politely responded.

"I can see that you are very personable. Eat and we will talk more."

"Thank you for taking time out for us to meet. I am grateful."

"How do you know that you're grateful? The meeting has just begun."

"But I am. I am grateful for things that you have no idea about."

"I am not suppose to know, but I must admit, I like this quality in you. You seem so opposite. You're in the street and still have faith?"

"Yes, very much so. I know that God is up there watching me. I noticed your religious medallion. It is beautiful. You also believe in God."

"I really think we will enjoy talking."

T was still stuffing his face and nodding his head and going, "Yeah, yeah, I told you Dragos, Carmen is mad deep. Carmen tell him about your service."

"Maybe later." I turned to Dragos and said, "I am having a small cook-out in Columbus, and I was wondering if you would like to come?"

"Only if I can come as your friend," Dragos said while patting my hands as a father does to reassure a child.

"I would be honored. I think you will enjoy it. Perhaps I can show you around Columbus and you could even meet my son."

I knew I was making some wrong moves. In the streets, you try to keep everything a secret, but I wanted this man to see that I was a woman in a man's role and that I was a human being in this life. I was just trying to make it. Not really as a Baller or a gangsta, but more or less as a businesswoman with big ideas that could be trusted. The approach worked so well for me that I wanted to try to make this family style, not Mafioso style.

He smiled more and more, and I liked this. I had already decided that when we took our walk, I was going to be real with him and not be something that I was not.

We arrived on the riverfront in lower Manhattan. The weather was warm, but windy. It was just Dragos and myself, all alone. Well, not really alone, his associates were several yards behind us. I had heard that he had bodyguards. But now I saw that he had watchful eyes. "Dragos, I can't really believe that I've met you. People in the streets dream of meeting someone like you."

"So, I've heard, and I can't believe that I am meeting with you. I wanted to see you for myself. What type of young girl does all that you have done and is trying to do?"

"Well, you are young yourself." Trying to hide my defensive side, I put the ball back in his court with the same questions. "What type of guy does all that you do and have all that you have?" I tried to pick his brain, but he avoided responding and asked me another question.

"True, how did you get into this…shall I say, line of work?"

I took a deep breath, closed my eyes tightly, and let it out. "I was turned out to the streets by my son's father. When I met him, he was a small-time hustler of sorts, mostly stealing clothes. Then, he went on to selling small quantities of cocaine and then on to the larger quantities of cocaine. We were very happy. Next, the relationship problems occurred. The usual, I suppose, but I learned a lot. He did the majority; I offered the support. When I was left with nothing, I got into some jams out of desperation. I just made every attempt to work my hand at a variety of things. I've had my hands in a lot of things. I don't like spreading myself so thin. I have some financial figure amounts I would like to meet. I want to buy a house for me and my lil' man. I want to move away from Columbus. Too many memories for me. I just want a new life. You ever wanted a new life?"

"Si, a nuevo vida yes," he said, smiling.

"I know a life is something you must work at, not work for, or wish for."

"So why Coca?"

"Because I have some outlets and I hope a resource. I want to take advantage of this opportunity. Things happen in rotations, and in life, everyone gets a chance. I think this is my chance. My turn to make a new life."

"Do you think of your salon?" he asked.

"Yes, but that is over. I don't even want another one. Not like I wanted that one. Dragos, I am prepared to move 20 to 25 kilos a week. I just need a good ticket and for them to be delivered to Columbus. I think you are the man that can make that happen for me."

"You really think that?"

"I am very serious about this. I think you can do that."

"Erik and T-Love have been in Columbus selling for the last three years. Why is it that you think you can do better?"

"Because I know I can. I am very good at business and I can make us a lot of money." I looked him dead in the eye having learned a valuable lesson from Chino. In business or any deal, the other person only wants to know what is it in it for him. I needed to show him that what was in it for him was an opportunity to make more money.

He looked at me, carefully searching my face for a motive and said, "I have a lot of money already. But, you want me to take a chance with you?"

"Yes, I do. And, for you to come to my party." With my perfectly lined strawberry lips, I gave him a confident smile.

He is rubbing his hands, now his head, and looks me in the eyes. He takes my hand and he says to me...

"Carmen, my family is the most important thing in this world to me. I don't ever want to leave them." *Is this a threat?* "Yes, I will give you a chance. I will have 15 kilos in Columbus for you by Friday afternoon, and *you* will be responsible for them. Not Erik, not Timothy (T-Love). We all work together, but please know, this is on your shoulders."

"I will need to explain this to T and Erik. I don't want them to feel crossed. They had been trying to work out this plan with you for a longtime. Now that I am on the verge of doing what they wanted to do, it is causing some ill feelings."

"Well, you must choose because I only deal with one person at a time. You brought this idea to me, not them. Whatever financial arrangement you three work out is still on you. But these are my terms. Be careful what you ask for Carmen because you've just got it. The question is, do you want it and at what cost?"

Of course I want it. I'll look after T and Erik. We just want to be plugged in right? "Yes! I want it."

"Do you have any people in your corner? Any men with you? The streets can be rough."

"No, I am alone, and I want it that way. But I will consider getting someone in my corner."

"Bueno, well, I will come to Columbus this weekend as your 'brother' to attend your party, meet your son, and bring your goods. Where are you staying tonight?"

"I'm not certain."

"You may stay at one of my apartments."

"I normally stay with T-Love, Erik, and his wife whenever I'm in the city. I just don't think tonight would be the right night to stay considering that things have changed." I looked off into the water and I admired the lights. He was still holding my hand.

"Dragos, don't laugh, but I'd like to stay at a very nice hotel in a honeymoon suite. A honeymoon suite all by myself. Chino always promised me this, but his promises never came true. Now I can stay there, and I can pay for it. That's what I want."

"No problem. I will have my driver arrange it for you." He kissed both of my cheeks. "Leave all of your contact information with Victor, and he will give you my contact information. He will also take you to the airport in the morning." With that, he began to walk off.

"Oh, Dragos. What is my ticket?" I asked, not really caring. I just wanted to be plugged.

"Carmen, your ticket is *Twenty.*" That ticket would put me in the position to stack thousands.

"Muy gracias," I replied in my best Spanish accent.

"Buenes noche," Dragos said impressed with my accent.

"Buenos noche. Adios," I said laying it on thick.

Chapter

ELEVEN

THE WALDORF ASTORIA

"OOOOOH-WEEEEE-AAAAAAAH!" This place had it going on, and I was here. I was here. I was in my very own honeymoon suite. All by myself. This suite was all that and a bag of chips, a six-pack, a twist, two snaps, and a swirl. I knew I should have brought a change of clothes. A complimentary bottle of 'Dom Perignon' sat upon the black baby grand piano. There was a huge bouquet of yellow roses. They were beautiful, and two big fluffy white Astoria embroidered bathrobes, a beautiful view of New York's skyline through floor to ceiling windows. In a dimly lit corner of the room, there was a fully stocked wet bar, a huge garden style bathtub, marble floors leading to plush thick wine-colored carpet, and a gigantic bed with silk linens of gold tones and goose feather pillows to rest my head.

I decided to take a long bubble bath. First, I would call T and tell him it was on. Then I thought no, maybe I should talk to T and Erik in Columbus. I decided to talk to them later because I did not want to spoil this mood. I called the airlines to arrange my return flight to get my son home to Columbus, Ohio. Then I called room service and just ordered up some shit! All sorts of food. Afterwards,

I turned on some classical music. I got ready to jump in the tub. I called guest services and ordered some bath products, although I already had enough in my room and in my Chanel shoulder bag. I had enough perfume and makeup to cover any slacking area. I turned my music up loud and was waiting on those strawberries I ordered. If Julia Roberts could eat strawberries and champagne, why couldn't I? I popped the top on the bubbly and poured me two glasses.

"Clink, Clink." To me, a toast for getting the plug! I did it, I did it! I'm plugged!

I jumped in the bathtub and just chilled, waiting for room service. I called and told the front desk to have the bell-person come on in and leave my bill because I was chillin' and I'd take care of it later. Yep! I had a phone right near the tub, right next to the toilet. Oh, I felt so relaxed, and this was what I needed, a nice bubble bath. Heaven has gotta be just like this.

Later, I called and checked on my son. My Mom said he was fine and enjoying his visit (hint, hint) playing with his cousins that never see him. "Well, Mom, I am coming to get him tomorrow. I may stay overnight with you."

"Oh, Pammy, that would be great. I miss seeing you, and since you are without Chino, you can come whenever you want. Not when he says that you can."

"Mom, please leave Chino out of this. I'll see ya tomorrow, and I don't need a ride. I want to take a cab. Put the baby on the phone."

"Okay, here he goes. Come on, it's your Mama."

"Hi, Boo. Hi, Boo. It's Mommie," I said.

There was breathing and slobbering sounds. "Halo-halo, Mommie." The sound of my son's voice sent chills up my spine. That's right, Boo, I am your Mommie, and one day, you will be proud of me.

"Are you having fun, Boo?"

More breathing and slobbering sounds. "Yes fun, Mommie."

"I love you and Mommie misses you."

"I wuv you. I wuv you." The phone dropped and kids were laughing in the background.

"Pammy, that boy is off and running. He is in there with those kids having a good time. Did you have a nice talk?"

"Yes, Mom, please be sure to watch him around the older kids, and he doesn't like milk and be sure..."

"Ms. Pamela, I do not need your advice on raising a child. I raised you and you came out straight, as you kids say. Didn't you?"

"Yes, Mom, you are correct. I just worry."

"You first-time Moms are a total trip. You got a hip mama, and for your information, he does drink milk and eat everything you say he does not. He is not made of glass. He will not break, bend maybe, but not break." She laughed

"Stop making fun of me. Just kiss the baby for me," I said.

"When will he stop being a baby?"

"See, I got ya because you have always told me that I will always be your baby, and so my son will always be my baby."

"Ha, that's right. It's true, you will," said Mom.

"I gotta go. Kiss him for me, okay? And I will see you soon. I love you."

"I will kiss him, and I love you too. Bye."

"Bye, Mom." Hanging up the phone, I remembered my childhood and what a wonderful mother I had. I really don't have much in this life, but my mom and my son, and for this, I am so grateful.

Whew! This champagne is good, I thought. And the strawberries were super deluxe fabulous. The seafood I ordered looked good too. It had been so long since I did anything for myself, and this was a nice evening. I was on a honeymoon with myself. I needed to start loving myself. This room had a gorgeous window seat. I wrapped up in my big bathrobe and cuddled in the window seat and picked over my food and drank half the bottle of champagne. I stared out of the window. The view was absolutely breathtaking. The more I drank, the more I gazed out of the window. I was having a serious buzz and was tired of the classical music.

I went to change the dial on the radio. Spanish music was play-ing and I decided to throw off my robe and do the salsa butt bootie-naked. Then I did the Macarena. Yes. La Macarena. I was pretty good at it, too. I love this music. I swear there is a Spanish person in me waiting to come out. I love tacos and burritos and plantains, all sorts of Spanish food. I did a few more dance moves and changed the dial again to the famous WBLS radio station. They were pumpin' Shabba Ranks remix of *Mr. Loverman,* so I sang along. I love jerk chicken, beef patties, curry chicken and some goat meat "mon." Then they started with the rap remixes. I love rap music. I swear there is a rap person in me waiting to get out.

Check it: *"I'm in the place where stars are born, and I am the only one that can't be worn out by anyone, anywhere, or any part of the world."* Now I finally figured out why I don't have a rap career, 'cause my ass can't rap. Then they were slowin' it down with the slow music. I love the slow jams. I swear there is a singer in me waiting to get out.

I put my robe back on, grabbed a rose stem from the vase of flowers and sang into it. The bottle was almost empty by then, but they were pumpin' my song by Teena Marie and Rick James, *Fire and Desire,* I sung every note off key, of course, but you couldn't tell me that. I swear there is a black person in Teena Marie trying to get out. All I know is if her and Rick ever hooked up again, it would be on and over for these other half singing entertainers.

I was tired of doing concerts with the rose stem, so I began to tear the petals off and throw them over my bed. I poured me a drink from the wet bar. I took my place in the fluffy window seat.

I just sat and looked at the twinkling stars. It was so lovely. The radio station continuously pumped the slow jams, and that's how it all started. Me, booze and music. It was only a matter of time before the memories rushed in. They played beggin' Keith Sweat, and he sang the same song Chino used to sing to me all the time.

He would call the salon and sing it over the phone to me. *"I would never do anything to hurt you. I'd give all my love to you, and if you need me baby, I'd come running. Life gets so rough on me, baby, and I need somebody that I can call all mine. I know that you are the one for me, baby, oh yeah, oh yeah."*

I could hear Chino's voice singing to me like it was yesterday and we were together, so I took another sip. They played all the slow songs. They even played Marvin Gaye, and it was over then; I was on memory lane. I sang myself silly. Then the tears came, and I started talking to myself. Sitting in the window seat, I pulled a pillow tight to my chest with my knees pulled up close and just started talking to my Chino:

Chino, I know you are not physically present with me now, but I know that you can still hear me and feel me. I know this because I can still hear you and feel you. I never meant to hurt you. All I wanted was for you to be happy. To love you is all I wanted and for you to love me, forever. I gave you all my love, my time, my life, my faith and my dreams. I gave you my heart. I couldn't accept the thought of you not loving me anymore and wanting someone else. I know I hurt you with my friendship with Erik. But it really wasn't what you thought. So many things went wrong. I accept our separation. We could never go back to the past again. We can't even talk on the phone without arguing, and we used to never argue. It is like we were never friends. Like we can't even stand to hear each other's voice. You resorted to sneaking and calling me on the phone so your wife and family wouldn't know that we still spoke to each other.

Then, to add injury, to insult, you told everyone that my son was not yours, yet you know I was always faithful to you. You also used to tell me that a woman would never come between us. You would say this about a thousand times, and I believed you. And in the event that you did not want me anymore, I always thought you would be decent. After all we had been through. After what I thought we meant to each other. You left me for a girl that didn't even want your fat ass. You knew her before you knew me. Yet, it didn't work 'cause you had no money. Now that your pocket is fat, she wants to be with you. This is what really hurts.

I struggled with you. I slept on the floor with you. I made twenty-five dollar runs with you. I was the one you turned out to stealing clothes and pulling capers. I was good enough for all that, but your wife was not. Then you married her when I was eight months pregnant and acted like a straight-up Bitch about everything. You held on so tight to material things. Why couldn't you leave me and walk away with nothing like I found you? I stepped with nothing, not even a car. You took our money, gave it to her, and then took my car and gave it to her and all we worked for.

Yeah, I was jealous because I am human. But I was hurt more because of your triple-cross. That's the real reason for all the drama, and you know it. I never had a problem with your wife. You know this! But I never meant to hurt you, and you know this also. 'Cause you my heart. Shit, Chino, you may be thirty-eight in the waist, but you still pretty in the face. Our shit just went haywire. And I could never really explain all that I feel. But, Chino, I know that you know, and I also know that God knows.

God, if you're listening, and I believe that you are, then all I ask is that you protect and watch over my son. God, I love my son so much, and when I look at him, I see the best of your blessings. I also see the best of Chino and me. So, I want to thank you for my son. And I want to thank you for the memories. I want you to bless Chino and his family. Watch over him and keep him safe from harm. And, me too. All I want is to be happy. Please keep Chino happy, too. All I want is for him to be happy and to forgive me for not being all he needed. Please forgive me Chino for my wrongs, and I forgive you Chino for all the hurt and pain you caused.

Dear God, one day, it is my prayer, that I'll be able to tell Chino how I feel today and that I am able to do something nice for him and bless him like he has blessed me in my life, through the good times and the bad times. I want to take my money and do something nice for him so he can sit back and remember and feel special about himself. God, I just want to make it. I don't know the way, but please walk with me and keep me and show me the way to happiness.

Damn, my glass is empty. Chino, wherever you are, may God bless you.

TWELVE

THE WEEKEND

The van, Dragos, and drivers arrived like clockwork, and I had all the fellas lined up. Everything was perfect at the party house. I had on a designer crimson linen sundress that melted against my honey brown skin. Of course, my hair was looking *fierce*. I wanted everything to be perfect, and it was. Everyone was there, and the music was bangin'. Dragos came looking all preppy in his crispy white Tommy Hilfiger short set. His drivers had on Tommy gear as well. Gabrielle was overjoyed, and China was working the room talking about, "Let that be the reason I makes three grand tonight." I had no doubt that she would do just that. She looked great in the swimwear that I got the girls. The boosters always came through.

I took care of my business the previous night, and it went well. I got rid of 15 of them thangs, and the quality was *all that*. Everyone I saw was pleased and the heroin was *all that, too*. I got $6,000 for one ounce. Hell, I only paid $2,500 for it. I just walked around and mingled. T even brought his wife *and* his hoochie to the party. Can you believe that? His wife had no idea of the hoochie. She just assumed it was another person at the party.

T and his hoochie went into the Jacuzzi together, and I swear it looked like she went down on him, under the water! I mean, he really liked this girl, and his wife just sat over to the side and acted unaware, like nothing was wrong. Maybe there wasn't. I was so into Chino back then that we didn't have this drama. Long gone are the days of the faithful-to-each-other couple. But everyone looked liked they were having fun.

I walked past China wiggling her ass with a plate of food in her hand, and she smelled like she was smokin' that stuff again, and at the party. I told them NO DRUGS. For a crack addict, she had a nice figure, so all addicts are not skinny. She also ate a lot of food. She ate all the time.

P and his crew arrived in freshly washed whips, lined in a row at the cul-de-sac entrance, rolling two and four deep to a vehicle. Delano, strolled in late, taking the breath away from Spice as she made her move to approach him. The sound system was bumpin' house remixes, and the air was filled with joy as Gabrielle celebrated her birthday in style. Toy was flossing an aqua blue swimsuit with matching laced sandals. Everyone made it, and everyone seemed to have a nice time.

Erik came also, but he never said two words to me. All he said was a dry, "Hi." He was still mad that I met Dragos. And even madder now that Dragos only dealt with me. I offered to split *all* the money three ways, but Erik had to put in some work and he did not like this.

It used to be that he was at home chillin' and T was putting in all the work before, but now I came along and changed the whole program.

Regardless of the fact that we had more money, Erik didn't want to do any work. I couldn't blame him, who likes to work? It was not an intentional double-cross. But I'd be damned if they were not going to put in some work.

T agreed to become a driver and share the responsibility of getting it here. In the seat cushion of the vans were hidden compartments that opened through a combination. Airtight compartments were lined with coffee grains to detract the scent from police dogs in the attempt of a search. Each van held 15 kilos, and on the return trip, it held the money. Thus, in the likely event that the police did their racial profiling routine and bogus traffic stop, they would not be able to find drugs or money in the van. A driver with a clean driving record and no warrants is home free. I agreed to move the product in the streets and meet people and count the money, which I learned is a job in itself.

All Erik had to do was help move the product, deliver and collect. He did not want that. Okay, so I offered to give him 30 thousand. He didn't want that. Well, he did want that plus a commission off each of them thangs. That shit was crazy. No way! So we couldn't agree, and Dragos refused to talk to him. Dragos said he was giving me a chance, and Erik was salty about this. So Erik just sipped on his Heineken all night and stared at me with a hateful look on his face. Erik's pockets were already fat. He still refused to talk to me. But I would try one more time. I decided to bring him a Heineken. I wrapped the beer in a white napkin and sashayed over to where he was standing. "Hi, Erik. How are you? (Silence) Are you still mad at me? Are we gonna make up and work this out?"

"Yo, Star! T, is my friend, not yours. And you would not have known him if it was not for me." He twisted his face in a screw-face grimace. You know the one you give a hater on the streets for looking at you the wrong way. He took another swig of his beer, and I continued my attempt to smooth things over.

"Yes, Erik this is true. But I thought after four years we were all friends. After all, I am godmother to your nephew, T's and your sister's son, and I have stayed at your home. We've been through a lot."

"Still, I just feel like you over-stepped your boundaries."

"Do you feel like I crossed you?" I asked already knowing how he really felt. I just wanted to hear him confess it.

"Not really. But, why can't you get money from Chino? He used to take care of you."

"Yes, but not anymore. I was nothing more than a drug dealer's girlfriend and that is all over. He won't support my son. I want this for myself. Like yourself, I want more for my son. Perhaps I'll go back to school. But in the meantime, let's work together."

"No, I can't work with this. I'm out of Columbus. After we split this weekend, I'm out! You're playing out of your league and you'll find out just how far out you are."

"Erik, I don't want you to be mad at me." I knew if Erik felt crossed, he might resort to something underhanded. He definitely had it in him to do some dirty shit, but I didn't think he would go there with me.

He took another swig of beer and continued, "Well, let's just say that all things have changed. Nothing is the same anymore. This is my last weekend. You know everyone. With your new prices, you'll have Columbus on lock down. I can't do nothing here no more. Look at T-Love, he's about to get a divorce, and he don't even know it. Just watch yourself," he said in an odd tone.

"I will and I won't be in this for very long. I promise."

He just looked real blank and stared off, drinking his beer. I just walked away. *Is this the price I must pay? My friendship?*

The birthday cake came. Renaye was singing with her beautiful voice, "Happy birthday to ya, happy birthday to ya, happy birthday." Underneath the singing, Carmen's voice told me Erik was sizing me up—but for what? I didn't know. He would not hurt me. *God, please tell me, what is it? What am I doing wrong?*

Across the room I noticed a guy I had seen all evening. He looked so familiar to me. He was with Delano, and I assumed that they were partners. But he looked so familiar, and he kept staring at me and watching my every move. *Where do I know him from? I just can't place him. Do I know him from Columbus or from someone? Who is he?* I decided not to approach him unless he approached me. Who was this dude in the jogging suit? Who was he?

Sunday Afternoon-

Everything went well. G got an attitude because he got no attention. He kept running up in everyone's face trying to be all that he could be. I wasn't mad at him, but this was not the appropriate place. These were Ballers like himself, not customers. He had absolutely no polish. A rusty brass-ass nigga. But he finally figured out the difference after he got dissed enough. Delano was disappointed that I did not spend time with him. I still don't think he understood how deep in the game I was. And I couldn't seem to discuss it with him because he wanted me to be a lady. It was like he had this image of me that was not true, and I didn't want to knock myself off the pedestal. He wouldn't let me be real with him. How would he take the service? Too many "what ifs." I couldn't deal with it right then.

After the party, Erik, T and I decided to meet at the condo to discuss our business. I was so tired of counting money. We made $6,000 off each kilo, and six times fifteen is$90,000. We split that three ways. We did it! I paid Dragos his $300,000. Three hundred thousand dollars! It was unreal. I was so happy with my $30,000. This was fair, and I was happy as hell.

T was like, "You did it, C! You go girl, you did this!"

All Erik could do was be mad. He said, "I can't believe that Dragos worked with you. I had been asking him for years to do this."

Easing in between the two of them I said, "Well, look at it this way, he finally did it. And we are a team. We made ninety thousand in a weekend. That should speak for something. This is about us. Now, are we homies for life or what?"

With a mouth full of food, T mumbled, "Yeah, Erik, she's got a good point. Carmen, you can be my homie and my Boo. Come here and give me a kiss."

"T, you are so silly. But, today I will give you that kiss." I kissed him smack right on them greasy lips.

Erik took another swig of his beer, stuffed his money in a bag and gave T a look that could kill. T-Love turned white as a sheet and stopped chewing and then responded. "I mean, I guess, I think you did good." I couldn't believe his switch routine. Erik looked in my direction and said, "Pammy, you taking this Carmen shit to heart, huh? You really think you are Carmen, the Baller." He shook his head and walked out the patio door.

I looked at T-Love and I said, "T, he acts like he is 'J'. He actin' jealous."

"I don't care. Fuck him." He gave me a high five and said, "I am not stressing this shit! Where is your phone? I'm calling my hoochie. The wife is at the hotel."

"T-Love, she is one lucky hoochie, sack chaser. T, what happens when you don't want her anymore?"

"Then she can look for another sponsor, and I can get me a new ho' to lick my balls," T said.

"See, that is why I wanted my own. True, I want a man with money. But at the end of the day, it turns back into money. God bless the child that got his or her own. That's got *her* own." With that remark, I handed him the phone.

Chapter

THIRTEEN

Friday. The vans came and went, and they came and went. Like the hands of a clock moves swiftly and surely, with equal certainty, the plan was executed. After three weekends, I had saved my "prayed-for" $50,000. Erik no longer came, but I still sent him his third in an attempt at a peace offering. After sending him $30,000, I decided I couldn't be a fool about it any longer. I stopped sending his third. I let go of any feelings of guilt I had. Shit! I was out there campaigning and trying to make it. Why couldn't he?

Two more weekends came and went, still no Erik and I still sent no money back. Then one weekend, he appeared and told me he wanted to put some work in. T-Love was with him, and he was real quiet. Normally, T was quiet, but that was only because he was eating something, and in that case, he would grunt once or twice. You could have heard a mouse piss on cotton before you heard a word come out of T-Love's mouth.

Erik and T left together to make a sale. Normally, T stayed around the house or stuck up under his girl, or shall I say, his hoochie.

This life was taking its toll on me. It was getting to the point that if I drove down the street, I was paranoid of rival drug dealers, the police, or stick-up kids. It seemed as if though the hoochies had all the fun. I always wanted my own, and this was the price I was paying. Dragos had increased my weekly supply to 25 kilos. I was now paying a fronted $18,500 for them. I was moving them, but with no problem. Erik told me that he needed ten kilos. Wanting to be in agreement with him, I gave them to him.

The drivers even looked surprised. We had all began to bond with each other, a family like old times when I was with Chino. The drivers were Ramon and Capo and occasionally Victor would come to scope things out, I suppose. When Erik and T received their ten kilos, they did not even look me in the face. They just walked out the door and left.

I delivered the remaining ten kilos and did some window shopping at the mall to relax myself. I felt so uneasy about everything. I dismissed it as fatigue and needing a vacation. Sunday came around and still no sign of T-Love or Erik. I paged them, and I paged them, and I paged them, and I paged them. I put 911-911-911-911-911-000(my code) and then I put my address 1104 and 911 to let them know to come to my home ASAP. I even put in T-Loves hoochie's code, which was 696969. I still got no answer. I called New York and that was when it was confirmed that I had gotten jacked for ten kilos. Robbed without a pistol.

"Hello?" someone answered with a Jamaican accent

"Hi, Ms. Fournier. May I speak with Erik?"

"Hi, Pamela, how are you?"

"I am well. Is Erik, Timothy or Diane home?"

"How is the baby, girl? Him be fine?"

"Yes, he is well and visiting with my Mom." *Damn why won't she answer my* fucking *question?* "I was trying to catch Erik before I went out of town. Is he there?"

"Listen 'ear, Erik, Timothy and Diane have moved to Florida, but they don't want anyone to know. They asked me not to tell anyone. You never know what they do. Do you know what is going on?"

"No, Ma' am. I don't." *I guess she doesn't know that I am the* *"anyone" that she was not supposed to tell, huh?* I hoped maybe they would contact me and tell me where they were. "Please tell them I called and that I wish them well."

"Yes, I do that for you, and you take care of you and the baby."

"Ms. Fournier."

"Yeah?"

"Thank you for the years of your hospitality. I love you."

"Pamela, you are welcome, and I love you, too."

"Bye!"

Because they were of Jamaican decent, with passports, they could be anywhere. I called the hoochie because I already knew that T told her everything. Pillow talk is deep. This is what she said.

"T-Love told me it was over last night and that I would never see him again. He gave me $25,000, told me to take care of myself and that he really loved me, that he was moving to England. He also said, Carmen, you be talking shit about me *(which I do)* and that they couldn't work with you. T said he got love for you, but Erik threatened to tell his wife about me if he didn't go along with his set up. Carmen, T never wanted to hurt you. But he said you got it going on and that you would be alright." Then the Bitch started crying and asking *"me"* if T really was gone.

All I could say was, "I believe he is." Then, I hung up the phone.

I just sat there in the middle of my kitchen floor and cried and cried and cried until my eyes hurt and all the snot in my nose was on my shirt. I could believe it, but I was just fucked up behind the shit. Now I was really all by myself. *Lesson #2: Don't trust nobody.* I also owed Dragos the money for the missing kilos. That being at my fronted $18,500, so that meant I owed him $185,000-out of my pocket. How could they do this to me and my son? To place me in a position like this. To place death upon my son and myself. I did not have it, and I had no way of explaining it. Dragos' words rang in my ears: "CARMEN, YOU ARE RESPONSIBLE, YOU ARE RESPONSIBLE."

As I sat on the floor, I realized I needed to make a decision. I just stopped crying and I got mad. I went to my closet, pulled out my stash and counted my money. I had almost $80,000

God... I know I said I would stop at 50 grand. *(Like God can't count)*. I was trying to do some things. *(Please, drop the act)* To be honest, it was time to lose the excuses. "I'm just plain old greedy like most hustlers get in the streets. Just plain old greedy." Whew! I said it and I felt better. I gathered all my money, except for $1,000 dollars. I figured it would get me through whatever it was I was about to go through.

I hit the streets. I collected all the money in the streets with each moment feeling numb. When I collected from Paul, he had a look on his face like he knew. Or maybe I was paranoid. It did not matter because he had the money. G-Money was giving me the "I'm mad at you" silent treatment, so he gave me the money with no words. I did not care. He could have thrown it on the floor, and I would have dove on it, picked it up and smiled. I would talk to him later. When I got to Delano, he wanted to talk. I refused to get out of my jeep, so he just stood there talking to me.

"Carmen, you looking kinda rough girl." I continued to trace the outline of my car door, the part where the rubber is that keeps the moisture and air from getting into the car. Tracing the door to keep from chewing it with my teeth allowed me to maintain my sanity at that moment. Moving my hand to gripping the leather steering wheel, I said through gritted teeth and a dwindling patience, "Thanks a lot. Just give me the money."

"So, I gotta pay to talk to you?"

"No, I'm just in a rush."

"You're always in a rush. I am going to slow you down one day. I'll give you the money after I tell you something." *Shit, just what I need, a lecture.*

"What is it?" I asked annoyed as fuck.

"Carmen, I am here if you ever need me." *I won't ever need no man.* "I don't have much, and I may not be able to live like you do, but I have my heart to give, and I want to be with you and your son. Give me a chance to make you happy." *These weak-ass lines.*

"Let's go somewhere for a vacation—my expense—while your son is away." Pamela was trying to break out, and I felt a tear forming so I turned to avoid eye contact.

♥

"Chino, please stop playing, let go of my hair. I am sorry." He tightened the grip on my hair as I felt the skin from my face pull back, widening my eyes. On my knees begging to end this game, he leaned into my face, looking me dead in the eye and said, "Now say something, talk shit now. You always thought that you were better than me. Your Mom always talking shit about me and how I feed my family. Thought you were too good for a nigga getting money. Look at you, fuck you and your fake-ass family."*

I grabbed his wrist, attempting to loosen the grip his hand had on my hair as I could feel the strands of my long hair being ripped in places. Suddenly, a migraine headache formed and piercing pains and white dots were seen every time I opened my eyes.

"Christonos, please baby don't do this, let me go."

I felt my leg going numb because the awkward position on the floor would not allow proper circulation of my blood. I called him by the name only his mother used hoping to bring back a memory and soften his heart. The look on his face did not change, and I realized using his real name, that only his mother called him, infuriated him more.

"How dare you call me that name? You ain't got it like that no more." He was seething mad and began foaming little slobber bubbles on the side of his mouth, spitting in my face as he continued to scream. Flinching at the flying spit, I had to make a decision. Continue to plead or begin to fight.*

♥

"No!" I said coldly. Here Delano was pouring his heart out, showing his willingness to do anything for me and my son, and I just didn't give a fuck.

"Carmen." Delano continued holding me longer than I wanted to be there. For a tiny moment, I thought of running what seemed like the good in my life over with my jeep. I placed my car in gear listening for a reason and said, "What?" He stood up straight, shoulders back and said, "I love you."

I snatched the bag from his hand and drove off. Who needs that shit? "Not I," said the brown cow. I had all the money, but I was short $75,000 dollars. I went to a payphone, and I called Dragos and asked him if I could talk. I decided to be a grown woman about things. I told him point blank: "Dragos, I have some problems with Erik and T-Love. They are out-cancelled, not with me anymore. I am on my own. I am a little short, but I want to keep going. Let me keep going. I am willing to do what I gotta do. I can come in person to talk more."

"Carmen, your sincerity always touches me. I understand about this life. Talk to my head driver Ramon. Time to say good-bye."

Dragos never talked on the phone over four minutes. He actually never spoke on the phone, only in emergencies and/or through someone else. So I had to talk to Ramon. I just wanted to ensure that those vans kept coming and that I would not receive a Colombian neck tie. Ya know what I'm sayin'?

With renewed strength, I helped the guys get off to New York. We packed the van with the money, and I briefly explained to them in my best Spanish what had happened. I was so grateful to have taken Spanish for three years in high school. This, combined with exposure to Latinos, really helped my conversational Spanish. We hardly spoke any English, only because they really could not. But they did know how to say some things in English like, "money," "count money," "yes," "no," and "kilos."

I sent them off and decided on a movie to calm my nerves. I

wanted to think that Erik and T were playing a joke on me, and they would re-appear. I knew they would not. They were gone, and it was up to me to repay their debt. "Our" debt. Besides, I was at point zero *again*. Plan A was that I had to bust my ass and pay Dragos and start saving all over again. Or, plan B, run and hide. This was not an option. I refused to live my life as a fugitive. I ain't going out like that. Every thoroughbred takes a fall or hit. I am a mother-fuckin' Baller, that girl. One thing for sure, I was going to spend some money this go around. I had to remember that failure pre-cedes success. Anyway, what is a smile turned upside down?—Nothing but a frown. And it always gets greater later.

Chapter

FOURTEEN

Ring…ring…

"Hello May I Help You?"

"Hi, Sweetheart." G always called me sweetheart, before he wanted something.

"Hi, Mr. G-Money."

Listening to the hiss sound of him blowing smoke from his cigar, he continued.

"Meet me at the hotel. I'm here with Tony and Marsha. They have something to show you. I think it will be worth your time."

"Where are you at?" I asked cautiously. I am on a come up trying to get these ends together for Dragos. Impatiently, I awaited his location, and he finally responded.

"The one on Morse Rd."

"I'll be there in an hour."

"An hour?"

"Yes, G or sooner."

"Please make it sooner."

"I will try. Bye"

Click! This mother fucker wants me to stop, drop and roll for his ass. No way! Hell No!

Ring…ring…

"Hello, May I Help You?"

"Bitch!"-Click Now who in the hell was that. Most recently I had become bitch to a lot of people, so I could not narrow down that phone call. I had other things on my mind. Today, I will be that bitch.

Finally, I would meet Marsha and Tony. I had heard a lot about this boosting couple. It would be interesting to meet them. I wondered what they were trying to sell. Maybe it was jewelry or perfume. I love perfume. Maybe shoes. Yes! They even boost shoes. I would know soon.

Can you believe it? I arrived there at the hotel, clean as a whistle, with a guess jean outfit, matching boots, purse, and smelling like a flower, and G wanted me to buy some tools. Yes, a bunch of tools stolen from a hardware store. They were valuable, I was sure, but no thanks.

"No, G. I don't want them." *These nickel & dime marks. I can't believe G called me here for this shit. I owe a king's ransom, and I am out here wasting my time on this weak loser shit.*

Interrupting my thoughts, he continued to question me,"Why, C?"

"Because what can I do with these tools?"

"Sell them."

"To Who?" I asked expecting an answer from this clown.

"I don't know. You're resourceful."

"Tools?"

"Yes, it's a good price."

"A trunk full of tools." My mouth fell open. *Where in the hell is a microphone when you need one. I need to scream a Flavor Flav wake up in the mic.*

"They've been waiting for over an hour for you. They expect to make this sale."

"How much?"

"$500."

"Hell No!"

"How you gon' play me?" He threw his hands up in the air with this question.

"I'm not playing you. You know I don't want tools. You need to talk to them."

"Come in." I parked my whip, and we walked into the hotel room.

"Tony, Marsha this is Carmen." G made the introductions

"Hi, Carmen (they said in unison)."

"First of all, how do you get all those clothes?"

Tony answered, "Well as you see, I am only 4'11" and my wife is 4' 9," so Carmen, the clothing racks are taller than we are. We just creep through them, and they never see us. They only see the empty racks when we leave the store. People call us the 'Littles.' "

Shaking my head no I said,

"I really like the clothes, but these tools, I can't do it." I offered a polite rejection.

"G said you would do it," Marsha screamed with an attitude.

"I just can't get rid of them." I repeated my explanation for rejecting the deal.

"Give them to your husband," Ms. Thang suggested.

"Nope! Tony, I don't have one. Look, I'll give you $250 for them, just because."

G, blurted out, "No way! Carmen, you got the money."

"G, can we talk for a minute?" We walked out the door, just far away from ear listening distance, and then I turned to him, got up in his face and said, "G, I'm out here trying to get money, and you call me out here to hustle backwards. Yo, I don't hustle backwards, and you had not ever in this life or the next, call me for some bull-shit. You've played yourself."

He tried to talk, and I continued, "I got money, nigga, but it ain't yours to spend. Understand?" I stood there until, like a kid, he nodded that he understood. I couldn't afford to go through this petty shit again.

I peeked my head into the hotel room and bidded my farewells, "Tony, Marsha, I can't help you, but it was very nice meeting you." I turned to leave, and as I walked to my car, G kept complaining in my ear.

"G, what's up? I just can't use the tools. But I will see if I can find someone who can."

"No, don't help me. I don't need your help." He started wailing and rolling his eyes like a 13-year old girl on the playground.

"G, it don't have to be this way. You catching feelings over some tools? What's really going on?"

"Nothing. You think you all that. You think you the shit!"
"All what?"
"All that. But you're not."

"No, I do not, but I hear how you feel. It's unbelievable that you feel this way. Check it, thanks for calling me. Call when you like me again." G began to laugh like a maniac from a horror movie. Silly-ass nigga. I detected something in his laugh. *This was about more than tools. It was old fashion jealously, and I thought only women acted 'J.'*

"Bye, Mr. G-Money."
He just stood there as I drove away.

Chapter

FIFTEEN

I was cruising the streets with my eyes glued on my rear view mirror looking for the Po-po, tail, or stick-up kid on my trail. I thought about how much I had been using my phone lately and was feeling weary of a phone tap. To relieve the stress, I decided to be good to me and pamper myself. I went downtown to the City Center Mall and I treated myself to a facial, manicure and pedicure. Inside the mall, there was a Caribbean bistro, and I had lunch with myself. It was very nice. I came to the mall prepared to spend and spend. All I did was window shop. Walking past Frederick's of Hollywood, I envisioned myself wearing the lingerie and a silk and lace panty set, feeling special as I stood before the admiring special friend in my life. Only, there was no one special in my life. The things I needed I couldn't buy. I needed things inside of me. I began to realize this. It was time to move on.

The City Center Mall has a fabulous perfume store called 'Grasse.' I loved that store, and I purchased several perfumes and had them gift wrapped for my mom and my four sisters. Next, I purchased a beautiful red Armani suit for my sister because she had just started a new job. Giving is a wonderful feeling. I owed money, but the last thing that was going to happen to me was that no matter what the future held, it would not catch me without spending some of all this hard-earned money. Be it death, the penitentiary or the grave, I am spending some of this money. Erik and T-love are somewhere spending all the money I threw bricks at the penitentiary to make.

I wanted to give Chino something, but what do you give a man who has everything? I know. A toy. You give a man that has everything a *"Toy."* Maybe, one day, I'll get Chino a motorcycle. I thought, whatever my Chino wants, he can have!

Moreover, for my son, "Don't worry, Baby. Mommy is out here getting down for her crown. You are gonna have more. I see that for you, and I am gonna get it for you-by any means necessary.

Chapter

SIXTEEN

Ring…ring…

"Hello May I Help You?

"Hello Pammy?" It was my Mom, and she never called me on my cell phone.

"What's up, Mom? Why are you calling my cell?"

"I was coming from the grocery store and noticed a car following me. Have you talked to Chino? Is he looking for you or something?"

"No, Mom, why do you think that you are being followed?"

"The other day I went to open the blinds in the dining room and noticed a car parked on the side of the house. A man was sitting inside, and I didn't really pay it too much attention. But when I was coming out of the grocery store parking lot, it was the same man and car behind me as I pulled into traffic. Now, the last time you and Chino were feuding and you took his money and left, him and some other thug came up here looking for you. So, what is going on?"

I had no idea, and I knew it was not Chino. I had only gone home once since I started hustling with the drugs, and I hoped to God no one was staking out my Mom's house or putting a tail on her.

Immediately wanting to calm my Mom's concerns I said, "Mom, don't even worry. You know that you ain't did nothing wrong, and if someone is tailing you, it is because of your cooking. Mom, maybe you have a stalker looking for your world famous Star B-B-Que sauce. Don't stress it, and stop thinking the worse. Okay?"

"Okay, Pammy, that is why I called your cell phone. I wanted to talk to you and see if you are okay."

"Mom, I am fine and was wondering if you would keep the baby?"

My Mom happily agreed to keep the baby for me while I looked for a house and continued to get myself together. My Mom had no idea about my career. I told her I was doing nails at home and was back in school. Nothing but lies. Mom didn't ask too many questions. I knew she didn't want to believe that I was in the streets. Many of my family assumed that Chino finally came through and was helping me out on the down-low. So I didn't have to answer many questions. I just promised to hurry, get myself together, and get back in contact with family.

As the weekend was approaching, I contacted the guys and told them of my new ticket. It was high post as usual. I decided to raise my tickets in an attempt to recoup after my loses. I didn't tell them exactly like that, but I did the usual. I told them that my prices went up due to a drought in New York. What else could they say? Droughts happen, prices vary, people get popped, people have falls, people take losses. Not to mention, the political aspect of the importation of drugs. That was the way of the streets. So I figured that I would have Dragos paid in about three weeks of steady pumpin'. Plus, I was placing an extra 30 G's on top of my pay off for GP, for being late, mending the relationship, and showing integrity. Shit, the bill collector gets interest if you are late, why not my supplier? I was like the mailman, UPS, and special delivery services: Rain, snow, sleet or hail I was coming through. The service was still bringing in about two thousand a week, so I was happy about that.

•

I went to a realtor that I had known in the past. I told her I wanted a house on a land contract, no questions asked. A nice home for me and my son. She dated a black guy that was in the game and instantly knew what time it was. He had been in the life, and by her being a white girl, she was able to get her foot in places that I could not get into. So I let her do all the foot and legwork, of course, for a discreet fee. I would occasionally go to house viewings, but she also had great taste and a good feel for what I wanted.

I wanted the American dream, though I was not sure if I would stay in Columbus. Remember, I was moving, but I was keeping my options opened. New York was out of the question. A small town anywhere would work. But it had to be mine. I increased my tickets by $1,000; even though there were gripes, everyone just rolled with it. I was on the look out for a driver and some corner men in my life to help protect me and my interests.

All I could think of was where was my Chino? If only he knew how much I needed him now. I had been dreaming of him lately. And in my dreams, *he* needed me. He was calling out to me. I didn't know where he was or what he was doing, but I know he was broke and he was in need of cash. I could feel it. He needed help and rest. Like me, he needed to know he had someone he could depend on. Yeah, he needed me. My dreams never lied to me. I spoke right into his spirit.

"Chino, I don't have much, but what I have is yours, and I am still here for you. Can you hear me?"

♥

Tightening the grip on my hair, I knew that I had to fight, but not with my fist, but with a woman's mind. I looked up into his face with eyes full of tears and said, "Chino, baby, please don't hurt me. All I wanted, all I ever needed to know was that you loved me. I miss you and how you use to make love to me."

He began to loosen my grip allowing me to take the posture of being on my knees in front of him. I began to caress his legs up to his groin area as I continued to plead, "Chino, don't do this to us. Please be there for us."

I began to bring my face near his knees and began to rub and talk to his "ego." "Chino, just hold me, baby, just make love to me." Knowing there is no better feeling than making up after a passionate fight, I tried to reach his "desire." He loosened the grip on my hair, but still holding the back of my head, he began to respond.

"Pooh, why you be trippin' acting crazy and shit." I began to unzip his pants and move my lips to his private area. Loosening his belt buckle, he placed the nine that was in his waistband in the chair on the seat cushion hiding my 380 underneath.

When I felt his grip completely release from my hair, that was when I made my move. As Chino relaxed and prepared to be sexed, I reared my hand back with a balled fist and punched him between his legs hearing the smack of his balls against the knuckles of my fist. He bellowed over in pain, holding his dick falling to his knees. I stood above him, grabbed his gun in the chair, shifted the gun placing one in the chamber and said, "Now, mother fucker, who is the Bitch? Looks like you the Bitch, Chino. If you only knew how to control your dick, we wouldn't be in this predicament in the first place. I wouldn't have bitches calling the shop, and we would be happy. Placing the nine to the back of his head I screamed, "Now, mother fucker, what?"

♥

Chapter

SEVENTEEN

"Chino, man, check it out! You will never believe what I found out. Okay. Remember I went to that party with Delano?" said the guy who wore the mysterious jogging suit at Gabrielle's party.

"Yeah."

"I went trying to mix it up and get us another hook-up since Joe Bub Baby got knocked and we fell off."

"Right, right." Chino nodded.

"Well, Delano is still trying to tax me. Shit, we wholesale not retail. But I went anyway because he really started blowing up when he got his new hook-up."

"How was it?"

"It was a small gathering, but it was real nice. It was at a party house up North. Remember everyone was talking shit about this new *Bitch* that's suppose to have it going on and serving up Ballers with high quality shit?"

"Yeah, real competition."

"Chino, if Joe Bub's ass wasn't so greedy and tried to cut a side deal, we would have never fell off, and he would not be on lock-down."

"So?"

"Well, I finally met that bitch, and she *is* as polished as we've heard."

"How do you know this?"

"Because I've worked with the best and that's you, and this bitch been schooled by the best. Problem is, she ain't really a bitch at all. She really is good people. Chino, it's Carmen."

"Who?"

"Carmen."

"I don't know a Carmen."

"Man all the shit coming through stamped with T.C.P. is from Carmen."

"T.C.P.?"

"Nigga, you forgot the Triple Crown Posse?"

"I know about my Triple Crown Posse, but no one else's."

"Man, the bitch slangin' them thangs is none other than your 'Pooh.' She is going by the name Carmen. She is a Baller and got some people in her corner. The party had several Spanish people and one she was introducing as her brother. But I know it ain't her brother. He's a Colombian, and she was kickin' it all tight and shit with him. Remember, Pooh speaks Spanish also."

"You don't have to tell me about my Pooh. I remember everything about her. Are you sure? What did she say when she saw you?"

"I don't think she remembered me. I wasn't around her that much. I'm sportin' my dreads now. I wish the police would forget my face, but I remembered her. She was looking at me like I looked familiar. But I just kept moving out of her full sight. I didn't want to get my ass thrown out of there."

"Maybe it was her man she was with?" asked Chino.

"No Chino, she's solo. He ain't her man. They just friends, business associates and pretending to be brother and sister. I watched her all night. Delano wants her, but she got him on hold, even though he is really into her. I noticed how he looked at her. Chino, Pooh was looking good, too. Just to see her laughing and holding her head up like she was, I was glad to see her like that. She had on a sexy dress."

"A'ight nigga, enough of that. What's happening with her? Was the baby there?"

"Why you want to know about her baby?"

"Fuck it, man. So what happened?" Chino reacted irritated.

"Oh, nothing you would want to know," Jogging suit responded playfully.

"Don't make me drop you. Keep your info. I don't fuck with her. She is crazy anyway."

"Y'all both crazy as hell and really need to squash that old shit. Delano said her son is cute and a good baby."

"She be letting that sucka around my... the baby? When I see that mark, I will check him about that. Don't he got enough baby mama's of his own to fuck with?" Chino began to shift his weight back and forth from one foot to the other. He always did this when he was getting impatient.

"Look, I got a run to make. All I am saying is she got it on lock down, and Delano ain't giving us no play."

"Was that sucka Erik there?"

"Yeah, but he was not with her, and to be honest, I don't think they were ever together like you thought they were."

"Who asked you that?"

"You know we boys, and I'm in your corner. But I ain't going into that shit. That's an old can of worms. You will never argue with me again. I just try to look out and speak on what I see. But, it is like this, either we take the ticket Delano is offering us or you step to your Pooh 'cause she got it going on and she is the one, or we keep taking a beating like we have been. You know Pooh got love for you and would help you. She would help anyone out."

"Fuck that. I won't ask her for shit. We gon' be alright. We can make it."

"I can't keep starving. It's about business. I don't want to deal with Delano, but I can't hold out either. We've been in a slump for six months. I love being on your team, Chino, but I gotta eat too. My pockets are hit."

"Right, right," Chino said blandly shaking his head up and down as if he understood where his partner was coming from.

"I gotta bounce and make this run. Get back with me. Oh, also that escort service we use from time to time. The one that has Ashley and China. Well that is Pamela's service also. Chino, Pooh done made a come-up. I gotta tell you, I like that in her because we all left her ass for dead. Go ahead and make that move. I'm with you until the end, and you know this."

"Yeah, Rock, I know this, and I'll talk to you later. Thanks for the info."

"Gone."

"Peace."

Chapter

EIGHTEEN

SHIT! Here I am taking a beating and Pooh got it going on. Well, I guess it is not Pooh anymore, but *Carmen*. Where did she get that name from? I kept hearing about this girl slangin' them thangs, but it never crossed my mind that it could be Pooh.

Well, it did cross my mind a little when I found out that she was doing good despite how I left her. Poo, got so much in her that I schooled her with, she can succeed at anything. I never told her this, but it is true. I'm not surprised that she is still floatin'.

One night I was hanging out with her brother. Her real brother, Young Ty. I named her brother Young Ty after my older brother. He was thirsty for knowledge, admired me, and was handsome like my older brother. So I started calling him Young Ty. We all decided to get us some girls, and Ty called an escort service that he said he was cool with the owner of. So, that was her escort service too that we used? She still didn't let on that it was her. I kinda missed her trying to get in touch with me. But she left my ass alone. I guess she's over me now, which was good. She needed to go on with her life. I'm sure as hell trying to do so. I still think about her all the time. Problem is, I can't tell nobody about it. Everyone would think I am crazy to even be thinking about her. They would think I was soft.

After the drama, I couldn't turn back. I still can't believe my Pooh played her hand the way she did. I knew she had heart, but damn! I almost left here over some bullshit. I am not mad at her though. I deserved it and had it coming. Anytime you cross someone, there is a consequence. My grandma kept telling me to be decent to her. She deserved that much. But for some reason, I just started torturing her, rubbing shit in her face, and acting like I owed her nothing and she didn't help me with nothing. It was too much drama. I drove her crazy.

All I wanted to do was let her ass know how I felt when I found her and that black-ass Jamaican Erik at that hotel that day. How the friendship that they developed in my absence affected me. She said they were friends, and he was someone she could talk to while I was away. A terrible feeling is to think that the next man is taking your place or taking up slack in any area because you were on lockdown. I just knew that when I got out of jail, it would be all good.

When we first met, I had my concerns. You know like, if her love was true. But it was, and she was always there by my side when I needed her the most, and here I am needing her again. No one ever knew how much Pooh did for me. Then I spread lies about the baby and how the drama happened to further help myself. I mean, why would she help me? I let her starve. Why should she help me? Would she help me? Shit just got fucked up. Then I went and got married on her while she was pregnant. I ain't really shit. What women need to understand about me is that I don't sweat them. Yeah, I like pretty, but pretty is what pretty ain't. You can't take pretty to the bank. I don't know why women wanted me, but they do. Or at least they did.

I saw Pooh rolling in her Jeep on the streets, looking good, head held high. I pulled up beside her and kept giving her eye contact. Either she saw me and kept on movin', or she didn't recognize my new car. I told her brother about it, so I knew that she knew that I saw her, yet still no word from her. Pooh knew I was going to come around, and we was gonna work something out. But no, she couldn't wait. Hell, she had been waiting for me to come home from prison. Then I came home and wanted her to wait some more. I got carried away, and Pooh got tired.

I was with my wife, and I couldn't look out the window over a minute or stare off in space without my wife naggin' me and asking me, "You still thinking about that girl?" Or "You still love Pammy, don't you?"

One day, I just told her point blank, "Divorce me if you can't understand. You should be happy I'm here with you." My wife got what she wanted—me, and she still wasn't happy. She wasn't happy because she had me physically, and Pooh still had me mentally. And the shit gave me a headache. Then I got me some more kids, two more boys. I love my kids, too. Problem was, how do I correct my wrongs and still look like a man. I got enough on my mind, and I wished I could just talk to my Pooh, because when I talked to her, it was like my spirit was at peace, but I couldn't tell nobody this either. So many people looked up to me and depended on me. I had mouths to feed, people to see, places to go, moves to make.

I want to open another salon. But I don't have the money to do it. Everytime I drive past our old salon, I get so mad, I could spit on someone. Pooh just walked away from the salon and said "Fuck it!" But what else could she do? So, I still ain't mad at her. She loved her salon, and I really wanted her to have it. Busted my ass so she could have it. But this ain't no memory lane, and I have got to get some money. So, God, you know I love my Pooh. I forgive her and I pray that she forgives me too. Can you have her get in touch with me? Pooh can you hear me? Remember, I always told you if you listen closely, that you could hear me in your mind. Pooh, I still need you. Can you hear me?

Chapter

NINETEEN

I ran into my baby brother, Young Ty. He was supposed to be in Ohio for school, but he ran the streets with his friends and Chino all the time. He had seen Chino at the Eight Ball pool hall where a lot of Ballers went and hung out. They started kicking it after seeing each other there several times. I didn't know what was up with Chino. He was in the streets all night and used my escort service all the time. His shit was really *fucked up*. Then he was trying to get Young Ty to start selling kilos, so they could work together. Anything not to deal with me. Ty tried to pretend that the request for drugs was for him, but I knew it was for Chino. Ty became fixed in the middle of our Drama. When Ty was fifteen, Chino and I became legal guardians of delinquent Ty. We were kids ourselves, but joined forces to save Ty from the streets, which is where he was being constantly kicked out of the house to go, due to his attitude with my stepfather. When Chino and I separated, we didn't know what to do with Ty. Ty would listen to my ranting about Chino, and when with Chino, Ty listened to his ravings about me. Ty was unable to offer his sincere opinion due to his loyalty.

Chino was like a father to him, teaching him to dress, what to do with his first sexually transmitted disease, and how to want more out of life. I was his big sis, and he wanted the best for me. He definitely wanted the best for himself, which had become our home,

156

security and family-like atmosphere. Ty, became our torn child in our divorce from each other. I felt so sorry for him, and responsible, as I could not pull our family back together.

I wanted to mend the fences for Ty and just give Chino some money. My family and everyone would think that I was stupid. We were still keeping secrets. It was just a part of our bond. No one knew what we were feeling or going through, but some wise old person out there knew, like my moms or his grandmas. But we did it all on the down-low. I still had a lot of old photos of Chino and the fellas from some of their cross-country trips. I was ready to let go of this life. That was the past. I had been making my own memories. I wanted to give him his old photos back. One day I hoped I would. I would not work with Ty to sell drugs, but I sent my pager number to Chino through Ty. This would let Chino know that it was all good, and one day he would call. When he was ready, he would call me.

One of my employees, Sheila, left to start her own service. A knock-off for sure that didn't have a leg to stand on. Shit, she barely got booked let alone book someone else. Also, she didn't realize that booking clients was the conversation that comes before the booking. I got to know my clients, and they were interested in a variety.

Still, everything was going well. I repaid Dragos, strengthened our relationship, and I saved more than enough money. Dragos was so pleased with my show of appreciation by offering the additional $30,000 for interest on the loss I had taken, even though he made it clear that I shouldn't make coming up short a habit.

I had a nice stash stacked, tucked away, actually, too much money. I purchased a new house in a very pricey suburb of Columbus. It was a nice house, too. It had four bedrooms, three and a half full baths and a two-car garage. My son had a wonderful room with his own bath with all Mickey Mouse fixtures. He even had a Mickey Mouse bath tub. He really loved his bathroom.

My large, beautiful master bedroom featured a walk-in closet finished in all lightwood. It was so big, it could be another bedroom. It had built-in closets and shoe racks. My closet was on full. I had been shopping like crazy, and the boosters had been very helpful.

I decorated my entire house all by myself. I purchased everything new and got rid of all my old items. I custom ordered one-of-a-kind furniture in breathtaking colors of greens and ivory. I chose Italian fabrics and leather. I had plush carpet that felt like I was on the moon. In my foyer and in my formal dining area, there were marble floors.

I finished off my great room with a large 100-inch screen TV that lowered from the ceiling, with a laser disc player and surround sound. I just went out and purchased all I ever dreamed of and all that was ever promised to me. They even have a store just for those items that add that finishing touch to your home like vases, rocks and black art paintings. I loved shopping there. I put all the touches on every part of the house. It didn't take very long to do it, but I had exceeded my prayer request. Not only had I made fifty thousand, but I had well over a million dollars saved, a house, and a new BMW. I was thinking of getting a sports car that went to 180 mph in nine seconds, but I was afraid to crash. I purchased myself a flawless three-carat stone ring and earrings to match. I had a cleaning lady to do my laundry. The entire nine. I had it.

The problem was that I was still not happy. I was happy with my accomplishments, but there was still something missing. The real high of hustling is the come-up. I had been working with various new shorties and must admit, I was jealous because it was *their* come-up.

I met this one shortie as I was walking down the mall, shopping bags in hand. He walked up on me and offered me lunch. I was flattered, but declined.

"No, thank you." I began to feel this stranger out for a rival gang member, store security, or whatever. The main concern was that I did not know him.

"Please. Lunch won't hurt you."

"Okay, I will have lunch with you." I only said yes because he reminded me so much of myself when I approached Dragos. He offered to carry my bags as we walked towards the mall food court. If you allow a person to discuss their favorite subject, themselves, they will tell you everything that you want to know.

"We can eat at one of the mall restaurants or go somewhere else," he offered pointing at the food court.

"The mall spot is cool." You think I would leave the mall with a perfect stranger so they could try to kill me? No way. *I feel like a celebrity.*

As we ate, he told me his story of how he had heard about me and how he was looking to make it in this life.

"Carmen, I work for someone, and they taxin' me. I don't even have a car or a place to live, but I've got heart. If you let me work for you, I promise to come up and do better. My folks live in the Windsor Terrace Projects, and I want out."

"Right, right." I just listened, and I enjoyed him because it's all about the come-up really, because the money will come. So I said, "I will think about it. " He refused to let me get away.

"Ms. Carmen, what do I have to do? Kill somebody for you?"

I thought, Fuck, this is 5-0! Then I realized, by the sincerity in his eyes, he wasn't. It was his heart, and he was going for broke. With that, he was in. Gave him the street name of "Cat" because of the color of his hazel green eyes. He was the best hustler I had ever worked with. His family was out of the Windsor Terrace Projects, and in no time, he was doing well.

He was married with a child on the way and stacking dollars in the process. I had no losses with him or anything. I had much material gain and my relationship with Dragos seemed great.

I even had a new driver named Wade. Yeah, Wade was nice. I met him at a Philly night club. The thuggish, ruggish, bone type. Pitch black in color with pearly whites that you never saw because he never smiled. Wore a poker face and cornrows to the back. Picked out his hair into a large fro, sometimes, to let it breath. Every girl needs a real thug in her life, once or twice. Probably won't be planning your future, but you'll be having some fun. He was always rapping and rhyming as he aspired to be the next Jay Z, always telling me, "Girl, you paid, spend that damn money. Smoke a blunt, have some fun."

He was a great driver, accurate and reliable. He was also a great bedroom partner. Wade was a brother that gave the best mind-numbing head. Say-my name-head, make-you-scream-head. Wade did total service: back rubs, suck your toes, take care of you.

In the bedroom he was like, "Lay down, baby, let me try my techniques on you. I am going to do the slurp, suck and bubble blow move. Tell me if you like it, Love."

If Wade were charging, I'd be paying. If he charged by the climax, he could retire a billionaire. I called Wade whenever I was stressed and wanted to be sexed. He handled me like a champion.

My first encounter with him was unmentionable. We were driving, and he suggested a detour through Franklin Park. "Park here." He directed me behind some trees, hidden from the view of cars passing by. Following his lead and pulling in behind the bushes, he began to caress my neck and shoulders with his left hand. Placing the car in park, I closed my eyes and let out a deep breath feeling instantly relaxed. It had been almost a year since a man touched me, and I was ready.

Wade continued, "Come in the back with Daddy, Baby."

I followed him to the rear of the van and watched him clear an area for me to lie down. Wade stood outside the door as I rested back on my elbows, and he removed his shirt revealing a six-pack mid section. Baby, had the body of a god and still ate everything in sight. He licked his fingers, sticking his tongue in between them and gave me a sexy grin. I thought, *Yeah Baby, let Momma see what you got in them jeans.*

He started with my toes, sucking from the baby toe to the big toe. Next, he slowly removed my clothing with his teeth. Turning me over, he began to lick up and down my spine. His licks stopped at the crack of my ass, and I felt the warm saliva from the tip of his tongue. Wade continued, circling my asshole, lifting one leg over his shoulder and turning me over. On my back he started giving me head as I squeezed the sides of his face, moaning with pleasure. His tongue felt so good that I did not want him to stop—*Ever*. Sliding his middle finger in and out of my vagina, I climaxed for what I believed to be the third time. It felt like ecstasy, and I forgot all about where we were and enjoyed the art of lovemaking.

I tugged at his belt buckle, anxious to feel him inside of me. I pulled down Wade's pants, and he was packing. Wade had no less than 12 inches of rock hard 100% beef. Taking every inch was a task, but it was fun attempting to take it all as I felt his thickness between my legs.

He moaned when he fucked you, and you knew he was into you. "Whose is it?" All I could respond was, "Yours Baby, it's yours," as I was moaning from pleasure, and licking the lipstick from my lips as I bit into my bottom lip with each climax.

Wade left me depleted of energy. I crawled into a fetal position beside him as he kissed my shoulder and covered me with the shirt he had been wearing. This man knew how to make love to a woman. He didn't ask dumb-ass questions like, "Is it good or did you come?" When a man has to ask, he should know that the answer will be a lying "yes."

Yeah, we got our sex thang on in-between runs, but I still missed my Chino. He hadn't called yet. I knew he was just being stubborn. That's how he was. His stubborn pride. He once told me that love was stronger than pride, and so is the love of money, and he loves money very much. More than anything. So I knew I would hear from him.

Sittin' up in my room and thinkin' thoughts of my life, I also started experimenting with drugs. Yes, I had gotten that miserable.

The more I had, the more miserable I got. I started snorting cocaine with Wade. He rolled up his blunts and laced them with cocaine. Since we were spending time together, I decided to try them. I was slipping, and then I let myself slip totally and began to snort cocaine. I preferred to snort by myself and this way I could listen to Marvin Gaye as loud as I wanted, and allow my mind to drift wherever. Some nights, I would sit up all night snortin', trippin', gettin' horny and snorting some more.

I wished Chino could see my home and see that I did well. To see that all he taught me really paid off. Noticing the stacks of 100 dollar bills on my dresser, the white down comforter on my bed, 300 thread count sheets, I have all I wanted, but all I knew was, "Damn, I miss Chino!"

Chapter

TWENTY

Two weeks passed, and I decided to call it quits with the service and the boosters. It was just too much, and although they were my first loves in the *life*, I had to let them go. I told the girls face to face, and they were extremely upset with me. They were so faithful to the service that they laid big guilt trips on me. I vowed to get them all settled before I left them alone. I told them it was over for me, and they should want out also. I was outgrowing this life. I gave each of the girls $1,000.

I especially helped Gabrielle. I helped her get her own one bedroom apartment. Surprisingly, she didn't want a car. She was still living in the hotel despite all the money she made. I offered the client list to Renaye because she had a great business mind. She was so excited and immediately took the reins and started her own service out of her home. I gave the other girls money and a farewell dinner, which was very, very sad. We all ended it with China's line, "Let that be the reason we all do great things with our lives."

China didn't show up, and no one had seen her. So after dinner, I drove around some of the areas that I knew she would be.

Knowing her, she was out getting money. I cruised the car wash noticing all the hotties kicking it with the local Ballers admiring the cars as they rolled off the drying line. Sammy's Car Wash was the spot in Columbus. They called it the Premiere Car Wash. If you wanted your car cleaned, you went there. If you wanted to meet some fine ass brothers, you went there also.

I pulled in and started kicking it with the fellas asking about China. The owner had a thing for China and allowed her to hang around the place as she hustled the men for twenty dollars. I told her to stop that shit, but China got twenty dollars for a conversation. I got my car washed and had to check one of the attendants about skimping on my shit. Girl or not, I want my shit armour-alled down, fingerprints on the inside of the windows removed and inside door jams cleaned. Plus, cherry smell good for the inside.

Next, I cruised over to Expressions Hair & Nail Salon on East Broad Street to see if China was getting her nails done. She wasn't. She didn't drive, so the next thing I thought of was who could pick her up. Then I remembered that China had started with a pimp named Mark. He was very hard on his girls. I heard he kept her full of coke and working 24 hours a day—straight 24-7. Something told me to try her grandmother's house.

I went to her grandmother's house, which was off of a main street in the heart of the inner city. When I pulled up, there were several cars parked out front. I was dressed very nice, so I didn't think she would mind, besides I had met her once when we came to bring China's daughter a birthday present of clothes and a beautiful cake. Tapping on the door, a woman looking like China answered and I walked in. Her grandmother just walked up to me, crying, and just held me. She turned to introduce me and said "Everyone, this was China's friend. She tried to help China. This is Carmen."

I just looked stunned, and I realized I was arriving after China's funeral! China's look alike younger sister, Gloria, led me to a back bedroom. China's sister told me that they found China in the alley. She had died of an overdose of crack cocaine and heroin. She had been beaten, and the police were looking for Mark, her pimp. I embraced her as tears flowed from her face. She reached underneath the bed and handed me a newspaper article about China's death.

The article included a coroner's report of her autopsy that said, "Woman's cause of death is combined with toxic level of drugs and asphyxia. Subject was strangled with human hands, as imprints were apparent, in addition to ripped skin below the right ear. Blood vessels were broken in both eyes from the pressure of strangulation." I could not read anymore as I began to join in with my tears. No human being should have to die this way. China would not hurt a flea. China's daughter walked over to me and she asked, "Can I go home with you tonight?"

All I could say was, "Yes." I got permission and sent her to pack. My heart hurt. It was too late for China. Let that be the reason I get my ass out of these streets. After that night, I never picked up another drink or indulged in another drug.

China's daughter had so many questions about her mom and her mom's lifestyle. Her innocent voice queried, "Is my mom in heaven?" I stroked her hair as I drove and replied, "Yes, your Mom was the best, and she is in heaven with God, looking down on you."

"Will I ever see her again?"

"Of, course, if you close your eyes you can see her. Plus you always carry her in your heart." I pointed to her chest to remind her that her Mom was in there. She rubbed her heart and closed her eyes and said, "Carmen I carry my Mom in my heart. I want to die to be with my Mom. Why did that man choke her?"

I wanted her to stop talking, because with every word, I thought of my son; how the tables could turn and it could be my son with the questions. How would my absence be explained?

I pulled over and looked into her eyes and said, "Listen, you have to keep living and make your Mommy proud. This is what she would want. She is watching over you. Always do your best. Your Mom was a strong lady, and that same strength is in you. She loved you very much, and you have to always want to live." The tears fell down her little blushed cheeks mixing with snot from her nose and slobber from her mouth. I wiped it all with my hands, not caring about the combination. I just wanted to ease her pain.

I returned China's daughter to her grandma's the following night with the promise that I would visit. I left her with some money and asked her grandmother if she wanted to move, but she refused to give up her neighborhood, although she would put the money away for China's baby. I didn't have the answers. I only knew that I didn't want that to happen to me and my son, for him to find out about me like this.

I told the other girls and gave them all copies of the obituary. That night I prayed! *God, Thank you for your blessings and please, please bless China's family.*

Beep…beep…Beep…beep…

Wiping the sleep from my eyes, I peered at the small screen of my pager but didn't recognize the number. Who was this paging me this early in the morning? This better be good. 832-2504228228. Who was this? 8322504228911911.

"Who's number is this?" I picked up my cell phone and dialed the number.

Ring, ring.

"Hello?" someone answered.

"Someone call a pager?" I asked.

"Pooh, it's me. You gave someone else my code 228?" I was speechless.

He whispered "Hey, how you doing? I got my white flag up. I surrender. I need you."

Without hesitation I responded, "Chino where are you? I'm on my way!"

Chapter

TWENTY-ONE

I jumped out of bed and was so happy that I felt like floating on air. My Chino finally got in touch with me. Thank you, God! There really is a God after all. Now I can quit this business, I thought. No more drug dealing, no more streets. I wanted to go back to school and get my degree. I was very intelligent, and I could move on with my life. I planned to meet with Chino and offer him his photos and some money to him, his new family, *and* his kids. I felt whole. I was going to see my Chino. I could do something for him that he would know was from my heart. Not because he was a drug dealer or because he did things for me, or because we were together, or because he gave me anything. It would be a 'just because' gift. We both knew he had never given our son anything. Yet, I just wanted him to know that he could have rest. That there was someone he could depend on with no strings attached.

This was not about a future relationship. That was over for us. This was about all we have been through.

I wanted to give him a gift to let him know all that we shared was for this: his time of need, just as he did for me in the past. After our separation, I remember speaking to him on the phone. I was crying and telling him how he never loved me. He said, "Pooh, be silent. All of that was for this, my phone calls now and to keep trying after all we have gone through." And sure enough, he used to sneak and call me on the phone all the time when others thought we never spoke. We tried to talk things out, but we couldn't because we were too busy blaming each other for all the wrongs in the relationship. Finally, I could close this chapter on my life. I would apologize and give him a gift that I prayed overwhelmed him like all the many things he had given me.

I thought: "Now...hmmmm? What will I wear, because I must look fabulous?" I walked into my closet, scanned my eyes over the shelves and racks of clothes, and picked out a navy blue Armani suit.

"No, this won't work. How about a yellow linen short set? No it won't work. Or a dress with some gator (alligator) sandals? Chino always liked soft and jazzy clothes. Wait, the perfect outfit. A Polo pullover with some jeans and loafers. Yeah, I'll meet him preppie style. Besides, every summer since I can remember, we always purchased a Polo jersey and dressed just alike. This outfit would be perfect, and to top it off, I think I will wear my old engagement ring he gave me. I always told him I threw it away, but I really didn't. So I'll wear it just to let him know that I still have it, even if it is on the right hand instead of the left. I will wear my ring that I purchased for myself with the flawless three carat stone in it, on my left ring finger. I am married to myself."

We were scheduled to meet at 2:00 p.m. at a seafood restaurant. This was just enough time to complete my weekly ritual of getting my hair done and nails French manicured, and running some errands. I was telling everyone that I quit! I was out of this life, and I would pass the scepter to Chino if he wanted. I knew Chino could handle my volume so maybe *he* could work with Dragos. Whatever Chino wanted, I wanted him to have it. Yes! I was out of this lifestyle.

I paged G-Money and prayed he would return my call. He

was becoming difficult. I saved my money, and the fellas spent theirs. G was upset that I quit the escort business. Even after China's death, he still acted like he didn't understand why I wanted out. I realized all G wanted was money and the streets. I wasn't trying to hustle forever. I had a son. I needed to be a responsible parent, and that involved more things than this life. Things that money can't buy. But here I was riding around in vans, sitting my ass on top of *Keys* in hidden compartments and placing my life on the line. And for what? Mo' money. This was crazy.

The previous week, a Baller named Nostradamus got killed in a drug deal gone bad. Someone killed him over two of them "thangs." Then Paul got robbed by the same guys that they say killed Nostradamus. Next one of Paul's boys, they called him 'Clockin' cause he stacked dollars, got "knocked" in a studio hotel.

The cleaning lady found a kilo of cocaine under the sink. When he got back to the hotel, he found his room cleaned, and looked under the sink. His package was gone. So he went to the front desk and asked for *his* package. Needless to say, they got him on lock down. So the game was getting whack!

To make matters worse, Dragos sent me some weak product, and I had major complaints and refund requests, and we all know ain't no refunds in the streets. So, I had to work through that mess. I became suspicious of everyone and everything. I even suspected a kid's skateboard as being a listening device.

Whew! I was tired. This definitely was harder than working a job. I don't know who said *"servin'"*was easy. It had to be said by someone who has never done it. It looks very easy, but it keeps ya on your toes, because as soon as you snooze, you lose. You hit. Finished.

It was very challenging, and I was relieved to be leaving that life. I had to think about my son and our life. Hell, what if they tried to jack me and my no pistol-carrying ass? So, I was unarmed. Yes, I wanted out, and G would have to understand. People will play all types of guilt trips on you. Like this was a real business with social security, and I was responsible if they ate. I guess it really was like that. Depends on your perspective.

I remember when Chino went to jail; all the fellas in his crew fell off. Rock, got evicted out of his apartment. Ant became a house-husband to some chick who was paying the rent while raising two kids, and their bills became overdue. They all fell like dominos.

It was time for me to leave. Everyone gets a chance, and it was time for someone else to get theirs. I would gladly step down. I knew when other competitors got knocked, it did more for me, and to be honest, I didn't want anyone in jail for two reasons. One, that ain't the place to be. Two, I didn't want the extra work. I wanted out, and I prayed that would they understand.

I did a T-Love move and called Wade over to the house for a booty call to relieve some stress. I showered, applied Bath & Body brown sugar vanilla lotion to my body and waited. Wade never rang the doorbell; he always did this sort of unique whistle when he got out of his low rider, signaling his arrival. I ran to the patio door wearing my birthday suit and let him in. He pulled from behind his back a can of whip cream, smacked my ass, and swooped me up into his arms. We were headed to my bedroom, and it was on!

Needless to say, I arrived a lil' late, and I could tell by the look on Chino's face he was pissed. After all, he never waited for anyone. People waited for him. But I smiled and we approached each other slowly. I knew he was thinking, *(Is she gonna hurt me again?)* I just walked towards him with open arms, and we embraced each other. It was a wonderful feeling.

"Pooh, step back, let me look at you. You look good."
"So do you. Shall we eat?"
"Yeah, I am starving like—"

"I know, Marvin. Right?" I responded completing his sentence.

"Yes!" His voice rang with a baritone sound.

"Two for dinner?" asked the maitre d'.

"Yes. No smoking." Chino took the lead.

"Your waitress will be with you in one moment. Enjoy your meal." He spoke into the air as we followed him to our table.

We placed our orders without saying a word to each other. Some young Ballers were eating and passed our table. One left me his pager number and said, "Baby girl, give me a call. I am trying to work out with you, yo." And I could tell the attention made Chino uncomfortable.

"So, Pooh, you're a celebrity?" said Chino while glancing at the tattered paper with the scribbled number written in blue.

"Nah, I'm just an entrepreneur, always for me, never for yours."

"Ha, ha, you got game in you." *I knew that would make him laugh.*

Our food arrived and we both started slamming, just like old times, when we went out eating dinner. He even took a couple pieces of food off my plate. "Chino, you are always eating my food," wiping food from my mouth and then he replied, "And you know it."

(We were breaking through ice.) We both were chewing with our mouths stuffed, and at the same time, looked at each other and repeated simultaneously, "I'm sorry." Then he winked his eye.

"Chino, forgive your Pooh," I pleaded.

"Done. Pooh, forgive your Chino."

"Done! I never thought this day would come. Did you?" I asked.

"I knew it would. It was just a matter of time. So what is this I hear about you in these streets? You know I never wanted that for you." He met my eyes dead center. Looking for signs of him regretting my position in the streets, I held his stare like a game of who-will-look-away-first-loses. He broke the stare and looked away first, and I spoke the facts.

"Well, I had to do what I had to do."

"How is the baby?" he asked.

"He is fine. How have you been?" I attempted to make eye contact as I tried to find out what was going on with him.

"Taking a real live beating," Chino confessed.

"Well, Chino, I am here to help you and give you the rest you need."

"Right, right."

"Chino, you can talk to me and you know this, man!" I said laughing. *(I am trying to keep the mood light because I know his pride is eating him alive. He keeps fidgeting).*

"I need some of them *thangs.*"

(Is this what this meeting is all about? Kilos?)

"Chino, you don't need them 'cause I have money saved up, and it is yours. How much you need?"

Instead of him being touched and overwhelmed, he got mad. "I don't need you to give me anything. I can work for mine, and I don't want no handouts. I want to work for mines. Get down. I want to make my own money. I don't want you to be able to say that you gave me anything."

"Chino, I am not like that, and you know it. Please don't feel like this. What is mine is yours. I can take care of you and your family just like you took care of me and mine many years ago. That is what I am talking about."

He just stared off into space and said, "Pooh, that means more to me than you will ever know. But the man I am won't allow me to accept anything from you. I do want a good ticket since you the *man* now." When he said that, he still did not look me in the eyes.

"I am not a *man,* but I feel like one sometimes," I said sadly.

"I just need some work. Some of them "thangs." I gotta get down for my crown!"

I don't want to do this. Why won't he take the money? He will sell the drugs for the money. I can just give him the money.

"What ticket do you need?" I couldn't believe my ears as I unthinkingly responded.

"I need to get 30 kilos at the ticket of 20 for each one."

That is a low price for delivered and fronted kilos. Don't do it. Stay in control, you know how you are with him.

"No problem, Chino, I can have them for you in the morning. Is there anything else you need?" *Instantly he mistook my willingness to help him as arrogance and got disturbed. This is not what I wanted.*

"Chino, you know I got love for you, and I just want to help." With that, I touched his hand.

"Pooh, I know. It is just fucked up that I got to come to you," responding and pulling his hand away from mine.

"Maybe next time I will come to you. But Chino, just this one time because I'm about to retire."

"All I need is this one time."

"I have transportation vans, and you may use one of them." *Those vans are not yours, you're frontin'.* This way you can be safe."

"That's straight, because I need to go to work in Cleveland."

"You still have Ant as your driver?"

"Yeah, all the fellas still with me. They just waiting on work." Then I remembered the dude from the party. He was one of Chino's boys.

"Chino, was one of your friends at a birthday party I gave?"

"Yeah, Rock was there with your friend Delano. I don't want to talk about that party," Chino said bitterly.

"Neither do I. I just wanted to confirm my suspicions. He looked very familiar to me. We don't have to discuss it."

"You didn't invite me to your party to meet your new 'brother.' "

"You may meet him, one day."

"Pooh, you've got to be careful. You're putting a million dollar hustle at the reach of a lot of suckers. If they get knocked, they will take you down and, that Columbian you fuckin' with will not like that. That may cost you your life."

"I know, that is why I want out. This will be my last run and only for you, Chino. Only because it is you."

"Do you want to ride to Cleveland with your Chino, just like old times?"

"Yes, I would like that. I am glad that you asked. I want to do some shopping."

"Pooh goin' cross-country with her Chino. I have one condition." I reached for his hand

"What?" Chino said suspiciously.

"That we will stay at the Tower City Hotel, and you will let me take you shopping and let me buy you something just for you."

"You don't have to." He shook his head resisting.

"I want to." I continued to give him eye contact.

"Okay, Pooh, let's do it."

"Thanks. Now let's order dessert," I shyly whispered.

Chapter

TWENTY-TWO

I met with my Pooh. That was not that hard. She was still the same Pooh, willing to give me her last. That was the Pooh that I knew and fell in love with. I only wished others knew her like I did.

I remember growing up in Cleveland, Ohio. Those were the good times of my life. I grew up in a family of hustlers. I had never seen my father work a job a day in my life. Rumor has it, he's never worked a job, but he stayed paid. He had various hustles from the drug game to women. My pops is doing time right now. I'll never know the truth of what really happened to my moms.

I lost my mom when I was twelve. I was sitting on our porch and waiting for my mother to come home and take me school shopping. Instead of seeing my mom, I saw the tears in my grandmother's eyes as she told me that my mother was found dead. Yep, someone murdered my mom when I was a shortie of twelve years old. They said she put up a fight, though not enough fight to save her life.

My parents were a lot like me and my Pooh. They hustled together. They caught a case together. My father took the time, and my mother took a deal. She made a deal with the Feds. We were supposed to be in the witness relocation program. We even moved away, but my mother didn't like it. She missed Cleveland. A lot of unanswered questions.

Shortly after we came back to the city, they found my mother dead in the alley. She had been beaten and shot. My mother was my everything, and we were very similar. I often wonder why in the fuck did my dad have her in the streets? She had six kids she left behind. My grandmother took up the slack and raised us, but I still wonder what the fuck was on his mind. That was my mom and the only woman I ever loved. She named me Chirstonos and was the only person allowed to call me that. My grandmother nicknamed me Chino when I was three, and everyone called me that. No one even knew my real name, but those I trusted, and that person was my Pooh.

I guess I am my father's son, 'cause I got Pooh out here in them streets. Yeah, Pops, I guess what the fuck was on your mind is the same thing that is on mine: Money. Getting paid by any means necessary. Anyway, I can't complain over spilled milk. See, that's why people think I am a cold person, 'cause I kept going. What else could I do?

She said it would be available in the morning. So as I laid next to my wife, I couldn't go to sleep. I got to see my Pooh and got to do what I love: make money. Thank you, God for answering my prayers. Good night, Pooh and thank you!

Chapter

TWENTY-THREE

Well, I saw my Chino, and it was nice. He looked really handsome, as always, with his honey brown sun-kissed skin. He still had those full, deep-set eyes that my son inherited from him. Even in times of despair, he kept those confident mannerisms that I fell in love with. The only problem was something inside of me didn't want to sell drugs anymore. I wanted out. Something was telling me, "No More!" But something was also telling me, for Chino, I must do this.

I called Dragos and asked him to add 30 more to my ticket. I listened hopefully into the receiver as he replied, "For you Carmen, no problem. There will be two."

I knew he had to send two vans to fill an order of 50 kilos.

"Will you please come see me? I need to talk to you."

"I will come soon." Which meant that weekend. I would tell him it was over when I paid him for this shipment. I would also tell the fellas when I made my deliveries that it was my last run with them.

The next morning, I picked up Chino and his driver Ant,

who kept staring at me. I just looked over at him and said," Please drive and stop staring at me. Yeah, it's Chino and Pooh in full effect."

Chino and I sat in the back of the van and talked up a storm. We talked about old times. We sang a few songs together, all offbeat, of course. He was still upset that he had to come to me. I tried everything to let his driver know that I would do anything and everything for Chino since I know they, all his boys, were still mad at me over the past drama. I just turned to Ant and said, "You know I got love for my Chino."

Ant replied by saying, "Yeah, I know that you both do." So, we were headed for Cleveland.

When we got to the Tower City hotel in Cleveland, Ant moved to the front desk and got us checked into a suite. Chino and I were inseparable—just like old times. We had some time to kill, so we went shopping.

The hotel was attached to the mall, and I knew just the store I wanted to go to. It was a men's store that sold nothing but the best. I told Chino that he could have anything in the store that he wanted, but all he picked out were two men's dress shirts. This was a special purchase because I purchased something for him, and not with his money as others shop for him, but from my heart. This made it all the worthwhile. We did more window shopping and then it was time for him and Ant to handle their business. Hit the streets handling business, moving that dope. I decided on a nap.

Chino was so smart. I only had to show him one time how to work the compartments on the van. *Place the car in park, put your foot on the brake, turn the a/c vent on, lift the rear window lever to open front seat cushion, and front window lever to open rear cushion. To close, do the opposite.*

He remembered the combination just like that! Before he left, he leaned, smacked me on my behind and said to me, "Be ready when I come back."

I knew what he meant. I just looked at him and said, "No, Chino, that is not for us. You have a wife."

"But you were my first wife." With that I turned and walked

away. This was supposed to be a happy time, and he had spoiled it by suggesting that I sleep with him. All I could think of was that I wanted more and that I deserved more than that. I would not sleep with him. Yes, I let Wade do me with no commitments, on several occasions. But those were a horny, toe-curling, eat-me sex sessions. I cared too much for Chino to sleep with him. I can't explain it, but I couldn't do it. I didn't want seconds.

I went back to my room and decided to call Delano. For some reason I was missing him. Maybe it was because I found so much peace with him. When I told him that I was getting out of the business, all he said was, "Good," because he was tired and he wanted more for me. Well, Delano, I want more for me too. So, I paged him and then ordered a steak & lobster dinner from room service. My room service arrived at the same time my phone rang.

"Hello?" I answered.

"Hi, Carmen."

"Hi Delano, how are you?"

"I'm fine. What are you up to?"

"I'm just in Cleveland chillin'." I chimed floating back into the fluffy pillows.

"I figured that this was where this area code was from. So, you thinking about me, huh?"

"I'm just chillin' out. Thought about you. As you know, I'm trying to make some changes, and when I get back to the city, I would like to spend a lil' more time with you—if you want to."

"I would like that very much."

"I don't care what we do, but I want to get to know you better. Delano, I apologize for being so difficult towards you and…"

"Shh, Carmen, it is no need to explain. We will work this out. Let's do something with our children. I want you to meet my sons." *He is a blessing.*

"My son is with my mom, but we can go pick him up."

"Cool! I can meet your mother also. It will be a smooth trip."

"Well my food is here, so I will talk to you later. I may page you again."

"I'll be waiting. Bye."

When I got off the phone, my message light was flashing indicating a message from the hotel's guest services. Following the instructions on the phone, I dialed 7. Ring, ring.

"Guest Services."

"This is suite 1310, I have messages?"

"Yes, from Chino. He is thinking of you and T.C.P. for life. That's the only message. Is there anything else, Miss?"

"No, thank you."

I ate my food and took a long hot shower. Then I called to check on my son. Next thing I knew, I was asleep. We would return to Columbus in the morning, so I figured I would get a good night's sleep. I planned to talk to Dragos in the morning and pay him. Soon this would be over. I was too anxious to do this. I wanted out.

Chino arrived at the hotel late that night, knocked on my door, and woke me up.

"Pooh, that girl-yayo, was excellent. I haven't seen that much dope in a long time. I was a lil' scared, but everyone liked that shit. The fellas that rocked it said it was just like butter. Can I get 50 next weekend?"

"Wait, Chino, you said just this one time and that was it!"

"But, why let a hook-up like this go?"

In total disbelief I said, "Chino, I will turn you on to my source, and you can deal with him."

"No, I like it like this. I don't want to meet no one. Why should I when I have you in the mix?"

"Because I'm not your front-line man anymore. You can step to him yourself." He began to pace back and forth a bit.

"Okay see, now you want me to look stupid in front of the fellas."

How could I tell him that, One, I was never to give anyone the van combination; and Two, that I really resent him wanting to keep me in this life for the sake of his own greed?

"Chino, I will give you some money. The more drugs I get, the more of my money will be tied up. Dragos already fronts me, but I must pay up front by a deposit. Dragos has a $2,000,000 deposit of mine which allowed me a credit line of unlimited amounts with him. I just want to pay Dragos, get my two million and get out of the dope game."

"Pooh, this could work for us. We can work out something with the baby. Somehow this could all work out." *Now he is bringing the baby into this. My weakness. I could never tell him no, and this was always my problem.*

"Come on, Pooh." He began to rub the sides of my face. This was not what I wanted, and he didn't want to let me out. Stuck!

♥

I looked down at my Chino kneeling before me as I pointed the nine to the back of his head and began to press the cold steel in against his skull. He raised his eyes to look up at me, and the look of hurt was on his face. Not one trace of fear was shown on his face, but the look of pain. I lowered the gun from his head and stood there in front of him as shame swarmed all over my body like bees swarming a hive. That look took my mind back to a secret that Chino and I shared.

Three years ago when I was in our bedroom, I heard sobs from my bedroom. I came into our living room and found Chino on his kness covered in blood and praying. I ran to him and checked him for injury as I noticed his face was bruised from what looked like a pistol whipping. Chino recalled the story of how he was abducted from some rival drug dealers, and they intended on robbing and killing him. He told me how all he thought of was me and how badly he wanted to live. They stripped him naked and had him kneel before them as they pistol whipped him and bragged. He said he never felt so humiliated in his life.

Wanting to live and thinking of the life we were building, he acted like he was scared to death, fooling his abductors into a false sense of security causing them to become too relaxed. He gained courage and snatched the pistol from the hand of one of his abductors. He killed all three of them with shots to the head, heart and stomach areas. Chino then jumped out of the second floor window naked, and ran streaking for help. He was assisted by an older white gentleman in a car driving by, and his story was safe. Only I knew what had happened, and we shared the secrets of those killings as we watched the news of the discovered bodies in an abandoned house on Woodland Ave.

Chino stressed how he never wanted to feel that way ever again in life, and if ever put in that predicament again, that he would fight instantly and choose death rather then to live with the memory of degradation and humiliation. I was the one who cried with him and wiped the tears from his eyes. I place my hurting baby in an Epsom salt bath and nursed his mind and body back to life. I whispered into his spirit that it gets greater later, that he was a king, and they used drastic measures out of jealousy—building my baby back up. Hurting with my sweetheart, I was sad 'cause I couldn't erase the pain. It was no different than a man consoling his woman after she had been raped. You know the person has been violated in an unmentionable way, scarred for life, but nothing that you could do. Here I was, having placed my Chino in that memorable position again.

Since that episode, Chino has always went for death, and the only reason he gave me the upper hand was because of our past. The fact was I was his Pooh. I dropped the gun and kneeled with him, holding him and saying my apologies, "Chino, I am so sorry, baby, I remember that night. I wasn't going to hurt you. I promise." I lifted my hand to wipe away his tears and mine. He was shaking and not responding. I hugged him closely, and he did not hug me back. I continued to try to reach him, "Chino, baby, I am here.

Please, what is wrong with us."

He abruptly pushed me back off him, backhanded me splitting my lip, snatched up his gun and stood to his feet. "How could you put me in that position after what I told you happened to me? I killed those niggas that did that shit to me, and now it is your turn to get what they got. So, now you a trick bitch, huh?

♥

We left Cleveland after breakfast the following morning and arrived back in Columbus. Everything went like clockwork. Chino was a little pissed that I made him get another hotel room to sleep in. I couldn't believe the brother tried to push up on some poom poom. He must have forgotten who I am, I ain't sleeping behind no bitch that I know about. I still had it in my mind that I did not want to sell anymore.

Dragos was impressed with the work that I had put in. But, when I told him I wanted out, he totally flipped on me with some story of how he was in debt from some other losses and people that he worked with, and how he needed me to work with him a lil' longer.

"Carmen, you can't do this. I need you to help me out now. On my end, I had some losses and I need you, who is a part of my team, to help move the product with me. How do you Americans say, 'Don't bite the hand that feeds you.' " Oh, now he a straight-up foreigner.

I spoke, "Dragos, that saying is good for anyone working together. How about this one, "Do you know the difference from a workhorse and a racehorse?' " He looked confused, as now I didn't even know what I was saying. So I continued to try to get out of this. "Or, this one, 'Give a sister a break.' "

He snapped in what seemed perfect English. "I gave you a break. When you wanted to be on, I was loyal and only worked with you. What was that worth to you? Did you think it came without a cost? Now, I want you to help me with my plans as I helped you with yours."

I listened in disbelief as this man now stretched our relationship to keep me in the position of selling. Dragos knew damn well he could get another one like me just like the other one to sell for him. Everybody was looking for a Columbian or Dominican plug to know. Now all of a sudden, I was valuable, indispensable. Did he forget I had to beg up on this position, cut side deals, and go for broke to work with him? More like *for* him, to help him repay a loss on his end. I couldn't believe it. These mothafuckas didn't want me out because it was benefiting them. Dragos evidently had a new supplier. His previous supplier ran into some problems on the customs end of things.

The yayo was coming into the country through "Dole" pineapple cans. I received cases of canned pineapples. When I opened them, the yayo was inside the pineapple cans. Then I had to repackage it. This was too much and too heavy. I was tired of all the lying to my mom and my family, not to mention all the stress. I had a feeling the cops were closing in. How long could I expect a run in these streets? For every thousand, eventually you paid the piper. Now Dragos didn't want to give me my deposit, nor did he want to let me retire. With every insinuation of ending my career, he had a response.

"Carmen, to end our relationship would make me very unhappy. This is a lifetime relationship, and now you want a divorce."

"No, I don't, but I need a break." My eyes welled up with tears.

"Get someone to help you."

I just wanted out, but talking to him was like talking to a wall. I had heard that these Colombians would get you to sell these drugs, then try to keep you selling, willingly or unwillingly. I was so tired that I had decided to go for broke. To make one last run and come up with enough money to bounce with no one's permission but my own.

"Okay, Dragos, I will be in touch." He left, but he left two of his associates with me, like I was trying to escape or something.

This made me nervous. Now I had chaperones. I phoned Dragos and said, "I need to take two weeks for a vacation."

He responded by saying, "Absolutely, a vacation is good. Please come to my winter estate in the Dominican Republic."

Squirming out of the offer I declined, "No, thanks, Dragos, I want to choose my own vacation spot and be alone with my son." Declining really made him mad. Dragos had been raising his voice lately, and this was a calm man. He said, "Carmen, why do you refuse me. I don't ask twice." Our relationship was getting off the hook.

"Cool Dragos, I won't mention it again. So you would not have to ask twice."

He cut off my reply and said, "I see, you've got deep pockets now. You want to take your ball home and not play anymore. The game is not over until I say it is over. You think you don't need me because you have saved some money. Carmen, think again. I like working with you. And I don't want to work with anyone else. Think about it." –Click the phone line went dead.

What had I gotten myself into? I was going to have to escape. So, in the meantime, I only dealt with Chino. I got him 30 kilos for the next two weeks and I left everyone else alone while I planned and plotted what I would do.

My world began to crumble. When I stopped dealing with the fellas, they started to take a beatin' because no one saved their money. In the streets, no one teaches you how to budget your finances. Make a sell, buy some sneakers, make a sell, buy some gear, make a sell, buy some pussy. Saving was unheard of. There are no 401K plans for hustlers, no retirement, nothing.

They all were pressed, and Chino had his boys on the streets really taxin' everyone since I was not doing anything. Next, G-

Money got word that I was supplying them. G took it personally, like I would help them, but not him. No one would fuck with G.

He was rumored to fuck-up money, and all the bragging about fuckin' crack heads had caught up with him. Chino told me that G-Money was getting fucked up his ass in the joint, so no one really messed with him because who could really trust a booty boy. Jay-Jay was too happy to see his ass crawling back to him. G kept paging me like he was desperate.

One day, he began dating the same girl that did my nails at this salon on the eastside of Columbus. He had her calling me also. I got weak and returned his call trying to keep my enemies close, and everyone on an even plane until I flipped and made my move. I agreed to see him one last time. My head was spinning around. I had so much going on inside of me.

Chino still had not done anything for the baby, and I resented myself for still helping him after I realized that he had not changed one inch. He was just out for the money, 'cause money was what was keeping his life together. All the substance had left him. He was a different person, and I was becoming a different person as well.

Then, one night I had a dream. In this dream, God showed me that I was going to be arrested. I saw myself on the news, featured in a pyramid line up of faces. At the top of the pyramid, I could clearly see my face as the other faces were blurred. In the background, you could hear a newscaster speaking and talking about a big drug bust, the largest in Columbus, Ohio history. I woke up in a cold sweat.

Chapter

TWENTY-FOUR

I've heard of people being unable to sleep in the middle of the night. They call this insomnia. Never did I think it would happen to me. Well it did. It was 3:00 a.m., and I couldn't sleep. I just couldn't sleep.

It was time, I supposed, time to face that which I feared. I wanted to see my salon.

I was going to see my hair salon. It had been over two years since I was there. I heard there were changes; The wallpaper was different, and the staff had changed. Something in me wanted to see it. Something in me was not afraid, ashamed or sad. Something in me wanted to let go. It was time.

I put on a sweatsuit and grabbed my car keys. I pulled out of my garage and rode in silence. If I had any thoughts, I can't remember them. The salon was 30 minutes away. I had refused to ever go past it. I would take a detour before I went past it. But that night, I was going there. It was the longest, yet, fastest drive I ever made.

As I pulled into the shopping plaza parking lot, I felt nostalgic, as if I were coming to work. Yep, there was my parking space. There was the dry cleaners, the computer store, and the pizza shop. Man, they had good pizza. There was the convenient store and the video store. It looked the same, but the feel was different. It was just not the same, and that magic was forever gone. Instead of park-

187

ing in the lot, I just pulled up in front of the salon. Everything was closed, so the lot was partially vacant. There was a new business in the shopping plaza, a bar or pub, and there were patrons in it. So, I just sat there.

In my Jeep, I could see inside because my Jeep sat kinda high. I could see that the new salon owner added a barbershop to the other side.

Yes, I was there in front of my salon. Carrying a different name, new owners, but it was still mine. Chino would come pick me up and pull his Blazer up to the door just as I pulled up then. If I slouched down in my Jeep, I would look like he did in his Blazer.

I had a box with some of my salon memorabilia. The Hair Show competition tape when I won first place, the newspaper article of our opening, photos from various workshops. I even have a salon bag with the logo that we used to put hair products in, plus a salon T-shirt. I didn't look at that stuff, though.

When I closed my eyes really tight, it felt like the past and I was in the salon doing nails. I heard the receptionist answering the phones, "L-O-Quent Hair Salon."

But that day I let go. I let go of it all. I felt the warm tears on my face. I started thinking about my son and how the money that I have set aside will afford his college tuition. Hopefully, he'll never go through what I have gone through. That my son, will not have to face the challenges of today's black man. Those gangs, the streets, and violence will not be an option for him.

Am I a good mother? Is this the only way? I want my son to be proud when he looks at me. I want to provide food, shelter and clothing. I need to devise a plan to do this legally. I don't ever want to leave my baby.

I heard my staff; we were laughing. There was Valerie at the first station. Val did great hair and was always there reassuring and supporting me. Valerie was like a sister to me. Valerie, thanks for your friendship. Remember those long hair nights? I miss you. Then Lenaye, fresh out of beauty school, trying to be a better stylist. And Ms. Jewell, she had clients lined up and kept everyone laughing with her jokes. It was her fault the salon windows stayed fogged up. She was an outstanding manager with the will to survive. I learned so much from her. Next, was Roger. He was one brother that did hair in a suit everyday, and if it was not a suit, it was a silk shirt and dress pants. He never got dirty, and turned out excellent hairstyles. Yeah, Roger came to work everyday smelling good just for the ladies. They loved him. Roger believed in the salon and stayed with me over the rough spots. Thanks, Roger. There was Marcia (Chino's cousin). And Yolanda, who did it all. She did hair, nails, eyebrows and makeup. My eyebrows have never been the same since she last did them.

There was Michael, who was from Detroit. He gave the best grip and short stories you ever heard. He wore a Jheri curl in the 90's and got it off. Yes, it looked that good. Then there was the salon's assistant that we all called "Baby." She was the salon's baby and kept everyone shampooed and prepared for service. She was a lifesaver on those busy, busy days. I can't forget my ever efficient receptionist/manicurist, Stacey. She kept my head on and the books in order. I also had another part-time receptionist named Selima, and I still don't know how she got the job. She only wanted free hair-dos and nails. She wore everything well. She was one of the models I used in the hair show that won me first place. She wore that black dress and award-winning hairstyle. Selima, we did that! She was like a lil' sister and was a horrible receptionist, but we all loved her and I kept her. She talked more on the phone than she did answering them.

There were others that came and went, but these were the ones that helped make the salon. These were the ones that believed in me and Chino.

Last, but never least, was Renardo. He was a grand 'Diva,' a Queen. I still believe he was to be a *she* no matter what the birth certificate said. Renardo and I went around and around over his ten-inch nails, but we got past that. He could keep the make-up if he lost the nails. So, we made it and soon everyone grew.

To the Staff, My L-O-Quent Family, I never got the chance to say good-bye to you. I just walked away. Had I known better, I would have done better. I thank you and I remember the fun. The salon is full. The lot is full, and our hard work is paying off. The clients are happy, and we are drinking Belinda's daiquiris on a Saturday—they even have the flowers I arranged in that black vase. It is still on the receptionist desk. But all this is no more.

I sat in my jeep crying, releasing that which I held onto from my past.

Let go! Pammy, it is time, just let go. Release and let go! I placed my hands to my lips, and I kissed them. Then I blew my salon a kiss Good-bye! This attachment is over.

I drove off and never returned.

Chapter

TWENTY-FIVE

Ring…Ring…

"Hello?"

"What that *Baller* life look like?"

"Hi, Chino."

"Pooh, I can't stop thinking of you—of us and what happened."

♥

I placed my head in my hands and cried, continuing to beg Chino to hear me. He paced back and forth cursing me and gaining momentum with his anger. Walking over to me, he kicked me in the side of my rib and continued the taunting going back to how much in love he was. Waving his gun around in the air, I slid my hand underneath the pillow and felt the small .380 caliber gun. I flicked the safety latch off, and Chino still did not detect anything due to his ramblings.

He began talking about the killings and how I was his weak link because I had that information on him. How he ran with the gun unable to wipe the prints off 'cause he was butt naked. Getting into the white man's car with the gun he used the change of clothes given to him to remove his fingerprints. Chino and I buried the gun together, sealing our secret. He began to talk about the location of the gun.

"Yeah, I went back and got that gun just in case you flipped on me. I can't even trust you no more. I have no more use for you. Pooh, your ass has got to go. Have you said your prayers, love?"

♥

"Did you really think we would see each other again?"

"Yes, I knew we would. Pooh, what happened at the hotel?" Chino pressed.

"What do you mean?" I asked playing dumb about his attempted booty call.

"You didn't want to be with me?" asked Chino.

"No, Chino, not that way. I don't want seconds."

"You had first's and didn't act right. All I ever wanted was someone for me."

Relaxing with our conversation, I commented, "Me, too. I don't know where we went wrong."

♥

Fearing the worse, I pointed the nozzle of my gun underneath the pillow at Chino and aimed. "Tatt!" He didn't' know what hit him as feathers flew from the ripped pillow. But as the warm hollow point became heated, he responded, "Pooh, where did you get a gun from?"

♥

"It all went so fast. We stopped believing in each other."

"Yes, I know," I sadly replied.

"Pooh, I'm sorry," he whispered into the phone sounding sincere for the first time since we hooked up.

"Chino, I know, let's drop it. Everything I do, I think of you. I know we can't be together, but I still miss you."

"I miss you too. We've gotta do something to work this out, to make this right."

"What can we do?" I got excited at the possibility of a solution, and that is when he offered his solution.

"My wife wants me to take a *paternity* test."

"You've got to be kidding! You constantly break my heart. We were together almost five years. The baby is yours, and you know, Chino, anything that is mine or of me, you should accept. I do for your kids and would give you anything to help them and your wife. Like now, even though we hustle together, I still ask you for nothing off the top for my son; your son, and I know that you're getting money. You have become *ridiculous*."

"Shit! I just don't know how to correct this," Chino said with desperation.

"Correct your lies you mean, don't you? I will never participate in a paternity test. I want my son even if you don't."

He didn't say anything, so I continued. "Chino, here we go again. You've got issues and so do I. All I wanted to do was help you and thank you for the memories and now the lessons."

Finally, he said, "I don't know what to say, Pooh. I do miss you."

♥

Shielding my face from retaliation, he just dropped his gun and said, "Pooh, don't shoot me, just drop the gun." I dropped the gun and ran to his arms. "Oh my, God, I'm going to call 911."

Chino held me tightly, "No, calm down and call my boy Darren."

♥

"I miss my Chino. I don't know who you are anymore." Fighting back the tears, I listened for a dream.

"I miss you, Pooh. Carmen is different," Chino said.

"Like Joe Bub Baby used to say all the time, 'I put the "M" on actin' and make it mackin'.' It is just a role. How is Joe Bub Baby?"

"You know I don't fuck with him after that triple-cross move he pulled," Chino said bitterly.

"Where's his girlfriend, is she standing by him while he is doing his ten piece x-tra crispy prison term?"

♥

I ran to the phone and did as instructed. Chino crept his way upstairs to the kitchen door leading to the garage. He raised the garage door with the remote from the kitchen.

"Chino, Darren said hold tight. He will be here in five minutes." I became hysterical asking him if he was okay and if we wanted to lie down.

He remained calm. "Don't worry, Pooh, it will be okay."

♥

"Yeah, you know his girl Chazz Baby Love is in his corner. Chazz asked me about you. You should call her. I saw her at the NBA All-Star game."

"Well, I am glad she is standing by her man. I just pray he don't do her like I got done when he gets out," I said this hoping that Chino would get my meaning and continued, " I should go see Joe Bub. We both should. He's doing ten years. Let the past be the past."

"Yeah, we should. I remember him being there for me when I got out of prison. Pooh, he used to ask about you all the time. He also knew you were getting money. Joe was for you. Believe it or not."

"Chino, we could reminisce forever. I'm living for today, and I'm trying to get my life together so my son's life is better."

He interrupted, "Despite what you think, I do care for the baby. I know with a mom like you, he will be fine. So, I don't worry about him. You've taken care of so many people, I know he is in good hands."

♥

It seemed like an eternity but Darren's Jag stopped at a screeching halt in our driveway. He ran inside and I fell into his arms, crying talking about how I shot Chino. He stepped back and looked at Chino for advice as to what to do.

Chino responded, taking the lead even injured. "Darren, I had a little accident, I need you to take me to the hospital."

I screamed, "No, I will take you."

"You can't drive, you're hysterical, besides they will arrest you for the shooting," Chino said in obvious pain.

♥

"He still needs a father. You had one."

"Maybe, one day I can be that father. Just not now. But I do know when he…one day… when he's a man and he talks to me, he will look in my eyes and see I got love for him and his mother."

"Love is what love does, Chino. Your love is doing nothing for him. Well, I have a date," I said

"Who?"

"What?"

"Who is it? Is it that Jamaican Erik?"

"No."

"It's that sucka Delano, isn't it?"

"As a matter of fact, it is. He's good to me, and he cares for my son."

"He can't replace me."

"I don't want to replace you. Replace means to substitute for the same."

♥

"But I want to, please, I am sorry, I sobbed."

Chino began to limp to the car holding his stomach area applying pressure. Darren wrapped Chino's arm around his neck and helped carry him to the Jag. I put on my sneakers and jumped in the backseat against their wishes. Darren gunned it, racing through red lights and headed towards Mt. Carmel East hospital's emergency entrance.

♥

"I don't want the same thing I had with you. I want more. I deserve more, Chino."

"Yeah, you do. I know you do."

The phoned filled with silence. Pendulum mood swings going back and forth.

"Pooh, you're growing up."

"Yes, I am, and I like it. I just want a family."

"Me too."

"You've got one."

♥

Arriving at the hospital, Chino continued to warn me, "Pooh, if you come into the hospital, do not say you shot me. Darren take her home."

I continued to plead, "No, I want to stay with you."

We ran to the entrance gaining the staff's attention. They ran to the car with a gurney and assisted Chino onto it. I began to kiss the sides of his face and pleaded announcing to everyone in ear distance that I shot him and how sorry I was and how they had to help him. Inside the hospital, everyone was racing as Chino began to lose consciousness.

♥

"How's your mom?" Chino said changing the subject abruptly.

"Fine, and your Grandmother?" I replied going along with his game and asking about his grandmother knowing full well that my mom and his grandmother's feelings were mutual about us respectfully.

"Lodie is fine. I think your mom hates me."

"And you know this is true, brother. " *After all, you left her daughter for dead and with no support for her grandbaby, dah?*

"I know, I know. Let's go to a hotel or let me come over."

"No! You've not heard anything I've said. You're still the same. I want to be courted."

"Courted?"

"Yes, like your wife received. You remember? How you would take her to dinner, buy her presents, take trips behind my back."

"Here you go."

"It's the truth. I never had that."

"We didn't have the money."

"But when you made it, you gave it to another."

"Here you go. I don't want to argue. Does Delano have any money?"

♥

"Pooh, go home. Darren take her home." Those were his last words. Darren pulled me by the arm and pushed me out of the door towards his car. He stuffed me in the front seat and drove off in silence. As we drove off, the sirens of an approaching police car sped past us onto the campus of the hospital. Sobering, I watched the police car go past us.

♥

"He's more than money. Just like I thought you were."

"Here you go."

"Well, sorry, no booty call here, buddy. Call my service-ha, ha."

"Very funny, maybe I will."

"Chino, I've gotta go. I'll talk to you soon."

As I slowly removed the receiver from my ear, I faintly heard his voice say, "Bye, Pooh, I love you."

♥

Darren reached over, patted my leg and said, "You know Chino let you go free. That's love baby girl. That's love." ♥

Chapter

TWENTY-SIX

I had done what is known in the streets as "booking yourself." That's right, I had booked myself. I had bit off more than I could chew, more than I could swallow. I didn't know what to do, and Carmen really did not have much to say those days. I was in an internal battle with myself, and pacing, cleaning and waiting for Delano's phone call. We were going to get my son from my Mother's home in Michigan.

Ring...ring...

"Hello?"

"Hi, Carmen, are you ready?"

"Yes, I'm waiting for you." *I hope his babies' mothers did not give him a problem.*

"I had a little problem with one of my babies' mothers. She doesn't want my son to go with us. She said she doesn't know you."

"I was afraid of this happening. Delano, I do not want any unnecessary headaches. I won't hurt the baby. Which one is it?"

"It is Karen, the youngest boy's mom. She has no drama."

"Why did you tell her I was going?" I asked somewhat confused.

"Because I don't keep secrets, and she needs to know that there is someone in my life. But we will work this out. I didn't realize it, but she still has feelings for me."

"Do you have feelings for her?" My heart pounded as I waited for the answer.

"Nothing more than friendship, but I will talk to you about everything this weekend. I'm calling you to tell you to come over to my cousin's home, and I will drive."

"No, thanks, I will drive. I don't think that your car will make it to Michigan."

"I will have you to know that I have another car. That was my working car, and I will drive safe. You live too far out, and I am waiting for someone to stop over. Plus, I am waiting for my older son to be dropped off so we can go. So come and leave your car here."

"Okay. Delano."

"Yes?"

"Thanks for going with me to get my son."

"Carmen, it is my pleasure. You don't have to do everything alone. You need to remember this."

"I will. Bye."

"Bye."

Twenty minutes later, I pulled into the driveway of his cousin's house. It was a very nice home with a shiny white luxury series BMW in the driveway. As I was pulling in, another car pulled in behind me. It was a young woman and a boy about six years old. The little boy looked just like Delano. *This must be the baby's mom and the son. Here I go. Please don't let me get played. Here comes Delano out of the house with his bags. He is putting them in the BMW. Nice car.*

Delano approached me and leaned close to the window. "Carmen, get out of the car. No one will bite you."

"Hi, D, help me with my bags."

"No problem." The little boy runs to Delano.

"Daddy, Daddy, where are we going?"

"It is a surprise. It is a trip full of adventure. Do you know what adventure means?"

"No. Can I have some ice-cream?"

"Where is my hug at?" *A man not afraid of affection. He is good with his son.* Holding his hand, he lead him to my jeep.

"Carmen, I want you to meet my son. This is Lil' D, Delano Junior."

"Hi, Lil' D or is it Delano?" I bent down to talk with his son.

"Everyone calls me Lil' Dee, but I am a big boy."

"Yes, you are. So what can I call you?"

"Mmmmh... call me Big Lil' Dee." He looked towards his father for approval.

"I sure will. I like it a lot. It sounds good." His baby's mama moved timidly towards us.

"And Carmen, this is Sheila, Lil' Dee's mom." We both held out our hands to greet each other with a handshake. Sheila was the prettiest dip-dark chocolate sister I had ever seen in my life. Instantly, my mind went to what happened between them.

"Hi, nice to meet you," I said politely.

"It is nice to meet you also. I have heard a lot about you."

"Good things I hope." I looked over at Dee.

"Too good actually, but I trust D's judgment, and I hope you all have a good time," said Sheila with a less-than-reassuring tone. "Come here, Lil' D, give Momma some sugar," Delano moved closer and placed his reassuring arm around my waist, touching the small of my back.

"Sheila, we have to get going. I'll call you tonight with all the contact information. Page me if you need me or want to talk to Lil' D," said Delano.

"I will. Talk to ya later. Bye, Carmen."

"Bye." And we were all in the BMW headed to Michigan. I couldn't believe how friendly that went. Now, that is how it is supposed to be.

"Delano, that was not as hard as I thought."

"No, Karen will be hard. Sheila is cool."

"We can work with it," I said.

"We? I like it when you say 'we.' " He held my hand as he drove. His son or shall I say Big Lil' D was asleep as soon as we hit traffic.

We arrived in Michigan just in time. My mom was so happy to see me. She was even happier to see me with a man. My son was so glad to see his Mommie. I just hugged and squeezed him so tight he couldn't breathe; smelling his scent, one that only a mother knows of her child.

"I missed you so much. I love you."

"I wuv you." Lifting him in my arms, I turned to my mother and said, "Mom, he looks heavier."

"And he is, I feed that boy things that will make him expel a turd. Not junk food, not canned food, not Mickey D's or Taco Belio, but home fried chicken, fresh greens from my garden. Need I continue? And who is this handsome young man?"

"Mom, this is Delano."

"Hi, Ms.—"

"No, 'Miss' here. Everyone calls me 'Mom' or 'Star.' This has to be your son. He looks just like you."

"Yes Mam—oops. Yeah, Mom, this is my son. Lil' Delano."

"Mom, he likes to be called Big Lil' Dee because he is a big boy," I added.

"Yes, he is a big boy. Big Lil' Dee. How about some of Mama Star's homemade ice-cream?"

"Daddy, can I?"

"After you eat, yes, you may."

"Mom, we are going to stay the entire weekend. I want to show Delano around."

"Sounds perfect to me. The guest room is all ready, and you all are welcomed. They have some sort of jazz concert downtown off the riverfront, and I know you like jazz. Get some tickets and go. I will watch the children. Your sisters are coming over with their kids. So there will be plenty to do for me and the kids."

"Sounds good, Mom."

"Now, let's get you settled."

We got settled in, and I was surprised when my mom put the boys in the same room, and me and Delano's things in the guestroom. She is old fashioned, but not naive. But I was not sleeping with Delano. I was too uncomfortable. I would let his son sleep with him, and I would sleep with my son.

"Carmen, your mom put your bags in my room. I can't disrespect her like this. How about if we all sleep together?"

"All of us?" I said surprised.

"Yes, me, you, my son and your son. It is a big bed, and this way I can still be next to you and my son." *Thank you, God.*

"Delano, I like that idea very much. Can I give you a hug?" I asked innocently.

"Of course, but why now?"

"Just because you make me happy."

"Can we throw a kiss in there because you make me happy too?" Delano joked giving me a sly grin.

"Maybe we can," I said. And with that, he grabbed me and gave me a big hug and kissed me on my forehead as he gazed into my eyes.

"Carmen, I want to marry you." I eased away from his embrace. The words a girl dreams of hearing, and then I was confused. My hands became clammy, and I felt the urge to panic inside. Was this my chance to be normal? I changed the subject.

"I want to go to the concert my mom mentioned tonight. Please be patient with me."

"I will. Let's check out the concert. But first, let's eat whatever it is that is smelling so good."

"Yeah, my mom can really burn in the kitchen."

Delano and I had a marvelous weekend, and we talked a lot. I still kept secrets from him. He mostly just talked about himself and his plans. He told me he would be honored to be in my son's life. That really blew my mind. I didn't know what to say. Then my mom gave Delano the thumbs up.

"Pammy, I see the way he looks at you. I like him. Let's keep him."

Delano never even asked about my alias *Carmen*. My mom only called me Pammy once, and I didn't even think he noticed it.

I started thinking: *Can I tell him the truth? Can I tell him everything about me? Can I tell him that I dated men for money and all about the drama with my son's father?*

And that I am a drug dealer, and that I sold clothes and that I am confused and that I have gone through hell? He thinks my association to the life is just from hangin' with my boys. He would flip if he knew how deep in the game I was. Can I tell him this? Can I trust him? Can I tell him about Dragos? Can I tell him and show him who I am without losing him? Would he want me still? Finally, I'm sitting upon a pedestal. I like it up here. No, it won't work. I'm afraid. I like how he thinks of me, and I don't want that to end.

God, When or how do I tell him all about me? How do I share myself with him? Please help me.

Chapter

TWENTY-SEVEN

Dragos requested that I come to New York. He didn't say why, but assured me there were no problems. When I arrived in New York, his driver, Victor, was there like clockwork. Waving my hand in the air, I spoke to Victor.

"Hola, Victor."

"Hola, Carmen. Como Estas?" (Hello, Carmen. How are you?)

"Bien y Tu?" (Good and you?)

"Bien." (Good.)

"?Donde es Dragos" (Where is Andre?)

"El es en Queens. Tu lo veras ai. (You will see him there)"

"?Me Ilevas por favor?" (Will you drive me?)

"No, tomaras el metro" (No, you will take the subway)

"?El subway" (The Subway?)

"Si, Dice Dragos que tu diviertas." (Dragos sends his love to you)

Victor dropped me off in front of Madison Square Garden. Standing before the arena, it felt as if I were entering into a new phase of my life. I raised my head and noticed the marquee announcing a sporting event and imagined my name in lights. Carmen got plugged on this day! Returning to reality, I skipped down the stairs to the subway and was off, headed for Queens.

The NY subway is an adventure. People singing, dancing, loitering and, of course, rushing. I got off the subway in Brooklyn, skipped up the stairs leading from the stop, and Dragos was waiting. We drove into Queens to an area with a large garage. We pulled into the garage, and I couldn't believe my eyes. There were over ten vans sitting chevron style, of various makes and colors. Above, there was a platform with men walking with guns surveying the floor below.

As we pulled into the garage, the door closed automatically. I was so nervous and kept asking myself, *you paid him-right?* My nervousness was obvious because Dragos grabbed my hand and reassuringly said, "Carmen, relax. It will be alright. I want you to meet my brother. Actually, he wants to meet you."

My eyes began to darting side by side, and I asked, "Why?"

"He's curious about you."

Shaking my head I said," I don't want to meet him."

"Too late, here he comes." Up walked a very handsome fiftyish older man. The door was opened, and I was led out.

"Hola, Carmen, Finalmente nos conosimos." (Hi, Carmen, finally we meet)

"Hola."

"Tu hables?" (you speak Spanish)

"Si, pero yo preferio Englise." (Yes, but I prefer English)

"Porque?" (Why?)

"Nada mas por que si" (I just do.)

"No te pongas nerviosa yo te tengo una sapresa para ti." (Don't be nervous. I have a surprise for you.)

"Un momentos. Como say llama?" (One moment. What is your name?)

"Adrian."

"Gracias."

Dragos began pulling me through the crowd. Workers were

stuffing vans with bundled cocaine like it was nothing. Adrian stopped in front of a new Toyota van and said, "Carmen, this is your surprise. A new van just for you. Do you like it?"

"Por trabaja o por placer?" (For work or for pleasure?) I queried.

"Trabaja."

?neccessitas un automobile?" (Do you need a car?)

"No, just trying to understand the surprise. I mean, sure I have a Jeep, but I'm not sure why you're giving me a van."

"This will hold twice the amount of one of the other vans. Plus, it is fully loaded. It has two car phones. One is a free hand. All you have to do is talk and drive, no hands."

"Really?" It was hard not to be excited with so much bling, blinging in your face.

"Really, check it out. The combination is easy to remember. It can even be any color you want."

"Really?"

"Really. I also have some cell phones for your use. Communication is essential. They have no phone bills and will last for at least three months."

"Three months of unlimited use?"

"Yes, a burn-out. So what color do you want your van because I can paint it if you don't like this color?"

"No, champagne is a nice color. It is fine. I'm not certain if I'll need it. I'm slowing down."

"No, don't slow down! Now is the time to move, to expand," said Dragos with a hint of panic in his voice.

Before I could tell him the same things I'd been telling Dragos, Dragos spoke to him, "Adrian she will be fine. Carmen, I can even work on your ticket." *Oh, so now he can work on his ticket.*

My hands were sweaty, and I couldn't move my mouth.

"I don't feel so well." I rubbed my face and closed my eyes.

"We've overwhelmed her, Adrian. Come, let's go eat and enjoy the city."

"Carmen." Adrian placed his hand on my back.

"Yes, Adrian?"

"We are here to help with anything you need. We are behind you all the way."

All I could think of was *great.* I wanted this. But at that time, I couldn't give it away. Gained by stolen conversation. Put shit together that I still don't understand. This is why old people tell you to be careful of what you ask for because you just might get it.

We went to Long Island City and devoured seafood. We didn't talk about the new van. Dragos began to get open.

"Carmen, I know this game, and if you follow my lead, you will make millions every month. I'm dropping your ticket again by $3,000. So now off each Kilo you can make an extra three grand."

I decided to pick his brain since he was putting a harness on my back in order to work the shit of me. I quizzed, "How did you get into the life. Is this an inheritance or what?"

He started laughing and responded, "You have been watching too many gangster movies. Not all persons of Hispanic descent are groomed for a life of crime. I have a sister that is a doctor. She graduated from Yale, and I have an uncle who is an attorney. He gives me a lot of advice."

I was impressed and felt a little embarrassed that I stereotyped him. "I feel you. People stereotype African-Americans all the time. Is your wife Latino?"

"Yes, she is. Her name is Daya and she's from Brazil, but if you ever saw her, she looks like a white American. She has blue eyes and light hair, but once she speaks, you will know that she is Latino."

I continued, "So, what made you get your hustle on?"

"I met the right person at the wrong time in my life. I was laid off from my state job as an auditor. I had been married for about three months with my first child on the way and was the sole provider for my family. A childhood friend saw me at a bar having a drink and thinking of my problems. He was in the life and had built a reputation for having money through the sell of coca. Make a long story short, he offered me an opportunity to make money. Like you, I wanted to do it, just until I could find another job or get on my feet. We became close, and he took me to make a buy with him. During that buy, the deal went bad and he was killed. After witnessing his death, I was passed the scepter of his business, and now I am in too deep to turn around.

"On this level, Carmen, out is death or the penitentiary. Can you understand this? It is not a hustle, but a way of life."

I sipped on my lemonade and just wanted to return to Ohio.

"Beep, beep." My pager went off.

"Dragos, let me use your phone. Paul is paging me from Ohio, 911." He removed the phone from his hip.

"No problem," he said wearily.

"Is this a burn-out also?"

"Yes, yours will be just like it." I called the number from my pager.

Ring...ring...

"U Next Barber Shop."

Damn, he's at that slow-ass barber shop

"Speak to 'P.' "

"Who dis?"

"Who dis? This is Carmen."

"Hold on... Yo, P! You got a phone call."

"C?"

"Yes." I said.

"Got a problem."

"Are you okay?"

"Yeah. I need some time. I took a loss, but it's all good. I'm ready to work-out. I mean, really work-out. Just tell me it's on."

"Yes, it's on. We will work out. I'm out of town, but I'll be back in the morning. I'll call you."

"Thanks, C."

"Bye, Paul."

"Peace." Click!

"Carmen, is everything straight?" Dragos asked curiously.

"Yes, it is, and I think I will need that van."

"Bien!" (Good!)

I handed him his phone, and he just sat there smiling.

Columbus, Ohio-

I was so glad to be back in Columbus that I could have done a cartwheel. My flight was on time and very smooth. Delano agreed to pick me up.

As I exited the plane, Delano was there at my exit with some beautiful roses. Two dozen yellow roses. He bent down and kissed me on the cheek.

"Dee, you're getting taller and taller."

He laughed. "Am I really, or are you shrinking?"

"Do you have any luggage?"

"No, just this carry-on bag."

"Here, I'll take that." He placed my bag on his shoulder

"Thank you."

"Do you have plans tonight?"

"No, not really. I am a little tired."

"Good. I've made plans for us."

"What type of plans?"

"Carmen, just relax and leave this evening to me."

Delano was the perfect gentleman. He opened the car door for me, and I was so glad to be in the BMW and not the hooptie that night. We left the airport parking lot listening to some jazz. Noticing his detour and needing to feel safe I asked, "Where are we going?"

"How was your trip?"

"Interesting."

"Is that good?"

"It's an 'I don't know?' I don't want to talk about my trip."

"Whenever and about whatever you want to talk about, Carmen, my ear and shoulder is always here for you."

"I know, Dee. So where are we going?"

"You'll see, Carmen, just relax."

We pulled into the parking lot of a very nice restaurant. We used valet parking and were escorted in. We both had on Karl Kani jean outfits with 40 belows (Timbs), and it was not suitable attire.

"Delano, we are under dressed."

"No. We are kicking it. I come here all the time. Relax."

The Maitre D' seated us in a secluded corner area. Delano had made reservations. All eyes were on us. But my eyes were on him. The room was dimly lit, and candles illuminated our table.

"Dee, I am so uncomfortable."

"Carmen, I have tried to tell you that I accept you just the way you are." He reached to hold my hand.

"I love my flowers."

"Good, I would have purchased more, but I couldn't carry them, too heavy."

"I have always wanted someone to bring me flowers."

"Here I am. Anything else?"

Ignoring his question and changing the subject I turned my attention to the menu. "No. How's the food here?"

"It is excellent. The Chicken Cacciatore` is great. I know you like Italian food. The spaghetti is very good, too."

"I've been searching for some good Italian food," I said optimistically.

"I believe you found what you've been looking for."

"Dee, I think so, and I'm starting to believe I've found more than just food."

He came close to me, embraced me and kissed me right there in the restaurant. I felt we were the only ones there. His kiss was very succulent. Then the waiter interrupted.

"Excuse me?"

"What's up, Charles? This is my girl I told you about. I got her to check out our spot. We are very hungry. Let's start with some champagne. Give me some Cristal."

"A celebration?" The waiter asked.

"Yes! She's just agreed to marry me."

"Congratulations!" And off he rushed.

"Delano, we are not getting married," I replied rather put off by his remark.

"Why not? Come here, there's something on your cheek." I leaned in and then he kissed me again. "Do you like my kisses?"

Blushing, I answered,"Yes, let's just eat."

"Fine with me, but you will be my wife."

Charles, the waiter, returned, and we shared a toast. We devoured delicious appetizers, and then we ordered the spaghetti with Greek salads. It simply was delicious. We even shared an ablazed banana foster for dessert. We conversed and playfully fed each other. Whenever I was with Delano, I felt safe and at peace. Our dinner came to an end, but not the evening. We left the restaurant for the downtown Hyatt Regency. In the lobby sat a baby grand piano. As he checked into the hotel, I wandered over to the piano. Enchanted by its appearance and feeling relaxed, I took a seat. I positioned my long slender hands over the keys as I had been taught from years of piano lessons. Something came over me, and I began to quietly play the melody by Stevie Wonder, Ribbon in the Sky, that I had learned when I was nine.

My parents wanted so much more for me. They invested in well-rounding me so that I could become something in life. First, to be a young lady. Second, not to commit crimes.

Delano stood behind moving my swing bob hairstyle to one side and kissed the nape of my neck. He then led me outside for a horse drawn carriage ride around downtown. Delano had everything planned.

When we got to the hotel room, he had a gift for me—a leather jacket. Matching leather jackets, his & hers. I loved it. This was so magical. We watched movies, and I will say, it was the most special time of my life. This man made me feel safe.

As we eased into the bedroom, Delano began to undress me, one layer of clothing at a time, until I stood before him with only a black thong. He positioned himself comfortably on the bed and glanced my body up and down. As girls do, I got a little uncomfortable with the pouch of my midsection and did the suck-in-your-abs routine. Placing his hands around my waist, he pulled his face into my midsection and kissed above my navel. I placed my hands on his head and held him there.

Slowly he kissed my stomach, the sides of my waist and then up to my breasts, encircling my nipples with his tongue. Chills covered my body as my nipples became erect and his tongue danced over them. Grabbing me tightly, he held my body, thrusted me onto the bed, and began kissing my mouth with full kisses. The taste of his tongue caused my thong to become soaked with juice from between my legs. Kissing my neck, his hands moved to remove the thong, and he began playing with my pussy and fingering me inside and out. I moaned with pleasure and wanted to taste him inside of my mouth.

I rolled on top of him removing his shirt, revealing a chest with smooth hair and began to kiss his neck, his nipple, and then I lowered my head to his pants to give him head. As I began to unzip his pants he spoke, "Wait, baby, I want to take care of you first. Come up here and sit on my face, I want to taste you and watch you as I make you come."

Music to my ears as I assumed the position over his face with the sides of my legs near his ears and felt his tongue between my legs. As he sucked on my clit with soft, even slurps, I began to pulse with sensation. Playing with my own nipples, as he sucked my clit and moving my head back and forth, I began a slow wind with the rhythm of his tongue as he gripped my ass. Reaching climax number one, I moaned his name over and over.

Turning around to a 69 position, I opened his pants and began to suck on his thick, smooth dick. Slow even strokes up and down the length of his thickness. It felt like silk in my mouth. Unable to wait any longer, I straddled his manhood and just worked it like a hool-a-hoop. Placing me on my back, he pumped up and down, moving in and out as I squeezed his ass, and we continued to kiss and suck each other's lips, tasting each other. As we came simultaneously, our bodies began to shake as he asked me not to move. "Don't move, Carmen, wait ummmh, wait, baby." I continued to moan with pleasure as I came, feeling of ecstasy.

We got underneath the sheets, smelling like sex and dozed off into a comatose sleep. I woke up in his arms, knowing that a man does know all the body parts of a woman. This man knew my body like no other, like he designed it himself. Remembering his unselfishness in making love to me, I moved my head underneath the covers to find his dick slightly erect and began to bring it to attention with soft kisses. Delano started to move and twist to find a more comfortable his position as I continued to lick and lick all over. My mouth made love to his dick. Sucking on his erection excited me, turned me on so much that another orgasm burst from between my legs.

Never had I come this way before with a man. I knew there was something different about Delano. He began humming my name as I continued to lap him up like a thirsty dog on a summer day. Twisting, squirming, moaning as he pulled my hair back off my face and pushed his dick deeper into my throat. Tasting every drop of his cum was like savoring nectar. Emerging from underneath the covers, he pulled me up to kiss him again as we embraced each other extra tight. Moments later, he began a soft snoring towards a deep sleep.

Now how do I tell Delano the truth about me? How do I tell him about the escort service, my real role in this drug trade...My past? I mean, what will he do or say when he realizes who I am? Who I really am. I haven't even told him my real name. I know it is selfish of me, and he will think it is deceitful. But I don't want this to end. Can I keep this fairytale for just a lil' while longer?

I just closed my eyes, inhaled the scent of his cologne, snuggled in close under his armpit and drifted back to sleep.

Chapter

TWENTY-EIGHT

Back in Columbus, I did my usual runs. I woke up early Friday morning, kissed my son good-bye, and dropped him off at daycare. No matter what, this was my last run. This was my last weekend selling drugs.

Dragos' boys were still following me. I stopped by an apartment that I used to hold the heroin. I needed a separate apartment because the heroin had to be refrigerated. Plus, this apartment was used as a dummy address. During times of entertaining, I took people to this address to make them feel like I was bringing them to my home. In the streets, you never take people to the address you rested your head. But when they thought they were at the place that you rested your head, they got comfortable with you, closer, and it strengthened your fictitious trust bond in the streets. I got the heroin, and then I met with G-Money. I gave G-Money two kilos and he gave me a bag of money. Later, I met with Chino and his driver and gave him his kilos. I went past my brother's apartment and made some phone calls. Then I went to a travel agency to arrange my plans to leave.

I was in the process of arranging a vacation trip for Delano and me. I would tell him everything at that time. We would leave Sunday afternoon, as soon as I am finished with this last shipment.

I had over a half million dollars in my trunk. The bag contained neatly stacked rubber band wrapped bills laying flat in a multicolored duffle bag. I stuck two tennis rackets on the sides of the bags giving it the look that it was filled with tennis gear for observer's sake. I had retrieved my stash and was getting ready to make a power move out of the city.

Pulling out of the shopping plaza listening to an R Kelly CD, my peripheral vision noticed a swarm of cars. Seven unmarked police cars surrounded me. My first instinct was too try and notice the driver's faces. In my rear view mirror, two cars came to a screeching halt bumping my bumper. They boxed me in with no recourse to move. Bystanders and good Samaritans came over to the arrest scene for a better view. I noticed one of the drivers from yesterday's breakfast at Bob Evans' restaurant. If only my car could go into jet mode, I would be safe.

My mind darted quickly to the possibilities. The raised guns indicated that any attempt to flee was a suicide choice. My next thought gave me some relief, as I knew I wasn't dirty. I had nothing on me but a pager, cell phone and couple thousand in my purse. This equaled at the most, criminal tools and $275,000 was in the trunk of the car. Without a search warrant, what could they do? It looks like I caught a case, but what type?

It was the Feds; The Federallies. An army of FBI agents with big ass guns.

I was ordered out of my car and placed face down. It was over. The policeman screamed in my ear, "You are under arrest!" I was on my way to jail, and all I could think of was my son. He continued "You have the right to remain silent,"

My lil' baby. Mommy is so sorry.

The Feds roped my hands behind my back. "You have a right to an attorney," He began pushing me to the car for transport.

Mom, I didn't mean to hurt you. I am sorry for lying to you.

"Anything you say can be used against you in a court of law."

216

God, help me, I don't want to be away from my baby.
"You have the right to an attorney."
Father, please forgive me. Is this a dream? Why? Why?
"If you cannot afford legal counsel, one will be appointed to you."
Who will take care of my son? Please, God, give me one more chance.
"Have you understood your rights as they have been explained?" He didn't wait for a response, he just shoved me head first into the back seat of the car. They searched my car, and they found the bag with the cash in it. All I could think of was that Bitch! G set me up.

G's story was that he was set up for a kilo by Jay-Jay. That Jay-Jay rolled on him for a case he had caught selling to an undercover policewoman, and that one of his workers set him up. So Jay-Jay was looking to set someone up, so he picked Greg and set him up to go free. Then Greg picked me to set me up, so that he could go free, and that was the way the ball rolled. Then, here I was on lock down with no phone calls.

I got down to the police station, and I saw Chino, Rock, my brother Ty, the driver, and Ramon. They had us all under surveillance. I had two sets of people following me. One set was Dragos, and the other was the Feds. I looked over at Chino, and he mouthed, "Don't worry, Pooh. It will be alright," and he gave me a wink of the eye. All I could think of was my son.

The Feds took my son and placed him in protective custody. They picked him up directly after my arrest from his daycare.

We were all booked in at the downtown police station. I later found out that the driver was stopped on the highway headed back to the house, and he had drugs in the van. My brother was arrested on a humble of my stopping by his apartment to make phone calls, not to mention the lies that G told on him. The Feds go on words, not evidence.

Chino was arrested because he was followed. He stopped over Rock's house, and the Feds found a kilo in a cereal box with a gun and some money. Rock just was at the wrong place, at the wrong time. They had me for the direct sell to the confidential informant, which was G 's, punk ass. He had turned me in. I couldn't even get mad. Yeah, I could feel betrayed, but G had lived up to his fullest potential—a lame-ass, snitch-bitch mark.

They booked us in, and because I was the only female, I was sent to the workhouse county jail in Franklin County. The Feds confiscated all my property. They didn't leave a penny on my books. They took it all, removing all my jewels from my fingers, neck and wrist, and placed my items in a Ziploc bagged marked with my name for storage. I was told to strip butt-naked, squat, cough and remove my hair tie. I was told to shower in a filthy shower and change into some jail greens. For three hours, I was stuck in a holding cell that smelled like a piss and shit combo. Still, no phone call.

Finally, I was allowed my one phone call. I called my sister Lori in Michigan. I gave her the information she requested, and she began to look into getting my son back. After my arrest, the Feds confiscated my son at the day care center. My sister assured me she would get me an attorney and that I would see her in court. I asked her not to tell Mom yet until we knew more. She agreed.

I was sent to a dorm and had the opportunity to see my dream become a harsh reality. On TV, with the evening news telecast, there I was pictured on the news. All my business in the streets, total and complete loss of privacy. Public humiliation at its very best. I was on another journey.

My new home, a two-room dorm was designed to house 15 ladies. There were no less than 40 persons, in the place. For the 40 persons there was one toilet and one shower. There were bunks in every square inch of space. Some of the bunks were in direct contact with the toilet. Privacy is not a priority. The percentage of women incarcerated and charged with prostitution is extremely high. Can you believe, once an escort service owner, now appalled at the thought of sharing a toilet utilized by someone who sells their bodies for a living? This raised the specter of AIDS and sexually transmitted diseases. No option other than if you want to piss, share a toilet with women infected with HIV, hepatitis, and STD's.

The single available sink was used by all the women to brush their teeth, wash their hands, drink water, wash out soiled undergarments, etc. The sink was a vector for a hybrid of contaminants. I found me an available spot on the floor in a corner and began to attempt to fluff out my mattress. It was full of lumps, one inch in thickness and falling apart with holes and cotton spilling out the sides.

I curled into a fetal position, placed my tattered sheet over my head and used my wool blanket for a pillow, and tried to fall into sleep. That night, I was called out of my cell by some federal investigators, and they asked me whether or not I wanted to talk to them. I again said, "NO! I will only talk to my attorney." I was living a Baller's nightmare: ON LOCKDOWN'.

Chapter

TWENTY-NINE

Because the state authorities arrested G, the motherfucking informant, bitch-ass nigga, they took us before a state judge Saturday morning for our bond hearing. There we stood, all five of us in a row: Chino, Young Ty, Ramon, Rock and me. It's not uncommon for the Feds to snatch entire households, family and friends. My sister, Lori, was there along with Delano sitting as spectators in the rows of the courtroom. They looked upon us as we awaited the judge's decision on our fate. My sister was surprised to see me standing by Chino's side and handcuffed. Chino's grandmother, and his wife looked with surprise at the sight of the two of us together, rather than the fact that we were busted. Just like I had told my family nothing of Chino, I was equally certain he told his family nothing of me.

My sister got me an attorney, and I stood before the judge awaiting the bond amount. I was called forward first. The judge went into a huddle with the prosecutor, and then she looked up and spoke my bond.

"Ms. Pamela Xavier, also known as Pammy Xavier, also known as Carmen, your bond is two million dollars cash." I almost fainted. I also heard some more words, but it was a blur. "Ms. Xavier, you are a menace to society, and you have raped the city of Columbus." Blah, Blah, Blah. It all translated into, I was not getting out. I would not be with my son.

The "Ho" continued to speak, "Ms. Xavier, it is of the court's belief that you are a flight risk. Your passport is revoked, and you are to remain in custody."

I was returned to the county jail. My attorney came to visit me and said, "Pammy, you will go for another bond before a federal magistrate because your case will be turned over to the federal government..so perhaps, we will have another chance at bond, now about money. Your sister gave me $25,000, but I think I will need more to defend you; you're in a lot of trouble. You could get life. So, do you have anymore money?" *Lawyers are fucking crooks. They are the real ones that get paid in the dope game. Plus they get to keep drug money. Can you believe it?*

"Attorney, check this out, I'll get back with you." Nah, he wouldn't work. He was in this to get paid. Buy a new jag or something. I wasn't the one. Nobody, even in jail, is going to make a come-up off of me. They invented money laundering as an offense for drug dealers. Isn't the attorney that charges five to six figures to defend a case from the unemployed, accused guilty of laundering drug money? This guy wasn't trying to be in it to win it. I didn't need his type. What I did need was an experienced Jewish attorney. Everyone knew that the legal system was managed by the Jewish attorneys, prosecutors and judges.

On the evening news, I learned that Chino and Will made bond of thirty-five hundred dollars. I couldn't believe it, and I didn't really know how to believe it, or how they received such a

low bond? I was happy for them because I knew how bad I wanted to raise up out of there.

They denied bond for my brother and for the driver. Our bonds were all two million cash bonds. Rumors flew everywhere that Chino was telling on people. That, that was how he got out on bond. He had a prior record, and I was a first time offender. This caused a lot of doubt. But I knew my Chino as one to do the right things, and he would never flip on anyone. I knew I was the target. They wanted me, but I didn't understand them keeping the others. Somehow this would work out. It had to.

I fired my first awful attorney. His ass was too sorry. A straight sell-out. I acquired another attorney that came highly recommended because he had defended some other drug dealers and gotten them good sentences, plus he was Jewish. So I went with my new hired gun, Myer Levin, and his price was also $25,000. Problem was, I was out of ready cash. I had a lot of money in the streets and at my home, not to mention the money that they caught me with. Over a half million cash. When I met with this attorney, I assured him that I would get the fee together.

"Don't worry, I will get the money to you."

"That is good. I will work with you. We have a lot of work to do. I've spoken with the prosecutor on your case. I've worked with him before. He is a no-nonsense prosecutor. We go way back. You need to take a DEAL. They want to give you life, and with these new drug laws, it is possible." *(What ever happened to "Are you guilty or did you do it?" Where's my due process?)*

"They want to take your son from you. They are prepared to play whatever game you want. They don't want to let you out," said Mr. Levin.

"Will you still try to get me a bond?"

"Yes, I will try, but it is doubtful. I will always be up front with you."

"Please do. I like to shoot straight from the hip. No games and no tricks. Are you a prosecutor in defense-attorney clothing? Will you sell me out?"

"I'm insulted. I'll always do my very best." He began to gather his paperwork placing it into his briefcase.

"I'll see you in court on Monday. Go do your homework."

"Pamela, I will do my best representing you. Stay positive."

"I will. Someone will be in touch. Bye." He left the pro booth, and I waited to be escorted back to my dorm.

My absentee father came out of the woodwork and offered his house for my bond and his retirement fund. My parents had been beefing for years. They got divorced when I was seven and could not stand to be in the same room with each other.

My mom offered all she had, and I was scraping together all I could. It was very tough collecting behind bars. I was limited to collect-calls only, and no one in the streets wanted to talk to me because when you get knocked on a drug case, you're hotter than a VCR in a crack house. I was soon learning how things went on the inside, behind the walls. Not to mention the horrible food, conditions, stealing, bulldogging, and the incredulous noise level.

You could barely hear on the phone. And if you requested that someone lower her voice, that was a provocation for a fight. I was in another world full of its own drama, and everybody trying to survive, missing their families and trying to get out, wanting to be free.

Chapter

THIRTY

My attorney told me that my co-defendants were already approaching the prosecutor for deals against me, and that is how they got out. Still, I refused to believe that Chino would leave me for dead—again. I had given Chino ten kilos, and he was only caught with one so I knew he had nine kilos out there, and he had money for me. So I had one of the girls, Renaye, try to page him. I gave her several ways to get in touch with him. Chino, never called her back. Renaye went and told his sister that I really needed to speak to him, and YEP! You guessed it—the mother fucker played me. I needed money to pay my attorney, and Chino had my money and he played me. He didn't give me nothin'. He didn't even try to get in touch with me.

"Renaye, are you sure?"

"Carmen, yes I am. His sister was snotty as hell and didn't want to take my number. But she finally did. But he won't call. I'm sorry. Is there anything I can do for you? I have a couple thousand."

"No. Thanks for taking my phone calls."

"Carmen, I am here for you girl, ain't nothing changed. My service is doing well, thanks to all you taught me, and if you need me or anything, I am here. We are all here for you. Me and Gabrielle want to come see you. Can we?"

"No, not yet. I am not feeling up to any visits yet."

"Well, keep calling me, and if you need me to bring you any-thing, let me know, it is no problem."

"Thanks, Renaye, bye."

Chino had done it to me *again*. I just knew Chino would con-tact me somehow, someway he would. He would use one of our secret codes or something. That mother fucker got out and ain't looked back.

The following Monday, we all went again for a bond hearing before the Federal Magistrate Judge, and as I stood before him, Chino refused to look at me. The Magistrate looked directly at me, and my attorney did his best representing my family and reasons for allowing me out on bond. We tried it all, from reporting bond, to ankle monitoring, to homes, to cash, to property, to retirement funds, yet the Magistrate *(Mr. Bitch at this point)* said,

"Ms. Xavier, you will remain in the custody of the U.S. Marshal Service. This is the prosecution's request, and you will remain until sentencing."

I leaned over to speak with my attorney and I asked him, "What does that mean?"

"It means they will not give you a bond, that they will not let you out. You are going from here to the county from the county to prison."

The words echoed in my heart as he continued. "Now we must just work on for how long, and that is where I come in. Let me do my job."

As they led me out of court handcuffed with a waist chain and leg irons, it was a feeling that I still can't find the words to describe. But one thing is for sure, prison has a sobering effect on the mind, and I began to think of all sorts of things. It was like my life flashed before my eyes.

All the lessons. All the warnings. All the mistakes. All the regrets. All the betrayal and the wrongs that I had done. All I want-ed was for my son to have a father. For my life to be happy. With a lil' flavor, a lil' bling, bling.

In the holding cell, thoughts floated through my mind. I can remember meeting Chino one day with the vans. So, I decided to surprise him and take the baby with me. I gave the baby a bath and tried to dress him so he'd be extra handsome. I brushed his hair and put lotion on his lil' face and just tried to make him look good. I did all this hoping, that if he looked nice, then maybe, finally, Chino would want him. My son was already beautiful, but I had run out of ways to get his father to love him. I thought maybe a new outfit would help in some way. Chino was happy to see the baby, but it still did not make a difference. He had no love for me and none for our son.

What does it take for a father to love his child?

THIRTY-ONE

My brother was held without bond and so was Ramon. Chino and Rock were allowed to remain on bond without any monitoring. They had reporting bonds. Now, call it skill or call it lawyer expertise, because he had a thoroughbred lawyer, but all I can call it is "Bullshit" because he left me for dead. I am glad he was out, though. I thought he could tie up business and look out for the baby. Maybe he could help me like I helped him, and we could continue to look out for each other. I even thought that now he would spend time with the baby, get custody of his son. Well I was wrong.

Chino got his Federal prints done as I waited in the cell. Glancing at him, he still refused to look at me, and then he turned around and bounced up out of there, a temporary free man. That was the last time I saw him or heard anything from him. My attorney told me things that Chino's attorney told him, and it was primarily about our past together. Chino told his attorney how I shot him, and how the baby was not his.

In addition, he said how jealous I was of his wife. Weak-ass bullshit like that, and it made me wonder, is that keeping him out on bond? Then his family accused me of setting him up. I would love to know a set-up that put me in jail and him out on the streets, free and with over $200,000 of my money in his pocket. Street bullshit at its finest. Money can't stop the drama, and money can't buy

227

you love.

I returned to the county, and my attorney came to see me that night.

"Xavier Pro (professional) visit," A correctional officer yelled.

"Coming." I was directed to the pro visit booth.

"Hi, Pamela, how is it going in there?" my attorney asked.

"Besides the usual complaints, it is normal. What ya got for me?"

"The Feds have seized all your property. As he shuffled through papers he continued, "They have a black BMW 525, a green Jeep, a white Jeep, a condo and a home in the suburb, Murifield. Sounds like a very nice home. You will get copies of all this. I will always give you copies of everything."

"Great, I can't really keep paper work in here. No lockers."

"I'll try to get you something to keep them in. It is a lot of paper work, but we will go over it at our visits. I have a lot of questions, but I need to tell you what you are facing. They have new federal guidelines that start at a mandatory minimum of ten years to life. Your drug sale puts you in the minimum, and they want to convert the money they found on you into drugs. We will get the 'Motion of Discovery' in a couple of weeks, and we will know more. But as it stands, you are at a guideline level of 34 based upon which you are facing 151-188 months in prison. Which is give or take 11 to 15 years." *I'm nauseated.* "I will keep giving you information as I get it. I will meet with the prosecutor to see what he wants to do with you."

"So, I am screwed?"

"That you are, but don't give up hope. (I just put my head on the table and laid there.) There is a light at the end of the tunnel, I doubt you will get life, and they are very interested in talking to you. They have been calling my office. My last client got twenty years and that was with a deal. I have got another client who plead-ed to six years with the Witness Relocation Program. You may want to consider a deal to help yourself before the others keep rolling on you, and you end up with no chance." *These are encouraging words?*

"Your name has come up with the kid that got caught at the hotel with some kids from the North side gang, and this kid that is in for murdering and robbing some drug dealer with a strange name. I forget it. Also, a guy name Joseph Jamieson, who got a case a couple years ago, mentioned your name and Chino's in relation to his case. So, they've got a folder on you and your son's father. Chino's name has been downtown for several years, and this is the same prosecutor that prosecuted him on his state case, so he is very familiar with Chino. They finally got someone to directly set you up. The Feds always hear things. They are the Feds, and now they got you. So just think about it, and I will be in touch. You've got my home number. Don't hesitate to use it whenever you want to."

I could not believe my ears and began to feel panicked, so I blurted out, "How long will this process take? How long will I have to stay in this county jail?"

"Mmmmmmmmmmmmmmh? Let's just say for about 15 months, give or take a few. My last client stayed for 19 months."

"WHAT! FUCK THAT! Just send me to prison. Why wait?"

"Don't worry. That is where they are sending you, and it is a process, be patient."

"No contact visits for 15 months. I have a baby."

"Pammy, it is a squeeze, and they know you have a baby and they know you want to see and touch him. But this is how they do things. I don't make the rules. Anything else?"

"NO! Keep me posted." *Fuck it! I want my Mommie.*

Chapter

THIRTY-TWO

I was escorted back to the cell, and I called my mom and gave her an update on everything that had occurred. I even tried to explain all that I had been doing to get into this trouble, but she just stopped me from talking and said,

"Nicole, I am your mother. I am not your friend. I don't care about the past because that is just what it is. We have to focus on today and tomorrow. We can't cry over spilled milk. I don't even care if you did what they are saying you did or not. You're my baby, and you can't do any wrong. I will always be for you. We will work through this. You are not alone (I began to cry). That's right, let it out. Momma will be there to see you and get my grandbaby. Them people are crazy. They're trying to take me to court about my grandbaby.

"Pammy, I will get him and bring him home, don't even worry. I will be there tomorrow. Your sister is coming too. After we get off this phone, I want you to call her. She has something to tell you that I think you will like. The God I know is a God of second chances and third chances. Your life is not over, and you will not do all the time they are telling you. Don't listen to them. Get on them knees and pray."

"I am praying all the time, Mom. I feel all alone."

"You are never alone, and remember that God is always with

230

you and that I am with you. You will be fine, and we will make it through this. Don't worry about your son. I will whip the Devil's ass before I let something happen to that baby." The tears poured as endless drops of rain.

"You and your brother stick together. Start writing each other, and do this together. It will work out. Just be strong, Baby. Mommas here every step of the way. You can call me everyday all day and talk to me. That is why I work. I can pay my phone bill. Don't let them pull you apart. I don't know much about the law, but I know about our Government, and they ain't worth shit!"

"Mom, you don't curse."

"When my baby is hurting, I am hurting. Now I am not condoning what you did, but you are not the criminal they are saying you are. Got you on the news and in the papers like you killed the President."

"It is nerve wracking."

"Stop watching TV, and God will take care of punishing you for your wrong. Pammy, we must all pay for our offenses. Retribution is inevitable. But forgiveness of others and ourselves, gives us hope for the future. I am sending you a Bible, and it will be fine. Your family got your back."

"Mom, you always know what to say to me."

"That's 'cause I am Moms. And that sorry-ass Chino, I told you he never meant you any good, and he never wanted anything. He will not change. It was always about what you could do for him anyway in some form or fashion. But God will take care of you. I am on my knees everyday praying for you, and don't make me get your Grandma on her knees. It will be over. You are protected. Come, let's Thank Him. Say it! Thank God right now in the bad and the good because it could be worse. You could have lost your life. This looks bad, but the God I serve will turn it into good. You'll see."

"I know, Mom, and I thank Him for my life, my health, and my strength. I feel Him with me because I have not fainted. I am still standing."

"Wipe them tears and hold your head up high. Cry if you have to, but don't feel sorry for yourself. You can make it."

"I know, and, Mommie, thank you so very much for everything. I Love You."

"I love you too. Do you need anything?"

"No, I am fine."

"Well, I am coming to see for myself. You know all I got to do is look at you and then I will be all right. So I am coming to see for myself."

"I am glad you're coming."

"Now, don't pray for freedom because that will come when it is your time. Pammy, pray for wisdom and strength to help you with this trial. So you can see with your spirit eyes, and hear what God wants you to hear. It will keep you grounded. Your spirit is free. Remember, no man can bound this. And your baby is in good hands. He is young. We will make it through this. Lori is there for you, and you two have always been really close. Call her as soon as we hang up."

"That's if I can get the phone. These phone lines are ridiculous."

"Do your best, but hold your ground."

"And you know I will. Okay, then I love you. I'll call in the morning."

"Pammy, I love you, and please keep your head up. You're not the first to be arrested, and you won't be the last. You can make it, baby."

"Bye, Mom"

"Bye, Baby."

There was no way I could get back on this phone without a fight or a bribe, and commissary day was not until Thursday. In county, snacks go a long way, and I did not need to get into a fight over this phone. I would call in the morning while everyone was asleep. Using the phone in the evening was almost as hard as gettin' out of jail. I would take a shower and go to sleep. A good cry in the shower would do me some good. In county, you cry in the shower so no one else will see you.

"Xavier! Visit!"

"C'O, Xavier ready!" Rubbing my hands on my clothes in an attempt to straighten them, I began to wonder who was visiting me? I hope it was not the girls, and my Mom wouldn't be here until the weekend. I approached the visiting room and noticed my sister.

"Lori! What are you doing here?"

"Well, you did not call, so I got in my car and here I am."

"I am so happy to see you. I was going to call today, but the phone situation is a mess in here. I was sleeping."

"Yeah, you look like it. You look good, even if it is in green." My eyes filled with tears. "Don't start crying 'cause you will make me cry. Be strong. Now is the time for you to be stronger. We need to talk."

"About what? Please not this case," I said and began to rub my forehead.

"No, I just care about you. Your friend Delano is helping me find an apartment."

"Really?"

"Yes, he called Mom. His baby's Mom, Sheila, had Mom's number from when her son was visiting, so Delano called to see how you were. He is really concerned and worried about you. I told him that you needed money."

"Why did you do that?"

"Lose the attitude, because you do. Anyways, he gave me what you needed. I don't want to say it; this place may be bugged."

"He gave you all I needed? All of it?"

"Yes, girl, plus took me to lunch. He is downstairs with Kristen."

"Kris is here? Why is my niece in Columbus?"

"Because this is our new home. I found a nice two- bedroom apartment."

"What? Why? What are you talking about?"

"Your attorney said you will be here over a year, and if there is a trial, it could take maybe two years. I am not leaving my baby sister in a city and county jail all by herself. No way! You need me."

"What about your job?"

"I'll get another one."

"I can't let you do this."

"Do I look like I am asking your permission? I'm like Nettie in *The Color Purple*. Nothing but death will keep me from you. I am here until you get sentenced. And I am going to get all the whites and clothing you can have and drop it off. I will be at every court hearing and in that attorney's ass. I will be at every visit. Mom won't let me keep the baby or I'd have him too."

"You know how Mom is about our children. Lori, I don't know what to say."

"You don't have to say anything. We are sisters until the end. I'll have a number for you soon. I am staying at a hotel, and Dee is showing me around. But he is real busy. I'll be settled in about two weeks."

"I can't believe this."

"Well, you need to believe it because you are not alone. I am here with you."

"Please don't sing, you're making me laugh."

"Here give me some (placing her hand up to the glass). I am your sister, and I love you, and you will make it through this. I promise."

"When we were kids, you never lied to me, and I still believe you." Placing my hand to the glass matching her smaller outline and mouthed,

"I love you, Lo-Lo."

"I love you too my lil sissy."

"Xavier visit's up," said the guard with an I-don't-give-a-fuck attitude.

"Lori, it is time for me to go."

"Don't worry, I will be back. Don't forget you are not alone. These people better get used to me. Oh, I drove past your home. The Feds got it wrapped up like a Christmas present. We will talk more. Delano told me to tell you hi."

"Tell him I said hi, and give Kristen a kiss for me."

"I'll bring her up next time. I have not explained why you are in here yet."

"XAVIER! Visit is UP! Move it!"

"I gotta go, love you." I quickly moved it, waved good-bye and was escorted back to my dorm.

I was very glad to have my sister with me in Columbus. She had become an important part of my legal team, and I looked forward to every visit. She tried to help me in any way she could.

I had lost contact with Dragos, but he stayed in touch with my Mom doing favors for my son. I didn't want him to, but it was his way of sending me a message. "You look out for me, and I will look out for you."

When the fellas I dealt with found out I was being held without a bond, they turned their back on me. Hey, that was the way of the streets. Right? On the outside you are tight like glue. Once you're knocked, all love is lost.

There was still no word from Chino. Rumor had him out spending all my money and having fun. Hell, if I were out, I would have fun too, especially if I were on my way to jail. But, I couldn't forget how he had abandoned his Pooh. I was haunted with the thought of how my Chino could leave me for dead; again. Sitting in a jail cell behind steel bars with no way out, allows time for reflection. Reflecting on how the two of us continued in such an unhealthy relationship. Keeping secrets, denying reality,and stuck wondering what kind of bond did we actually share. How was it developed? I pulled out my yellow stationery pad and penned a letter to the missing-in-action Chino.

To My Dearest Christonos,

Others call me crazy, stupid and dumb for helping you. I too, call myself these names. I could have gotten out of the dope game, but I chose to stay. Partially, I stayed out of greed. Some, out of low self-esteem as the dope game gave me power. Power over poverty. It, coca, gave me control. Hustling hard, climbing the dope ladder of success in an attempt to make you proud. That was always important to me. In the beginning, I wanted, no I needed, to care for my son. In the end, I wanted to impress you. When I am questioned on why we are co-defendants in a Federal Drug Case after our separation, I draw a blank. Then I go back to our bond. It was not the baby's Mama or baby's Daddy drama, as you don't accept my or our son. Was it the love you professed to me everyday we were together and even apart?

Perhaps, our bond, came from the good times. The gold, diamonds, jewelry and cars. Was it from the bad times? Times of lack, infidelity and forgiveness when I shot you. I believed your forgiveness came out of your love for me, beating impossible odds. Even in the dope game, there are odds. What were the odds of each of us stacking the dollars that we did? Did the money bring you back into my life? It sure seems like that. And that really hurts me. I hoped time would change you, so I made excuses for your behavior. I loved you so much. Chino, you have failed me in love. You have failed me in friendship. But I failed myself, as I need to love myself. Love, I have learned is not always requited in relationships. Couples sometimes love at the same time or pace and with the same intensity. Couples, other times, love at different intervals. We were unequaled and unbalanced. As we both sought wealth, I extended to you the greatest treasure, unconditional love. My love was never wealth for you. I don't regret loving you. I do regret the choices I made as I live the consequences.

Consequences that now tax my son. I realize as I face my federal trial, I must love myself. I must love my son and be strong and do what I gotta do for me. I did my very best, and I know that you can still hear me, inside. One day I will understand. One day we both will.

Always,

Pooh

I folded the letter placing it with my legal mail next to my bunk. Maybe I would mail it to him, maybe not, but it was closure to write the letter. I just missed my son so very much. This was the hardest part about jail. Yes, the conditions are terrible. More than 30 women share one exposed toilet and one unsanitary shower. The food is slimy, cold and often unrecognizable. I have never seen bologna salad with green chunks? The food sucks. But like my Mom has always said, if you're hungry, you will eat it. And after so long, the food doesn't taste so bad. Ideally, at mealtime, the deputies are to bring trays of food to the inmates, who must eat the meals in their room dorm. The deputies return to pick up the empty trays. Many times the deputies order the inmates to pick food off their trays and eat it with their hands so the staff does not have to make a second trip to pick up the trays.

At first, I gave all my trays away. Later, I traded things for commissary. Still had me a hustle. I guess it is just in me. I had good days, and I had bad days. In the Franklin County Jail, there was no light of day because the windows were covered with paint and no outside recreation privileges.

I spoke to my son on the phone often. I still have not seen him because there were no contact visits, and I did not want to see him behind a glass. Maybe he would not have understood why Mom couldn't touch him or hold him. The price, in addition to length of time I was paying for my offenses, included the lost chance of mothering my son. So, I was just trying to get out of here and to prison so we could have a contact visit. My attorney said I would be in the county for two years going to trial, but I took one day at a time, and it was all right. You still cannot complain; you had to keep campaigning on all levels. No matter what you are going through, you have to keep pushing. I am a survivor, and I knew it gets greater later. One day, I would have a chance at a new life. Everyone gets a chance. I could start over. I had done it before.

I got scared, but then I remembered that God was still with me, and He forgives me, and He really was all I needed, and it is about the right things in your life. I saw the effects of drugs. I was seeing women withdraw from heroin and women in crack comas and tracks all over their bodies. This was up close and personal. I couldn't believe I had my hand in contributing to this. Putting this poison in people, especially my people. I was being educated on a whole new level. A spiritually conscious level. I was learning about myself and my life. They say your twenties are your learning years. This is very true. I read a lot in here and I wrote a lot. I started writing my story. After all, stories are sold, not told. Right?

"XAVIER, VISIT."

Hey this was early for my sister, and no one else comes to visit me.

"C.O., is it a pro visit or personal visit?" I asked, and got a nasty attitude response. I felt like spitting on half these C.O.'s. They needed to sell baseball bats in the commissary.

She continued to snap at me, "No, it is a regular visit. Do you want it?"

"Yes, I do. Here I come."

"Hurry up."

I wondered who this could be. The girls sent me some money and a card, but that was three months ago. At least they thought of me. I understood that they were doing their own things. In fact, Toy came through the county on a whore case. She was out on the streets even after what happened to China. I talked to her for a brief moment at the county jail church.

I still didn't know who this could be. I walked up to the glass and it was Delano. Let That Be The Reason you always keep your faith! He was still looking very good, and I couldn't believe he was here to see me.

I was feeling slightly embarrassed by my appearance. My relaxed hair was gone, and I was wearing my shoulder length hair straight to the back in French braids. I picked up the conference phone and sat down in the booth. He had his hand held to the window, so I placed mine up to the glass. My palm rested upon the glass matching the outline of his stronger over-empowering hand. I yearned to touch it and feel his warmth just one more time. I loved the way he touched the side of my face and the nape of my neck as he caressed me ever so gently down my spine. Remembering our night together, I just closed my eyes and imagined his scent in my mind. His voice brought me back to reality.

"Carmen, just because I am in here and you are out there..."

"Wait, Dee, I am in here, you are out there."

"You know what I meant. But I miss you, and I think of you, and I want to be your friend."

"Delano, you know I am hot. I can't believe you are here talking to me." I could feel my heart beating fast as I became more-comfortable with my appearance and relished in the moment of this visit. A visit, so sudden, so strange and so needed.

"I am not afraid. I want to be here for you. Do you need anything? I left some money on your books," Delano said.

"This is not wise. You should not be here."

"I know you will not do anything against me. I am not worried. You will be all right. Do what is best for you and your son. You know what I mean.

"You got a good lawyer, and I feel good about that. I saw Chino at the downtown mall with his crew, your co-defendants. They are not thinking about you."

I began to cry as tears formed in my eyes, and the evidence of being played continued to get next to me. I had to get past this and stay strong.

He continued, "Carmen, don't cry. You in jail, but you gotta think like you still on the streets. I was going up the escalator to the Marshall Fields level, and they were riding down, and it was a starefest like in the wild wild west to see who eyes moved first. It was obvious that they were strapped, but I was too. I would love to run into Chino's ass alone, like at the carwash or somewhere. Where does he get his hair cut at? Where we could talk, ya know?"

"Yeah, I hear ya. Just leave it alone. I am fine, thank you."

Delano became furious at my nonchalant attitude. "No, I don't care. I am gonna handle my business. Why? Fuck that nigga! He left you for dead, and you still give a fuck about him?" He was frustrated throwing his hands in the air wondering what was up with me.

"I don't care." I wiped a tear from my face.

He screamed into the receiver. "Well, I care! That mother fucker is going to get handled."

I pleaded, "Delano, if you love me, just leave it alone."

"Don't try that bullshit. I love you. That's why he's gotta be talked to, and when I see him, I am going to split his…

I cut him off stopping him from saying the unmentionable, "split his wig back." This meant murder in the streets and who knew who was listening to us.

"Delano, watch yourself, be careful, we on the phone love."

"Carmen, I miss you." He continued to yell. "And if you think this is a fuckin' walk in the park, you're mistaken. They about to slam dunk your ass, baby! The feds got a place for you." A tear welled up in his eyes, and I saw the painful expression on his face.

A tear inched down his face at a snail's pace. We sat holding the phone as he sat not ashamed for me to see him cry, and I watched the tear descend and rest upon a trembling lip.

Our eyes met and he continued, "You still got somebody out here that is for you. I got heart, just say what you need done, and I got you." Immediately my mind went to what I need the most, and that was to know if Chino moved the gun he used in the killings.

"Dee, listen, I left something somewhere, and I need you to go and find it for me. I need to know if it is still there. Can you do that for me? Check to see if something is still there."

I could not really tell where Delano was coming from. I didn't even want to go there. But it was good to know that if I had to, I still had a trump card in my back pocket. I would sit and decide how to proceed from here. Play my hand and pull my information card, elimination card or fold and do 15 to the door. The cards dealt before me were not easy on the eye, but I knew that once studied or watching the game unfold before me, I would get a chance to make a play.

The guard approached the booth signaling the end of our visit. I gave direct eye contact and kept smiling wanting Delano to hear positive words in his head, I whispered into the handset, "I miss you, too, Delano." I winked my eye at him, carefully choosing the remaining words spoken. Our visit time was running short. We sat for the remainder of the visit, tracing our fingers on the glass and giving each other the look of "handle your business by any means necessary." He asked, "Okay, you left something somewhere. Tell me where you want me to look?"

All I can do is smile.

Carmen is awaiting her federal trial in the franklin county jail. Her sister, lori, still comes to visit her faithfully every week, and her mother has custody of her son

THE END FOR NOW

AFTERWORD;

It was very challenging for me to write this book. The events that have transpired in my life are very personal. I've exposed myself with the prayer that my life can be used as an example to warn others of the awful dangers of the drug Game. I've tried to keep my terminology as close to the streets as permissible; because it is for the people in the streets that I write. I was approached and had many opportunities to write this story in several ways. Because I did not want sensationalism, I chose to write this story, myself, in Novel form – for the purpose of being enjoyable reading for many. Attention definitely needs to be given to the federal Mandatory Minimums that are in effect as "Justice". The Mandatory sentencing Guideline is inhumane. It imposes punishment that does not fit the crime. Granted, drug trafficking in itself is indefensible. It defies God's Law. It is against the human spirit. Next, it violates man's law. Therefore, retribution is inevitable for this offense. However, what is in dispute is the astronomical amount of time given to persons found guilty of this offense. The first-time offender is given no relief. Not to mention the disparity in the Crack Law verses Powder. This 100 to 1 ratio is a further outrage. It is a biased law and evident by whom it effects the most—People of Color. The conspiracy charge places too many innocent persons at harm and unfairly responsible for another's actions. The accused is represented by attorneys whom themselves are not knowledgeable about this mandatory nightmare. The Judge is rendered powerless. The accused is left in a corner of sacrificing their life for virtue. The guidelines, conspiracy laws and relevant conduct, all enhance guideline points that leave many at the highest end facing life terms. Some attorneys even disbelieve that any human could be given the sentence merited by the guidelines. Soon, they and their clients are made believers. Those attorneys that do believe "advise" their clients of Plea-agreements (Deals). Oftentimes, rightfully so. Because there is absolutely nothing else they can do for them. The accused ends up with still a lengthy sentence—after partaking in a plea-agreement. Sometimes worth the exchange, sometimes not. The individual can only determine this. In the streets there is a saying: "FAIR EXCHANGE AIN'T ROBBERY". Please realize that there is no fair exchange for your freedom. Consciously choose Freedom for your life from the beginning. I implore you to become aware of the laws governing your actions and the actions of those you love. What you find may amaze you. These guidelines have been law since 1987. I came face to face with them in 1994. As an accused, they became my reality. Do not allow my mistakes to become yours. Please become cognizant. Your awareness may save someone else. The Federal Prisons are filling at a rapid pace with young promising men and women. Men and Women deserving of a sentence reflective of a second chance at life. I Humbly Thank the Creator for another chance at life, and it is with my new opportunity that I dedicate my life to Him and this cause. To the unheard victim; the children of incarcerated parents. My prayers are with you. May God strengthen me to be your voice. To the addict, my family and my community: forgive me because I knew not the extent to what I did... To you, nor myself. To those whom have never done time, nor experienced any of this, I'm certain it is difficult to perceive. But I ask you to "Imagine This". For those who have experienced this, I know it was very difficult imagining yourself in "This". Know that this (your past, your present) was for that (your future). There is a purpose for your life. You are strong, continue to be strong. I am at work on my second Novel, which is the sequel to this book. I invite you to continue reading about Carmen's journey. It is a journey for her of awareness, self-love, purpose, strength, the justice system, the media and courage. Most importantly, an experience with the power of God.

TO ALL THE PLAYERS PICTURE ME ROLLING

AN URBAN INCOMPROMISING NOVEL

I would love to hear from you. I welcome your thoughts and responses to my first Novel.

Vickie M. Stringer
P.O. Box 7212
Columbus, Ohio 43205

VickieStringer@aol.com

ORDER FORM

Upstream Bestselling Titles.

Name: _____

Company _____

Address: _____

_____

City: _____ State_____ Zip_____

Phone: (_____)_____ Fax: (_____)_____

E-mail: _____

Credit Card:　　Visa　☐ MC　☐　Amex ☐ Discover ☐

Number _____.

Exp Date: ____/____Signature: _____

DESCRIPTION	PRICE	QTY	TOTAL
1. WHEN DAY MEETS NIGHT　Ramadhan Nanji	$ 12.00		
2. DAMN !　　　　　A. P. Ri'Chard	$12.00		
3. BAGGAGE CHECK　　Curtis Bunn	$13.00		
4. SASHA'S WAY　　　Scott Haskins	$13.00		
5. MY FRIEND MY HERO　Jerald Hoover	$ 5.99		
6. Sometimes I Cry　　Grosvenor	$ 6.99		
7. Let That Be The Reason Stringer	$13.00		
...SHIPPING CHARGES	Subtotal		
Ground　　　　one book　　　$ 4.95	shipping		
each additional book　　　　$ 1.00	8.5% tax		
	(NY/NJ)		
	Total		

Make checks/money orders payable to
A&B Distributors
1000 Atlantic Ave, Brooklyn,
New York, 11238
(718)783-7808